I0613517

Fire and Ice

by

B.T. Polcari

A Mauzzy & Me Mystery

This is a work of fiction. Names, characters, places, and incidents are either the product of the author's imagination or are used fictitiously, and any resemblance to actual persons living or dead, business establishments, events, or locales, is entirely coincidental.

Fire and Ice

COPYRIGHT © 2022 by B.T. Polcari

All rights reserved. No part of this book may be used or reproduced in any manner whatsoever without written permission of the author or The Wild Rose Press, Inc. except in the case of brief quotations embodied in critical articles or reviews.
Contact Information: info@thewildrosepress.com

Cover Art by *The Wild Rose Press, Inc.*

The Wild Rose Press, Inc.
PO Box 708
Adams Basin, NY 14410-0708
Visit us at www.thewildrosepress.com

Publishing History
First Edition, 2022
Trade Paperback ISBN 978-1-5092-4295-5
Digital ISBN 978-1-5092-4296-2

A Mauzzy & Me Mystery
Published in the United States of America

As I tiptoed around the sectional, my pounding heart did its best to alert the intruder and simultaneously foretell my impending doom. But nobody lurked behind the furniture or, for that matter, anywhere else in the room.

That meant they were upstairs. With Mauz.

Either that or I was being overly paranoid, which has happened on occasion, and the alarm wasn't tripped for a reason. Because nobody broke in, and Mauzzy was sleeping in our bed.

I spun back toward the kitchen when a flash of movement and a sound startled me so much, I took a quick reflexive step backward and flipped over the ottoman, my purse flying off into oblivion, the back of my head cracking into the hardwood floor. Bright white stars exploded in front of me, the brilliance beyond blinding. I fought to bring the pepper spray to bear, which miraculously was still in my hand, but couldn't move my arm. I tried to stand, but my lower legs were casually stretched across the ottoman.

Suddenly, I couldn't breathe.

Also by B.T. Polcari

Against My Better Judgment, Book One in the
Mauzzy & Me Mystery Series

Praise for B.T. Polcari

The first Mauzzy & Me Mystery, *Against My Better Judgment*, received the following:

2021 Eric Hoffer Awards—Honorable Mention, Mystery/Crime category; Grand Prize Finalist; First Horizon Award Finalist

2020 Heart Awards—YA Romance Finalist

A coveted "Recommended" rating by The U.S. Review of Books

"Polcari's debut novel…the first book in a series, is a winner….spot-on dialogue and characters…laugh-out-loud funny…a mystery of plot twists and adventure. Readers of all ages will find much to like in this page-turning offering, keeping them reading into the wee hours."

~ Kat Kennedy, The US Review of Books

"Readers who enjoy laugh-out-loud moments and the winning combination of a clumsy but effective amateur investigator who stumbles into unfamiliar territory will find *Against My Better Judgment* wonderfully entertaining, refreshingly different, and just the ticket for a lively read."

~D. Donovan, Midwest Book Review

Dedication

To the love of my life, Mary. Thank you for your endless, unwavering support and being there every step of the way on the long road to getting a book dreamed up, written, revised, revised again, edited, and published. It's a journey I look forward to taking with you on many more projects.

To my children, Michael and Maria. Thank you for being the best kids ever. I couldn't be a prouder father. And a special thank you to Maria for letting me bounce ideas off you, especially in the early days of this book, when I got wrapped around the axle as I searched for the perfect plot. Your clarity of thought helped me immeasurably, then and now.

To our pups, Jack and Wiley. Thank you for being with me every day as I wrote this book. It was a comfort having you at my feet even as I banged my head against the desk when the right word eluded me. Which happened all too often.

To our friend, Karen. A big appreciative thank you for your input regarding a certain feisty character.

To my fantastic editor, Lea Schizas. Thank you for everything, including your support and encouragement.

And finally, to Mauzzy, the only real-life character in the book. Thank you for allowing me to immortalize you in these pages by bringing your personality to the world so people can enjoy what you have brought to our family each and every day.

Author's Note

On pages 59 and 104 of this book, the characters access two websites. These are real sites and provide additional information for an enhanced reading experience, including a printable page on one site for future reference throughout the story. Enjoy.

Chapter One

If only…

If I could pick my superpower, it would be the ability to see how my day was going to unfold—while it was still folded. In a nice pretty package with a glittery purple bow, hopefully full of potential. But only one day at a time. More than that and I would never get out of bed lest things get too complicated.

Which is exactly what I should have done today.

My name is Sara Donovan. I'm a twenty-year-old college student home in Annapolis on summer break before starting my third year at the University of Alabama. And unfortunately, I don't have my desired superpower. Or for that matter, any superpower, except for maybe my observation skills. So today, with no clue as to what waited for me, off I went to work at the Carlton Museum, the oldest private museum in Washington, D.C.

Had I known how the work day was going to end, I would have stayed in bed.

****

Today was an unbearably hot and humid Tuesday, which was saying something for mid-July in D.C. And it wasn't going to get any better because severe thunderstorms were supposed to roll through right when

1

the evening commute began. Nothing like jockeying for position on New York Avenue in the middle of a monsoon with lightning flashing, horns blaring, and gestures flying. Although, the latter two are just a staple of commuting in the District.

My job entailed working in the museum's main vault, deep within the bowels of the building. If it wasn't for the entrance being a three-foot-thick steel door with a security grate called a day gate, the space appeared like any other workplace: drop ceilings, fluorescent light fixtures, cubicles, workrooms, and private offices. Next to the row of offices loomed a valuables vault with another three-foot-thick door with two combination dials and a large spoked wheel. And another steel day gate. The valuables vault held high-value jewels, artifacts, and irreplaceable documents like the Oliver Carlton Papers. During the day, both doors stayed open, with the day gates remaining closed to prevent unauthorized entry. A legion of cameras kept a continual eye on everything and when the workday ended, security closed both vaults and activated various sensors and alarms.

On the first day of work back in May, my typical exuberance hit an all-time high when I got my own cubicle, complete with gray-veneer cabinets lining one side and an off-white work shelf attached to the panel behind me. Very professional. In between training sessions, I spent the rest of that first week decorating, although while putting up glittery fabric over my workstation, my arm came down, smacking the monitor.

Hard.

The rude tech guy said in twenty years he'd never

seen a new employee destroy equipment on their second day of work. Unperturbed, having been there many times before in my life with unusual computer mishaps and rude tech people, I finished decorating my cubicle to the nines, including a small desktop reading lamp with a purple shade, various figurines and placards with funny office sayings, and of course, multiple pictures of me with Mauzzy, my college roommate who happens to be a miniature red dachshund.

On cue, a whine floated up from beneath my desk. Followed by a second whine and short yip.

Instead of being home today, Mauzzy was under the desk because he got into a bottle of ibuprofen early this morning, so he couldn't be left alone for twenty-four hours. The bottle may have been child-proof, but not Mauzzy-proof. Naturally, he pulled this feat off *after* Mom and Dad left for work. And leaving him at the vet for observation was a nonstarter. Last month, when he was in for a teeth cleaning, he escaped from his crate and wreaked a little havoc in the cat area. Okay, plenty of havoc. And now he can no longer be dropped off at the vet. For anything. Ever. Fortunately, I called Boss Lady, Chief Curator Evy Langston, and convinced her to let me bring him to work after assuring her, repeatedly, he would be quiet and remain throughout the day in Louie, a faux designer pet carrier that fit him perfectly in so many ways.

I bent under the desk and hissed. "Shhhh. Quiet, Mauzzy. We'll be leaving in thirty minutes."

He responded with a huff followed by a loud fart.

Typical.

Part of my job as an archivist intern was to organize

the wide-ranging collection of papers of the museum's benefactor, Oliver Carlton, for a new research room the museum was opening in September. He was a wealthy landowner in North Carolina in the 1800s who was also a scientist, inventor, botanist, cryptologist, and numerologist. In 1880, he established the Carlton Museum with a gift of one million dollars, and when he died in 1888, the balance of his estate went to the museum, including all his correspondence, maps, notes, and a vast collection of journals filled with his observations and experiments.

With Mauzzy silenced, I became engrossed in my work. I was sorting through Carlton's correspondence and typing up a chronological listing when a voice from the top of my cubicle startled the crap out of me, sending my chair rolling backward, crashing into the work shelf, and rattling the attached cubicle panel.

"*Hey*," came a voice with attitude from behind the accosted panel.

"Sorry, Victoria," I called back, but I wasn't really sorry.

Every office has that one conniving person who will do and say anything to advance in the organization. In our department, that's Victoria Finkle. She was such a parrot, constantly stealing people's ideas about everything and anything and proudly spouting them off later to Boss Lady, or during various staff meetings. Although, I did get Victoria good one time when I told her in "absolute confidence" about an "idea" I had for revising the layout of the cubicles to free up more space for worktables. Within ten minutes, I overheard Boss Lady's voice erupting from her office, asking Victoria where on earth she got such a harebrained idea and the office parrot's subsequent stuttering and sputtering. *That* was a great day.

I looked up. Peering over the top of my cubicle was Danielle Rollins, my friend and another cubicle neighbor. She was going to be a junior at the University of Maryland, majoring in graphic design. We had both started the same day in the internship program, although Danielle was an exhibit design intern. We got along so well and looked so much alike, quite a few employees at the museum thought we were sisters.

"You think it's happening today?" she asked, her soft brown eyes bugging out in excitement.

"It's four-thirty. Not looking good."

She frowned. "But it was supposed to get here last week. The museum has been advertising tomorrow is the grand opening."

The Carlton was hosting an amazing diamond and ruby exhibit called *Fire and Ice* for a three-month stint in the final stop of a two-year national tour. It was coming from its most recent appearance in Philadelphia, having also been to Los Angeles, Houston, Chicago, Atlanta, New York City, and Boston. The star attraction was a one-hundred-seventy-five carat flawless pear-shaped diamond called the Star of Midnight, one of the world's largest cut colorless diamonds worth an estimated fifty million dollars. There was also a twenty-carat heart-shaped ruby called the Heart of Fire, worth twenty million dollars. In total, the collection contained twenty diamonds of various sizes and colors, plus ten rubies. They were on loan from private collectors throughout the world, sponsored by the exhibit's organizer, London-based Bancroft and Culpeper. The tour was wildly successful and the exhibit coming to town was the talk of D.C. for weeks.

I shrugged. "Maybe they didn't want to make the trip from Philly with all these storms today. I sure wouldn't want—"

An electronic buzz followed by a loud metallic click caught my attention. I rolled to the edge of the cubicle and poked my head out. A group of people led by the museum's gargantuan chief of security, Mickey Fraser, passed through the main vault's open day gate. He wore a cheap navy-blue polyester jacket with a stain on the lapel, a half-tucked blue shirt, loosened tie, and scuffed brown shoes. Right behind him were four serious-looking armed security guards surrounding a trim man of average height I never saw before, sporting a bad comb-over of white hair with a platinum-colored metal briefcase—handcuffed to his left wrist. Unlike the disheveled Mickey, the man dressed impeccably, rocking a black blazer with a bright-red handkerchief in its breast pocket, starched white shirt with gold cufflinks, gray slacks, and polished black shoes. Next to him strolled a long-legged, classy-looking lady with shoulder-length satiny black hair in heels and a gray business suit with mid-rise ankle pants. The trailing person was the museum's evening security supervisor, Tony Carlucci, who slammed the day gate closed after he passed through it.

The *Fire and Ice Exhibit* had arrived.

I leaned back and gave Danielle an enthusiastic thumbs-up. Her mouth popped open before she disappeared and within seconds was at my cubicle. Victoria stood frowning with folded arms at her cubicle entrance as the procession approached on its way to the valuables vault.

Boss Lady bolted out of her office and intercepted the group in front of my cubicle. Mickey's massive six-foot-five frame towered over the diminutive lady. She wore a two-piece light-blue business suit and black blouse, with reading glasses hanging from a silver chain around her neck. Gray-white hair fell to narrow shoulders in a swoopy layered bob cut.

Addressing Mickey, Boss Lady snapped, "You're late."

"Not his fault, ma'am," drawled the white-haired man. "Those storms slowed us down a spell. Made it just in time. Another big one is fixin' to hit, too." He stuck out his untethered hand. "Name's Jefferson Scott. I'm responsible for the exhibit's security."

She acknowledged him but made no move to shake his extended hand. "Evy Langston. I'm the Chief Curator."

The man pulled his outstretched hand back, tipped his head, and flashed a smile. "Ma'am. Pleased to meet you." He motioned with his head toward the tall lady in the suit. "This here is Ms. Dana Wainwright. She's Bancroft and Culpeper's representative."

Wainwright stepped forward and offered a hand. In a proper English accent, she said, "Mrs. Langston, I'm so pleased to meet you. We spoke on the phone several weeks back after the fire at the National Museum."

Boss Lady brightened and shook her hand. "Ah, yes, so we did. That fire was dreadful, wasn't it?"

"Indeed," she replied. "Fortunately, we had time to make adjustments."

"This here's why we red-teamed the Carlton's security way back when," Jefferson added. "Always gotta have a backup site selected well in advance. You know, in case something goes all sideways."

"Certainly." Boss Lady glanced at her watch. "Yes, well, let's get with it. I have to pick up my granddaughter from camp."

She spun around and the group followed her to the valuables vault. Danielle and I fell in behind Tony, hoping to get an early glimpse of the jewels.

Boss Lady stopped in front of the valuables vault, swiped her museum ID card through a card reader, placed her right hand on a biometric scanner, and the day gate lock released. She opened the gate and stepped back. "Gentlemen."

Jefferson and Mickey each took an identical black fob from their jacket pockets and entered the vault, followed by Boss Lady and Wainwright. The guards closed in around the open vault, forming a barrier, as two loud clunks sounded in rapid succession from inside it.

Danielle and I pressed forward, craning our necks to see over the guards.

"Ladies, please step back," Tony said, signaling for us to move away.

"We were hoping to get a sneak peek," I said.

He hooked a thumb toward the vault. "Not my call. Take it up with them."

We waited, and after five minutes, the group emerged from the vault.

"Excuse me, Mr. Scott?" I asked.

He stopped and considered me. The metal case was no longer attached to his wrist. "Yes, ma'am?"

"My friend and I were wondering"—I gestured toward Danielle, her face pleading with the man—"if it would be okay if we got a quick sneak preview. We've been so looking forward to seeing the exhibit."

Jefferson shook his head. "Sorry, but that ain't gonna be possible."

"Absolutely not," Wainwright added in a snippy tone.

"C'mon, Jeff," Mickey said. "Give her a minute. She's okay."

"Please, sir," I begged. "We'll only take a minute."

"Shoot," Jefferson said. "Guess I got no problem with it so long as it's quick. That is, if it's okay with Ms. Wainwright?"

"You've got one minute," she said tersely. "I don't want the vault staying open any longer than that."

"Thank you so much," I said. "We'll be quick."

Danielle and I eased past the group into the vault.

The display case was set in the center of the space. Heavy steel shelves lined the back wall. Half were filled with labeled boxes and brown leather-bound books. The Oliver Carlton Papers. The entire left wall contained small locked metal doors resembling safety deposit boxes. On the right, narrow sliding metal drawers, also with locks.

I stared into the display case. The stones were dazzling, all sitting on small round black pedestals. In the center of the display was the Star of Midnight. It was by far the biggest diamond I had ever seen, almost the size of a golf ball. A very *expensive* golf ball. Danielle and I marveled at the glittering stones from multiple angles, several times putting our noses inches from the glass.

"Time is up." Wainwright's shrill voice cut through the air like Mauzzy's recent fart.

I took one last look, taking my phone out to—

9

"Hey, hey," Mickey called into the vault. "No pictures."

"Oh, I'm so sorry," I sputtered. "In the excitement, I totally forgot."

"Not a problem. Just put it away," he replied.

Remembering phones must be on silent when in the main vault, I surreptitiously fired off several quick pics of the stupendous diamond before slipping the phone back in my pocket.

"Okay, ladies. Let's go," Boss Lady said. "I need to close this up."

After we exited the vault, she secured the day gate, swung the thick vault door closed, cranked the spoked wheel, and spun the combination dials.

Mickey took a radio from his pocket. "Control room. Fraser."

"Yes, sir," a male voice crackled over the radio.

"Exhibit is secured. Activate all sensors in the valuables vault."

"Sir? All sensors? What about the main lobby's night renovation work?"

"Ah, right, forgot about that," Mickey said. "Activate everything but sound and vibration."

"Roger. Done."

"Thanks. Fraser, out."

Tony checked his watch. He was a trim six-foot former marine with an elaborate tattoo on his right forearm depicting an eagle with spread wings perched on a globe in front of an anchor. Beneath it were the letters USMC. He produced a Shazam chocolate bar out of his breast pocket. I recognized the wrapper. It was my favorite kind of Shazam. The one with hazelnuts.

"It's almost closing time down here," he said. "I'll

hang around to clear the place and lock things up in fifteen."

"Sounds good," Mickey said.

With the jewels safely secured, the *Fire and Ice* team quickly exited the main vault, followed by Boss Lady and Mickey. Tony disappeared toward the exhibit design offices on the far end of the vault. Fifteen minutes later, the staff straggled out past my cubicle as the time neared five o'clock, which was when security ordinarily came downstairs to clear the vault before closing the outer door and activating the alarms. Tonight, Tony was already in the back, clearing people out.

I was getting my things together when Danielle stopped at my cubicle.

"That was fabulous, wasn't it?" she gushed.

"Oh my gosh. The red and blue diamonds were amazing, but the Star of Midnight—man, that thing is huge."

"I know, right? Well, gotta run. And you do, too. See you tomorrow."

"Okay. Have a good night."

"Thanks," she said, taking off for the vault door, calling over her shoulder, "You, too."

I stuck my phone in my purse, picked up Louie and—uh-oh—the carrying case was way too light. The front door was still zipped and toggles locked, but a side door was unzipped. I looked through the front door's black mesh window, dread creeping up from the pit of my stomach.

Crap.

He was gone. The little dude was beyond tricky.

"Mauzzy," I yelled, dropping both purse and Louie

on the desk. I exploded out of the cubicle and dashed around the room in a panic. "Dammit, Mauzzy, now is not the time."

Silence.

Running from cubicle to cubicle, I searched under each desk. "Mauz, now is *not* the time. Tony will be here any minute."

He wasn't hiding in a cubicle. I shot into Boss Lady's office and was checking under her desk when—

Everything went black.

Chapter Two

The night the lights went out in...D.C.?

An eerie silence filled the air in the windowless, pitch-black vault. No humming from the air conditioning. No buzzing from office equipment. No noise whatsoever. And with my phone securely stowed in my purse back on the desk, I had no flashlight during a power failure. Talk about a recipe for disaster. I couldn't even see my hand in front of my face.

With hands out front, I felt my way out of Boss Lady's office, only cracking a shin once on what I believe was a guest chair.

Just as I made it to the doorway, Mauzzy began pitching a fit off in the distance, yelping hysterically. Something was wrong. Horribly wrong. I needed to get to my phone. Fast.

I picked up the pace, perspiration working its magic in all the wrong places as the air grew stagnant. Hugging the wall, I pushed through the suffocating black toward the faraway hyperventilating Mauzzy. My brain issued the alert to slow down because there was a—

Oof.

—copier coming up along the wall. That I was now draped over, hugging it like an overindulged sorority girl clinging to the porcelain throne.

Sliding to the ground, I crawled on hands and aching knees toward what I prayed were the cubicles. As I inched across the filthy tile floor, I debated what was more important. Getting my phone and using its flashlight to find Mauzzy, or grabbing the hand sanitizer in my purse and saturating my hands with the lifesaving gel.

Oh my God, what the *heck* did I touch? Anything that's slimy under your hand as you're crawling along a floor can't be good.

The debate was over. Hand sanitizer shot to the top of the list.

Mauzzy's yelps became frantic screeches, so I scooted across the floor, mimicking an ambitious infant making a break for it. Sweet Handsome maniacally scratched away at something, and this time, it wasn't his butt. He was pawing at some kind of hard surface. Like a wall. His screeching became more of a—

Crack.

I found the cubicles.

With my head.

I felt my way into the offending cubicle and hauled myself up into the desk chair. My fingers slid around the desk surface, looking for telltale signs it was mine. As luck would have it, they ran into my purse and Louie. I tore into the purse, extracted a bottle of hand sanitizer, and wiped my hands and arms down, rivaling a redhead putting on sunblock before a long day at the beach. Fortunately, it was a brand-new bottle, because otherwise…yeah. I can't even begin to deal with that thought.

With priority one taken care of, I dug back in the

purse for my phone. Activating the flashlight, I took off in the direction of Mauzzy's hysterics. I rounded the row of cubicles and reached the front corner of the valuables vault when a blaze of lights blinded me.

The power was back on.

After my eyes adjusted to the brilliance, I spied Mauzzy in the back corner, pawing at the valuables vault's outer wall, which was painted drywall. "Mauzzy, stop it. Get over here."

He stopped his antics and stared at me.

Not good. I knew that look. This was going to require some finesse to corral the little fella.

"C'mon, Handsome," I crooned. "We really need to get out of here."

Mauzzy twisted his head sideways, eyeballed me, and—smiled. Crap. He was formulating a plan, meaning seconds counted.

I rushed him and that was all it took.

The little man twirled around and barked once. He lowered his head and waited for me to get close. I bent to grab him, but he jumped to his left and darted away from my flailing hands toward the door of the valuables vault.

With an exasperated groan, I whirled around and chased after my fleeing dachshund.

When he got to the vault door, he skidded to a halt as his little body went into a sneezing fit. That was the break I needed. I snatched him up, secured him under an arm, and charged back to my cubicle. Between his failed dash for freedom and sneezing convulsion, he must have been exhausted because for once, he didn't fight being put into Louie. I threw my purse over my shoulder, hoisted up Louie, and legged it for the main vault door.

No sooner had I slammed the day gate closed when from behind me, a deep voice spoke. "Sara, everything okay?"

I wheeled around. Mickey Fraser stared down at me. Behind him, the entire *Fire and Ice* crew.

"Um, sure. Just hurrying because, you know, it's going to be a real mess on New York Avenue."

"Were you in there during the power outage?" Jefferson asked.

"Yes, sir. I was about to leave when the power went out for like ten minutes."

Mickey chuckled. "The power was only out one minute."

"No way," I said.

"It was one minute. Trust me. That's how long it takes for the emergency generators to power up and kick in. One minute." Mickey finished with a smile.

"Well, it seemed like ten," I said.

"Anybody else in there?" Jefferson asked, eyeing me intently. The kind, southern temperament in the man was gone, replaced by a hard edge.

I swallowed. "Pretty sure it was just me."

Tony strolled up to the closed day gate from the inside. "Incorrect. I was in the back working through lock-up procedures."

"Anybody else back there?" Jefferson asked.

"No, sir."

Addressing me, Jefferson said, "Okay, miss, you're gonna have to come with us 'til we verify the display case wasn't compromised."

"*What?*" I appealed to Mickey. "I didn't do anything."

Mickey put out a reassuring hand. "It's okay. We're following the exhibit's security protocol. If there is ever a power interruption, we're required to check the case and hold anybody in its vicinity until we can ascertain the exhibit is safe." He gave me a warm smile. "It's no big deal, but you're going to have to stay with us until we can check things out."

With a huff, I whipped back around, swiped my card, and opened the day gate. "Let's get this over with so I can go home," I said over my shoulder.

Everybody filed into the main vault, and Tony closed the day gate.

I stomped toward my cubicle, fighting the urge to tell these security folks off. Like, how in the heck could I get into that vault with the door closed? Only a couple of people have the combinations, and this museum intern certainly wasn't one of them.

"Ma'am," Jefferson called out to me.

I stopped and turned. "Yes?"

The exhibit security man sauntered up, with Mickey right behind him. "You're gonna have to stay with us 'til we sort things out." He bent down and peered into Louie. "Whatcha got in there, some kinda lil' pup?"

Mauzzy erupted into another sneezing fit.

"I'm so sorry," I said, mortified.

Jefferson straightened, pulled out his handkerchief, and wiped his face. "No worries. You just set the little fella on your desk and come with us. We're waiting on Ms. Langston to open the vault."

While we waited for Boss Lady to show up, Mickey talked on his radio. "Control room. Fraser."

"Yes, sir."

17

"Have we determined why we lost power?"

"Facility maintenance thinks the storm knocked out power to the building. He's contacting the power company to confirm. But backup generators are working fine."

"Okay, keep me posted. Fraser, out." Mickey clicked off the radio and dropped it in his jacket's outer pocket.

After five minutes, the main vault's day gate opened, and in stormed a livid Boss Lady. The woman could be a sixty-year-old version of my best friend, Zoe. Wee and feisty. "Not only did I have to turn around in that horrendous storm, but it was bumper-to-bumper all the way back up Fourteenth. My wipers could barely keep up." She stopped in front of Mickey and glared straight up. "And I'm going to be charged extra by the day camp for watching my granddaughter until I can get there, which judging by the logjam out there, is going to be tomorrow."

"Sorry, but like I told you over the phone, it's the exhibit's security protocol," Mickey said defensively.

"Were any alarms or sensors tripped?" she fired back.

"No, ma'am," Jefferson said. "But we still gotta—"

Dana Wainwright cut Jefferson off. "We're terribly sorry to inconvenience you, Mrs. Langston. The exhibit's insurer insisted on this protocol. Any time there is a power interruption, the exhibit must be examined right away. I'm sure the case is fine, but we still must check it."

Boss Lady must have a thing for English accents because her anger evaporated. "I understand. Okay, Mr. Fraser, you're up."

Mickey took out his radio. "Control room. Fraser."

"Yes, sir."

"Deactivate all sensors in the valuables vault."

"Roger. All sensors deactivated."

"Roger. Stand by." Mickey stepped up to the vault's door, peered into a small display on top of a dial, and spun it back and forth as he entered a combination. When finished, he took a step to the side. "Your turn," he said to Boss Lady.

She approached a second dial, looked down into the display, entered a second combination, and cranked the spoked wheel. With a hefty yank, she tugged open the door, swiped her ID card, and placed her hand on the biometric scanner, releasing the day gate's lock. "Gentlemen, do your thing."

The two security experts entered the vault, followed by Wainwright.

I angled closer for a better look. Something didn't feel right. Mauzzy's reaction was way out of character. The only thing he paws at is his bed or chair when he's settling in for a nap. And even then, nothing like he did earlier to the wall.

"The stones are all there and the glass is intact," Jefferson noted. "Confirms why the pressure sensors under the stones didn't trip." He gripped the edges of the case. "Electromagnetic locks still activated. One last thing." He edged around and inspected the back of the case, his head of white hair disappearing. A voice rose from behind the case. "Both sensors still operating." He straightened and addressed Wainwright. "I'm satisfied the case was not compromised. This jibes with the lack of any alarms being triggered."

"Excellent," she replied. "I'll need your report to

file with the insurance company."

"Yes, ma'am. You'll have it in the morning."

Mickey's powerful hands tugged up on the top front of the case. "Sorry. Have to perform my own check." He leaned over the case and inspected the back. "Confirmed. Sensors operating. We're good here."

Boss Lady clapped her hands twice. "Okay, everybody. Out. I have a granddaughter to rescue."

The group moved away from the valuables vault and Boss Lady closed the day gate, heaved the door closed, cranked the wheel, and spun the combination dials.

Mickey produced his radio. "Control room. Fraser. Activate all sensors except vibration and sound."

"Yes, sir. Sensors activated."

"Roger. Fraser, out." He clicked off and dropped the radio into his jacket pocket.

As we headed for the main vault's door, I stopped at my cubicle and peered inside Louie. Mauzzy glared back. Satisfied he hadn't pulled off another Houdini escape stunt, I picked Louie up and fell back in the procession.

At the day gate, Jefferson stopped and faced Boss Lady. "Now, ma'am, remember, y'all gonna have to be back here at…" He looked at Mickey. "What time y'all gonna have the museum cleared?"

"Should be by eight."

With his attention back on Boss Lady, he continued. "Y'all gonna have to be back here at eight tonight so we can move the exhibit upstairs, get the case secured to the floor, and tie everything back into all systems. That still okay?"

Boss Lady pressed her lips tight. "Yes, I remember.

I'll be here."

Jefferson smiled graciously. "Okay, good. Only need you to open the valuables vault. After that, we got it. The rest of y'all best get some supper 'cause it's gonna be a late night."

"Except for me," I said. "I have nothing to do with the exhibit."

"Yes, of course," he replied. "You and that lil' pup of yours have a fine evening."

Chapter Three

Coincidence?

As I turned into the driveway outside my home, another furious thunderstorm announced itself. Rain pounded my car, an ancient hatchback more the color of gray primer than its original black, as lightning flashed and thunder boomed. I debated waiting it out until my stomach spoke up.

A piercing yip from the passenger seat jolted my senses. I glanced over. Mauzzy sat on the seat, imploring hazel eyes locked onto me.

"Mauz, you've gotta stop sneaking out of Louie," I scolded. "That act almost got me busted today with Boss Lady."

No response. Just an unblinking, intense stare.

I revisited his earlier jailbreak. The *Fire and Ice Exhibit* arrives. It's secured in the vault. Everybody leaves. The power goes out. And soon after, Mauzzy manically scratches at the vault wall like it was full of treats.

"Sweet Handsome, what'd you hear inside that vault?"

He obviously didn't hear the question. His stare remained unrelenting. The message unmistakable. *Feed me.*

I set aside my budding theory about today's events. For now. It was already seven o'clock and my stomach was clamoring for food. "Okay, we'll make a break for it, but first, get back in—"

Mauzzy dove headfirst into Louie, spun around, and poked his head out the unzipped door.

"—Louie." I eased his head back into the carrier and zipped it, as if that really mattered.

I hefted Louie over onto my lap, a groan from Mauzzy telling me he didn't appreciate the hard landing. Grabbing my purse and gripping Louie tight, I sucked in deep and shoved the door open. Ice-cold rain hammered my face. Kicking the door shut, I made a run for it, Mauzzy banging around as Louie bounced off my thigh with each stride I took. Unfortunately, lugging his fat butt made what was already a challenge for me, as in running, much more difficult. And as some "friends" have suggested in the past—dangerous. To my physical well-being.

I charged along the walk toward the front door, only slowing when my feet hit the steps leading to the wraparound porch and door. It made no sense to race up them because I was already soaked. Plus, the risk of a catastrophic fall was too high and I would probably crush Mauzzy in the process. Sometimes, taking your time is the prudent course of action. Sometimes.

Before I could get my key in the door, it opened and Mom stood there, looking radiant as ever. And dry. She was as tall as me, missing six feet by a quarter inch, with short salt-and-pepper hair and high cheekbones anybody would kill for. "I heard you coming up the—oh, my goodness, you're soaked."

I stepped inside. "A bit."

"We were finishing dinner. Go on upstairs and get dried and changed while I fix you a plate."

I set Louie down, unzipped it, and a concussed Mauzzy stumbled out. He gave me a disapproving look before tottering off for the kitchen.

"Thanks. I'm starved."

When I got back downstairs and entered the kitchen, a perturbed Mauzzy sat by his empty bowl. "I'm sorry, Handsome, but I needed to get changed first."

I picked up the bowl and headed for the laundry room. His precious food was kept in a sealed plastic container stored on the top shelf of an upper cabinet. That was done out of necessity because otherwise, it would be an unsealed *empty* plastic container and I would be taking Mauzzy to the vet to have his stomach pumped. Again. And it had to be sealable plastic containers. Three years ago, I quickly learned after bringing him home from the rescue shelter that putting his food in sealable plastic bags was a major mistake. The little guy would be the perfect drug dog because he could sniff out *anything*, including treats, in a sealed double-bag. That particular day he was sick as a, well, dog. And so, he would also be the *worst* drug dog ever because he would eat the evidence.

Mauzzy followed me into the laundry room and when I extended my arm for the cabinet door, his little front paws pitter-pattered on the floor in unbridled excitement. I filled his bowl and did the two-step back to the kitchen to keep from tripping over my starved Sweet Handsome, who danced around and between my feet, his eyes focused on the bowl the entire time.

After setting the bowl down, I sat at the table

where a plate with two vegetarian stuffed peppers waited for me. The aroma, mesmerizing. Dad and my younger brother, Matt, had already left the kitchen, but Zoe still sat at the table. She lived near us in Annapolis for five years before her family moved back to Tuscaloosa after our junior year in high school. She was living with us for the summer because she had a summer internship with the NSA over at Fort Meade, where Dad also worked. We were both business majors at 'Bama, but that pretty much ended what we had in common. In fact, we were complete opposites. I was tall, curvy, with boring brown eyes and long dirty-blonde hair. She topped out at five feet and was wee and wiry, with shining green eyes and vibrant red streaks in tousled black hair. I was polite to a fault. She was feisty, and at times, also to a fault.

I leaned over the steaming plate of food and breathed in. "Mmmm, I love your peppers, Mom."

Smiling, she took a seat next to Zoe. "When you called to say you were going to be late because of a situation, I knew right then what to make for dinner."

Zoe sat up, her head whipping around toward Mom. "Situation?" Without waiting for a response, she eyed me suspiciously. "What situation?"

Dad's voice boomed from the adjacent family room where he was reading the paper. "Situation? *Sara?*"

And obviously, eavesdropping. No wonder he worked for the NSA.

I told them about everything that unfolded after the *Fire and Ice Exhibit*'s arrival.

Zoe blew out. "You call that a situation? Losing power for a minute is suddenly a situation?"

Mom watched me closely. The sound of a newspaper crinkling reached me from the other room. Out of the corner of my eye, the tall burly figure of Dad stood and faced the kitchen.

"No, it's what I think happened during the power outage."

"But you already told us what happened," Mom said, a hesitancy in her tone. "Mauzzy threw a fit over being in the dark."

I shook my head. "That's not it. He reacted because of what was happening *inside* the valuables vault. It had nothing to do with the lights being out."

My gaze shifted to Dad. He took three steps closer to the kitchen, his eyes narrowing.

"Inside the vault?" Mom asked. "You said it was closed up."

I took a healthy gulp of ice water. "Um, it was. Boss Lady closed the door and locked it."

Dad folded his arms. "So?"

Zoe chimed in. "Yeah, so?"

"I think the vault was robbed." I scrunched up my face, waiting for the reaction.

After a moment of silence, Zoe spoke up. "You're crazy. You even said it, the security folks came back and checked the vault. Everything was cool."

I caught a glimpse of Dad, who was another step closer. "Something's not right. Don't you find it strange that right after the exhibit was delivered, the power went out? That sounds too coincidental to me."

Zoe cocked her head. "Any of the gems missing?"

"No."

Her eyebrows raised. "Display case broken?"

"No."

She smirked. "Uh-huh. I assume they have alarms and shit. Any of those go off?"

"I already told you. No."

Mom pointed at Zoe. "That's a dollar for your jar."

Zoe pulled her head back. "For what? I didn't curse."

Mom decided this summer she was going to work on Zoe curbing her language. Every time she cursed, it was a dollar in the jar. At the end of the summer, the money would be donated to a charity of Zoe's choosing. The way she's been going, some lucky charity was going to have quite the windfall come mid-August.

Mom smiled gently. "You said the 'S' word."

Zoe's mouth fell open. "No sh…kidding."

"Now you see why I suggested this little project for you?" Mom asked.

"Yes, ma'am. Sheesh. I never realized."

"Good one," I said.

By now, Dad stood tall over the kitchen table, his lips pinched together. "You know I don't believe in coincidence, but in the absence of evidence, why do you think the vault was robbed?"

"Because Mauzzy went nuts after the power went out, and when it came back on, he was scratching like crazy on the vault's wall. I think he heard something inside it."

As if on cue, Mauzzy padded proudly past Dad toward the family room. Seconds later, he jumped into his purple child recliner on the far side of the room, spun, and sat up, eagerly watching me defend his actions. Something I always seem to be doing.

Dad rubbed the back of his neck. "We've had

strong thunderstorms all afternoon. I can't believe I'm about to say this, but that power outage happening right after the vault being closed was pure coincidence. Best you keep this one to yourself." He gave me a wink and returned to the family room to continue reading his paper.

Mauzzy sighed and rested his head on the recliner's arm.

Mom stood. "I agree with your father. Now eat your peppers before they get cold."

I turned my attention to a grinning Zoe. "You're loving this, aren't you?"

"Yep, sure am."

"I'm telling you, someth—"

"Isn't Mauzzy afraid of the dark?" Zoe asked.

"No, he just can't see so good in the dark."

"Uh-huh. And you don't think that's why he was going off, because he couldn't see?"

"He heard something. I know it."

She squinted at me, her grin dissolving into a hard smile. "So, you're basing your latest theory on Mauzzy? *Mauzzy?*"

I refused to break eye contact with her.

Zoe settled back in her chair and let out a derisive little laugh. "Girl, this is one of your craziest theories *ever*." She paused. "And that's saying something."

Chapter Four

Grant

After last night's suggestion by Dad that "*in the absence of evidence*" I should drop my vault robbery theory, I decided if I was going to be considered neurotic, then I was going to be a neurotic with evidence. I set off for work today with two missions—collect evidence a jewel heist occurred, and finally get the name of Hot Lunch Guy. I only see him on Wednesdays because he's the rice bowl and taco toppings guy for the cafeteria's Mexican Wednesdays, so it was either today or wait yet another week for that magical moment to occur. To improve the odds for success on this daunting second mission, I went with my nice-butt black jeans and a super-cute but business-classy black sleeveless shirt. It was paired with a purple jacket and layered gold necklaces with purple accents because—jewel tones are my thing. I felt great about the look and left for work ready to crush it.

And now, I just left the cafeteria's serving station where I failed miserably on my second mission. In my defense, it's pretty crazy on Mexican Wednesdays with famished patrons and employees jostling for position in long lines at HLG's service station. Unfortunately, this kept the pressure on to keep the line moving, limiting the time available for me to strike up a proper conversation. Things started off great with his gorgeous dark eyes asking me if that was my rice bowl next up to be filled. I answered by making eye contact, saying yes, and asking how his day was going. But from that celestial high point, it quickly dissolved into him telling me the day was going better than yesterday, after which he proceeded to talk about his doctor's appointment and how he waited over an hour—for a fricking mole check. He then handed me my rice bowl topped with grilled chicken, beans, guacamole, and cheese, and addressed the next in line with his dang beef tacos.

As the line pressed forward into me, I took one last shot at accomplishing the mission but totally panicked and asked HLG, "Excuse me, what's your...doctor's name?"

With my utter humiliation complete, I slumped off in search of an empty table, leaving behind a line of people throwing me weird looks and HLG staring at me with a confused smile. Pulling off this mission was going to take some serious planning. And possibly a wardrobe upgrade.

After lunch, on the way back to the main vault, I stopped in the Gem and Minerals Hall to check out the *Fire and Ice Exhibit*'s grand debut. A decent crowd milled around the display case, but eventually I got up close and took in the dazzling spectacle without a fussy Englishwoman named Dana Wainwright putting a timer on me. I read all the information cards and examined every stone from different angles, marveling at the incredible varying colors and shapes of the diamonds. There were rare blues, pinks, yellows, even a green and an orange one. The Heart of Fire was the largest ruby

I'd ever seen, as if I see rubies all the time, but the Star of Midnight was the star for good reason. It was even more captivating than when I saw it in the vault. The striking pear-shaped diamond caught and refracted the light into a blaze of colors. As I circled the case, never taking my eyes off the bedazzling bauble, the gem pulsated with a surreal effervescence of life itself. It was as if—

I froze.

Something caught my eye. About the Star of Midnight.

I brought up the gem's pictures on my phone from yesterday. That I took in the valuables vault. When I wasn't supposed to be taking pics. I stared at the photos, then the display case, then back to the photos. Adrenaline surged as my mouth went dry.

The Star of Midnight in the display case was *not* the same Star of Midnight from yesterday.

The one in my photos was a perfect pear shape. Fat and rounded in the bottom, tapering up to a single point. I scrutinized the stone in the display case. It was pear-shaped-ish, but not a perfect pear shape. The bottom half wasn't as rounded as it should be. It was really close, but not perfect. If I hadn't seen it yesterday and didn't have my photos to confirm, no way I would have known it was different.

But I did. And it was.

The Star of Midnight on display was—a fake.

I snapped a pic, tore myself away from the exhibit, and hustled through the museum for the main entrance. I needed to get outside and make a call.

When I hit the sidewalk, I brought up Grant Doherty in my contact list and placed the call. Grant was a special agent with Homeland Security Investigations of the Department of Homeland Security, aka DHS. He was also kinda my boyfriend, maybe, sorta? We met a year ago in Tuscaloosa where he was working on a case. It was because of Grant I landed my current job. That's because he called Mickey Fraser with a recommendation for me since they knew each other from when Mickey worked at DHS. Although I've known him for over a year, Grant and I have only been on a couple of dates because I'm either at school or he's out of town. It's not like we're exclusive or anything. Yet? We were looking forward to seeing each other this summer to see where things went, but he left town in early May on another major investigation.

After a series of strange clicks on the line, Grant answered the call. "Hey, Sara. I was just thinking about you."

"All good, I hope."

He responded with a light laugh. "Of course."

"Is now a good time?"

"Yeah, I've got a few minutes."

"Okay, so first, how's it going?"

"We're making progress, but I probably won't be getting back until the fall sometime."

"Well, that sucks," I grumbled. "I'll be back at 'Bama by then."

After several seconds of silence, Grant spoke up, his tone low and soft. "I know, and I'm so sorry about that. It's not what I planned for the summer." A pause. "For us."

I softened. "Me neither. Maybe in the fall I can get back up for a weekend, or you can come down and see me?"

"It's a date. I'll have some comp time after this thing wraps up. Hey, I've only got a few minutes, was there something you needed?"

I glanced around. A steady stream of pedestrians flowed along Constitution Avenue, keeping pace with creeping traffic in the street. I stepped off the sidewalk and placed my back up against the museum's wall to keep an eye out for any nosy people getting too close. Or perps surveilling me.

"Did you hear about the big diamond exhibit that was coming here?" I asked.

"Yep. Something about it being moved to the Carlton because a junction box fire impacted the National Museum's security systems. I hear the FBI is getting involved with that fire."

My stomach tightened. The thought of the FBI brought back some not-so-great memories from Tuscaloosa. If they're getting involved again, maybe I should listen to Dad and drop this whole thing.

"Sara? You still there? Hello?"

I startled. "Um, yeah, sorry. Just hearing *FBI* kinda gets me nervous."

Grant let out a short, easy laugh. "They're the good guys. Everything worked out for you, didn't it?"

Unpleasant memories flitted across my brain, eliciting a groan. "Eventually."

"The exhibit?"

I told him everything, except for the photos of the real Star of Midnight on my phone. I didn't want to worry him since he got me the job and I broke vault protocol when I snapped them off.

"What makes you so sure the diamond was stolen?" Grant asked. "It makes zero sense."

"You gotta believe me," I implored. "I don't know how they did it, but that diamond is a fake."

"You run this by Mickey?"

"No."

"Why not? He's the museum's chief of security."

"Because he might be in on it. You know, an inside job."

"Wow, you watch way too many movies."

"That's beside the point. Inside jobs happen, right?"

Grant breathed out into the phone. "True, but not with Mickey. You can trust him."

"We'll see."

"Okay, to get you off this thing, I'll call Mickey and run it by him."

"Pay close attention to how he reacts," I cautioned.

"Don't worry, I will. But I'm not expecting much other than him thinking I might have lost my mind."

"Thanks."

"I'll call you right back."

Several minutes later, Grant called.

"Hey. What'd he say?"

"That there's no veracity to your theory. And he thinks I'm crazy."

"Look, someone broke into that vault during the storm. I know it. Mauzzy is never wrong."

Grant's voice hardened. "Let's leave Mauzzy out of this. The vault wasn't compromised, nor was the display case. No alarms have tripped ever since the exhibit first arrived and no incidents have been reported. Mickey said it's impossible to get into the case without him being alerted."

My cheeks burned. Things were slipping away

from me. My mind raced for a rebuttal. Something. Anything. "How do you know he's not lying?"

"Because I know Mickey."

"I'm not so—"

"*Sara, listen to me.* You're wrong about this. The case has two tamperproof sensors. Neither one has sent an alert. The case wasn't busted up, the locks were intact, and the sensors have been silent. Mickey doesn't want to get the FBI involved unless there is clear evidence of a robbery because the insurance company would likely pull the policy and kill the exhibit. Besides, there is not a scintilla of evidence."

"Except Mauzzy," I countered.

"I said *evidence.*"

"But Mau— "

"I've gotta go, but Mickey ended the call saying it's best you left it alone and dropped the idea of a heist. It didn't happen."

"But—"

"We'll talk later. Be smart."

Chapter Five

Why is it always in a parking garage?

That crappy call with Grant did nothing but spur
me on to uncover the evidence and prove I'm right and
everybody else wrong. A position throughout my life I
was all too familiar with, unfortunately.

I spent the rest of the day finding excuses to stroll
past the valuables vault. Hit the coffee station twice.
Popped into Boss Lady's office with a question about
how best to cross-reference Oliver Carlton's
correspondence with Samuel Morse and Cyrus
McCormick. And, of course, numerous trips to the
copier. With each pass, I frantically scanned the outer
walls for signs of a hole being patched up and shot
desperate glances through the locked day gate searching
for any kind of disturbance inside the vault. But
everything appeared normal.

By the end of the day, I was left questioning myself
as I trudged along Constitution toward the public
parking garage. Maybe Dad was right. The power
outage was pure coincidence. Exiting the elevator into
the garage, the smothering smell of oil and car exhaust
overwhelmed me, made all the fouler by the heavy
humidity. A typical July day in D.C.

I navigated my way through the grody garage in

search of my car, a daily routine for me. Parking garages always mess with me because everything looks the same. Not to mention the stench and filth. Just a fricking maze of concrete pillars and walls, with signs and arrows pointing every which way. Except the right direction for finding your car and the way out of the dang place.

After several futile minutes of searching, I hit the panic button on my key fob in hopes of my car signaling its presence. Multiple blasts of a car horn reverberated off the walls. On the other side of a stairwell, flashing lights danced on the low ceiling in perfect time with the blaring horn.

Score.

I hurried toward the flashing display of—

A sturdy voice called out from the inner recesses of the stairwell. "Hello, dear."

I jumped sideways, stopped, and spun toward the opening. I recognized that voice.

A scratching sound followed by a metallic click and more scratching emanated from the dark void. A walker emerged from the black, a head of snowy white hair floating above it.

Peering at the ghostly image in the gloom, I called out, "Mrs. Majelski?"

The walker pushed further into the garage, and the jowly image of a very short, very old lady came into focus. Like a four-foot-eight, eighty-five-year-old lady. It *was* Mrs. Majelski. What the heck was she doing here? I knew her from Tuscaloosa. We met at the gym at the beginning of freshman year, where her iron-pumping, treadmill-dashing, and elliptical-cranking routines put me to shame. Zoe has always been suspicious of the mysterious octogenarian, and she's never missed an opportunity to remind me. Never. And now Mrs. Majelski is up here? When Zoe finds out, she'll go ballistic.

"In the flesh," she declared.

"What…what are you…doing here?"

Mrs. Majelski flipped a hand toward my car. "Shut that racket off."

I fumbled with the fob, and after two failed punches on the button, turned off the alarm. "What are you doing here?"

"Visiting my twin sister. The old girl is getting on in years," she cackled.

"You never mentioned you were a twin."

"I didn't?" She flicked a thick, gnarly hand. "Pish posh. Not important. What's important is you think a robbery occurred at the museum?"

My head jerked back. "How do you know that?"

She wheeled forward two steps. A crooked smile appeared beneath soft white curls and a droopy nose. "Let's say a little birdie told me."

"Who called you?"

The old lady's gaze swept the garage before turning back to me. "Again, not important." Another step forward. "What's important is why do *you* think there was a heist? Nothing was out of place. No alarms went off. So…"

Mrs. M was freaking me out, although it's not the first time she's done that to me. "How do you know all this?"

She stared up at me, her slate-gray eyes boring into me. "Just answer the question, dear."

"I had Mauzzy with me in the vault when the

power went out. It set him off and when the lights came back on, he was barking and scratching at the wall of the valuables vault. Pretty sure he heard something going on inside it."

Mrs. Majelski arched an eyebrow and chuckled. "That's it? Because your little dog was scratching and barking? Like a dog?"

"He's never wrong."

She snickered. "Didn't realize he's an expert on museum heists."

I winced. "He has very good hearing."

Her dubious smile vanished, replaced by a stern visage. "Anybody else with you in the vault during that outage?"

"Just Tony Carlucci."

"Who is…"

"He's the evening security supervisor."

She hesitated. "That his normal post, inside the vault?"

"No, he's usually upstairs. He stayed behind after they locked the exhibit away to clear everybody out and close the main vault at five."

The squealing of tires echoed through the garage.

Mrs. Majelski scanned the area, then made a break for my hatchback.

"What are you doing?"

"Let's get in your car."

I hit the fob's unlock button and headed for the car. By the time I got there, she was sitting in the passenger seat, the walker folded and stored behind her.

"Man, you move fast," I said.

"That's why I work out." She looked at the floorboard, then into the back seat. "Looks like you live in here, dear."

I grimaced. "Commuting two hours a day does it."

"Mmmm hmmm."

"Why did you find me?" I shuddered. "Here, in the garage of all places."

She checked her side mirror, then fixed on me with an unwavering gaze. "Because I need to tell you a few things. Look, I know I can't stop you from doing what you're going to do. Lord knows I learned that about you back in Tuscaloosa. So, you need to know this. If that diamond *was* stolen, and that's a mighty big if, dear. But if it was stolen like you say, then there are only a few crews in the world who could get past the security measures and into the vault in the short time available and pull that job off."

"You gotta believe me. The Star of Midnight on display is not the same one I saw in the vault yesterday."

Mrs. Majelski put out a hand. "I believe that you believe it. I'm just not convinced. However, two crews jump to mind when I think of sophisticated high-value heists."

"Like who?"

"You heard of the Pink Panthers?"

"From the movies?"

"No, but they got their name from one of those movies after the cops found a stolen blue diamond ring in the bottom of a jar of cold cream, a trick similar to a scheme used in the second movie. They're legendary. INTERPOL believes they're responsible for a half-billion dollars in robberies all over the world. They're highly disciplined and use military-style tactics to hit targets hard and fast, getting in and out in less than two minutes and sometimes in seconds." She paused. "That fits your timeline of the power outage."

I gasped. "Oh my gosh, that's it. It's them."

"Could be. The brashness of the heist, hitting the vault during broad daylight, fits their M.O." She raised a crooked forefinger. "However, many of their jobs are smash-and-grab hits. Sophisticated in terms of planning, pure speed, precision, and execution. But I believe the Carlton job would require a level of sophistication beyond their capabilities."

"You said two crews. Who's the other one?"

"The Antwerp Diamond Center crew." A look of admiration washed over her stern face. "These guys were good. An Italian crew. I believe the mastermind was from Turin. They committed what was called the heist of the century, stealing over one hundred million dollars in diamonds, gold, silver, and jewelry from a vault considered impenetrable. They took eighteen months to plan it. The vault was two floors below ground level and had heat, seismic, and motion sensors. Magnetic fields. Doppler radar. A three-ton door with six layers of security including a door lock with one-hundred-million possible combinations. A special one-foot-long door key considered impossible to copy. And of course, cameras. A total of ten layers of security had to be bypassed." She angled her head and threw me a mischievous smile. "Sound familiar?"

I stared back, slack-jawed. "Uh-huh. You think they did it?"

She shook her head. "Remember, I don't think anybody did it. That Antwerp crew ransacked the vault and left several key pieces of evidence that got them busted. With the Carlton, there's zero evidence anything happened. But in the very off chance you're right, I think somebody handpicked a team of pros and recruited a few key people from these crews to defeat the security measures. They also probably had somebody hack the power grid, or maybe a power meter or substation."

"Who could put together a team like that?"

"Don't know. Could be anybody. Maybe this Carlucci fellow."

"Seriously? Him?"

"Look at what you're saying happened. A vault within a vault was robbed during the day and probably within a minute or two. That tells me someone had advance knowledge of the systems they had to get past. Complete knowledge of both vaults was required. Maybe even knowledge of or access to blueprints, that kind of thing. And they had to know how to defeat that display case without smashing it. Carlucci might have access to some of that intel."

"You really think he did it? Carlucci?"

"I don't think anybody did it. Don't forget, the crew also had to have a perfect forgery of that diamond. This is beyond high-level stuff."

My shoulders slumped. "When you put it that way, it sure sounds impossible."

"Exactly, dear. That's why I'm extremely skeptical and strongly advise you to drop the whole thing. But"— she let out a half-laugh—"I also know you. So, if you decide to pursue this silly idea, let me know if you need my help."

"How do I contact you?"

"Start the car, but keep the lights off."

Mrs. Majelski jumped out of the car, retrieved her walker from the back seat, and wheeled around to my window, which I lowered. She rummaged in a purse sitting in a white basket strapped to the front of the walker, produced a small folded piece of paper, and handed it to me. "Call this number and immediately hang up. I'll find you."

"I...hang up? Like...I don't talk with you?"

"Precisely. I'll find you." She curled up her lips, wheeled the walker about, and slipped around the wall toward the stairwell. Her voice called out from the darkness. "But I think you're wrong."

Chapter Six

An early start

Despite Mrs. Majelski's skepticism and recommendation, I was jacked because she gave me some angles to look into. I got up early the next day to make sure I was at the main vault when security opened the door at seven-thirty. Most of the people working in the vault didn't arrive until eight, which gave me enough time to examine the valuables vault.

When I got to my cubicle, sitting on the back shelf was a set of keys plus money wrapped around something and secured with a rubber band. I dug out a sealable plastic bag from my purse, snagged a tissue from the box on my desk, and using the tissue, picked up the keys and money and placed them in the bag. For all I knew, the money was wrapped around anthrax or something, and I wasn't about to put my fingerprints anywhere on it or the keys. No way Sara Donovan was getting framed for a crime. I made a mental note to get the bag to Mickey, right after accomplishing the whole reason for coming in early.

I grabbed my phone and ran to the wall where Mauzzy freaked out the other day. Turning on the flashlight, I bent down and pored over the painted drywall, looking for anything out of the ordinary. But other than scratch marks, everything appeared norm—

"What on earth are you doing?"

I lurched forward, cracking my forehead into the wall. With a big push off the fiendish drywall, I stood and faced my inquisitor—a frowning Boss Lady.

Crap.

"Um, looking for what caused Mauzzy to go crazy on Tuesday."

With hands on hips, she leaned in toward me. "Mauzzy? Your dog?" She caught sight of the scratch marks. "I made it quite clear he was to stay in his pet carrier."

"Yes, ma'am, you did. But he escaped. And then the power went out and—"

"Escaped? How? When?"

"After the exhibit arrived, when we were over at the valuables vault. He somehow unzipped the carrier. I'm so sorry."

Her eyes went cold. "Well, he's no longer welcome here. I understand it was an emergency, but I simply cannot have an animal roaming free around the office."

"I understand."

"Good." She whipped around and marched smartly toward her office, heels clicking a rapid staccato on the tile floor.

I know everybody told me to drop my theory, but since Boss Lady was responsible for the vault, it was my duty to let her know something might be amiss. Then I'll drop it. Maybe.

"Excuse me, Evy?" I called out.

Boss Lady stopped and made an about-face. "Yes?"

"I think Mauzzy heard something inside the vault

when the power went out."

"Like what?" she snapped.

I swallowed. "I don't know. Maybe somebody inside the vault? After the exhibit was put in it?"

She raised a manicured eyebrow. "You mean after I closed the door and locked it?"

My chest tightened. "Uh-huh."

"Preposterous," she said curtly.

"Are you sure?"

Boss Lady's eyes bored into me. "Nobody was in there when I closed the door. Nobody was inside when we opened it after the power outage. The vault itself is fully intact. And the instant that door is locked, security activates the sensors inside it. So, you see, it's simply impossible for anybody to go undetected once the vault is secured."

"What about the power outage? Would that knock out any of those gizmos?"

"My dear, there was a hellacious storm going on outside."

"But would it?"

She broke eye contact, her gaze shifting to the right for a brief second before returning to me. "I don't believe so, but I don't know how everything is wired." She stuck out a cautioning finger, her face reddening. "This notion of yours is ridiculous. Do *not* take this any further because it will only reflect poorly on you and I can't afford to lose you. There's too much to do getting the Carlton Papers organized. The opening of the new research room is only two months away."

I sucked in a quick breath. "Lose me?"

"Indeed. We take security very seriously here, and someone spouting off about a supposed robbery will create quite the ruckus and disruption. Something the Carlton does not need." She paused and leveled her gaze, cold blue eyes drilling into me. "I won't be able to protect you. Understand?"

"Yes, ma'am."

"Good." She put her back to me and disappeared into her office.

I shut off my phone's flashlight and staggered to the coffee station with the fancy-schmancy self-service dispenser to make a much-needed mug of French roast. Beside it sat a locked shred bin with a two-inch slot for depositing important papers for future destruction. With one hand, I picked up a white mug while the other set the phone on top of the bin.

Thud.

Seriously?

With my focus on the coffee station, the hand holding my phone was clearly not paying attention, resulting in the phone catching the top of the shred bin's slot and being dislodged.

From my hand.

Into the locked shred bin.

Panic tore through me. I crammed a hand halfway into the slot in a desperate attempt to rescue my lifeline. Unfortunately, that thud sound reminded me today was Thursday. And the bin gets emptied on Wednesdays. Meaning, my phone fell to the bottom instead of sitting within reach on a pile of discarded papers near the top.

"Looking for something?"

With my hand stuck in the slot, I looked over my shoulder. "Um, my phone?"

Boss Lady stepped up to the coffee station and made a cup of tea. "I'm not going to ask. But you'll need to call security to open it for you."

I extracted my hand. "You can't do it?"

She picked up her steaming teacup, a restrained smile on her face. "Sorry. Call security."

As Boss Lady walked away, a part of me wondered if this was payback for me getting her all riled up about the vault. How could she not have a key to the bin? She runs the fricking place.

Whatever.

Armed with an extra-strong French roast, I returned to my cubicle and called security.

"Security, Fraser speaking."

"Hi, Mickey. It's Sara. I have a little problem."

He sighed. "What now?"

"I, um, dropped my phone into the shred bin."

After several seconds of silence, Mickey spoke up. "Say that again."

My cheeks burned as I repeated my mishap.

"And now you need security to retrieve it for you." Smugness dripped with every word spoken.

"It would be appreciated."

"I'll send somebody over."

"Thanks." I eyed the plastic bag on my desk containing the keys and money. "Oh, and somebody left a set of keys and a wad of money in my cubicle last night. Can I give it to the person you send here so you can find out who they belong to?"

"Wad of money? How much?"

"Don't know. It's wrapped around something and held by a rubber band."

"Put them in an interoffice envelope, seal it, and give it to the guard."

"Thanks."

I hung up and while waiting for Mickey to send someone to rescue my baby and retrieve the keys and money, I ran through the last two days. Dad advised me to keep my hunch to myself. Zoe said this was one of my craziest theories ever. But that wasn't the first time she's said that over the years, so she doesn't count. Grant told me to leave it alone in no uncertain terms. Mrs. Majelski shows up out of the blue and recommended I drop the whole thing. And now Boss Lady gets all up in my face and threatens me with termination if I take things any further.

I leaned back, taking care not to flip backward like last week, and focused on a series of Mauzzy pictures clipped to a black string draped across the panel over my desk. In one, lounging in his recliner, staring off in deep thought. Either that or planning his next move. In another, looking resplendent in his glittering gold tux and top hat, a black bow tie tucked smartly beneath a sly mug. And in yet another, partying, wearing his birthday sombrero. Sweet Handsome was many things, including quite the handful at times. But he was also never wrong. I've learned that the hard way too many times to count. Okay, "learned" might not be the best word choice, but the point being, the little guy was never wrong. He never pitched a fit without a reason. Just like he never got out of bed without a purpose. Or turned down a meal, regardless when or what he's being fed.

Edging up to the desk, I scribbled down the vault's security systems. Studying my notes, I remembered the control room told Mickey back on Tuesday they couldn't activate the sound and vibration sensors because of lobby renovation work going on at night. I

B.T. Polcari

scratched through those items. *No evidence of a heist* kept pounding in my head. No evidence. Except for the pics on my phone proving the Star of Midnight in the exhibit is a fake. But how did they do it? No evide—

I checked the Carlton's internal phone directory and picked up the phone.

"Facility maintenance," a gruff voice answered.

"Hello, this is Sara Donovan, from Archives. Is this Mr. Barton?"

"Yeah. Call me Jake."

"Perfect. Jake, my phone directory says you're the facility maintenance manager. Is this correct?"

A pause. "Yeah. What can I do ya for?"

"I'm curious if you know what's outside the back wall of the valuables vault."

"Valuables vault?"

"You know, the one inside the main vault. It's where I work."

He hesitated. "You mean the one with all the valuable stuff?"

"That's it."

"Strange question coming from somebody with Archives."

"This is a special project I'm working on. So, do you know what's on the outside of the back wall?"

"Yeah."

A buzzing filled my head. I was onto something. "*You do?*"

"Yeah."

"What?"

"Dirt."

"Excuse me?"

Hoarse laughter came through the phone. "I said

50

dirt. That whole vault is probably twenty feet underground. Ain't nothin' but dirt on the other side of that wall."

"Nobody can access it from the other side?"

More laughter. "Not a chance."

"What if somebody dug a tunnel?"

The laughter stopped abruptly.

"What's this special project about?" he asked, his tone laced with suspicion. "Sounds awfully fishy."

I swallowed hard. "Just a routine internal review of possible soft spots in security."

He snorted. "Who came up with the absurd idea of a tunnel?"

"I did. Why do you find the idea absurd?"

"We're in the middle of the city. Go outside. There's concrete everywhere. Ain't no place to start digging from."

"What about in the Mall across from Constitution?"

Barton roared with laughter. "Sounds to me like common sense is chasing you. But so far, you're beating it."

I fumed but wasn't about to let 'ole Jake rattle me. After a deep breath, I said, "So, your rude answer means it isn't possible to tunnel to outside the vault."

"Got that right."

"Well, thank you for your—"

"Hold on."

"Yes?"

"Mickey Fraser know about this special project you're working on?"

"Not exactly. It's an Archives initiative."

"I kinda figured. He ain't gonna be happy if he

finds out you're snooping around and poking your nose in security business." A beat. "*His business.*"

Crap.

Chapter Seven

Vindication, maybe

My phone call this morning with Jake Barton bugged me all day. I couldn't get his warning out of my head to stay out of Mickey Fraser's business. Why would Mickey get upset if I could help him uncover a major heist? He should be grateful for my assistance, not angry. Or was Jake trying to dissuade me for other reasons? Personal reasons. I made a mental note to dig deeper into Jake Barton's background.

I scooted back from the kitchen table and stood. "Dinner was great."

Mom beamed. "Thank you. I wasn't sure how that recipe was going to work out. First time I tried the instant pressure cooker."

"You nailed it," Zoe chimed in as she jumped out of her chair.

"Sure did," I added.

Mom turned to my brother, Matt. "Did you like it?"

Matt was two years younger than me and a brainiac. In August, he heads off to college in Cambridge, Massachusetts, on a math scholarship, a fact that kept Dad smiling for a week after he received the notification letter. Matt was also proof positive a distinct tradeoff existed between smarts and common sense.

He shrugged. "Sure, I guess. What was it, pork or something?"

Mom chuckled lightly. "Close. Chicken Pad Thai." Turning to Zoe and me, she said, "What are you two up to tonight?"

I flipped a nonchalant hand. "Not much. Just going to head upstairs and research some stuff."

Zoe's eyes bugged out before narrowing. "Research? Some *stuff*? You're not taking any summer classes."

Mom gave me a questioning look but stayed silent.

"Research is probably the wrong word. I heard about some pretty amazing jewel heists and it got me interested. No biggie. I like reading that kind of stuff."

Zoe folded her arms and cocked an eye at me. "Mmmm hmmm. Sure, you do. Especially after Tuesday's non-event event?"

I peeked over at Mom, who was watching me closely. "Nope, nothing to do with it. Mrs. Majelski told me about them, and it piqued my interest." I broke for the hallway leading to the stairs going up to the bedrooms. "Some fun night reading, is all," I called over my shoulder.

Mauzzy jumped off his recliner in the family room and scampered past. He must have sensed it was his favorite time of night. Bedtime.

Zoe caught up to me in the hall. "Majelski? When?"

I charged up the stairs after Mauzzy, Zoe right behind. "In the parking garage. Last night."

She zipped past on the fourth step and was waiting for me at the top of the staircase. The girl was so wee and jackrabbit-quick, I should have known better than trying to outrace her.

Zoe's eyes were ablaze, rivaling the intensity of the fiery red streaks in her hair. "The old lady is here? In D.C.? Are you serious?"

"Yep. Said she's spending time with her twin sister."

She followed me into my bedroom. "And you believe that shit?"

I sat on my desk chair and spun around to face Zoe, who flopped onto the bed, disturbing an already snoozing Mauzzy. "Why would she lie?"

"For real, Sara? You *know* I don't trust her."

"I also said—"

Zoe thrust her hands at me, palms out. "I know what you're gonna say, and I still don't believe it. I've been telling you for over a year now, there's something about her. She has a knack for showing up right in the middle of shit. I'm just saying."

"You're crazy."

"You should know."

I twisted up my face. "Ha-ha. Hilarious. And that's two dollars for the jar."

Zoe flashed an exaggerated smile, then a look of concern. "What exactly did she tell you?"

I told her everything, sparing no details.

Zoe propped an elbow on her leg, rested chin in hand, and stared at the floor. She blew out hard. "Sh...oot, I can't believe I'm about to say this, because it's going to get you all spun up. But...I mean...she comes up here from Tuscaloosa and tracks you down to a parking garage right after the diamond exhibit shows up here? Which you suspect somebody robbed?

Doesn't that sound suspicious?"

"I admit it's quite odd and I was shocked to see her. But I don't know."

"Why would she care about something she said was 'a silly idea'? I'll tell you why. She's involved, caught wind of your suspicions, and now wants you to think she's available to help so she can keep tabs on you and steer you in another direction if you get too close."

A satisfied smile spread across my face. "You hear what you said?"

Zoe stiffened. "What?"

"You said 'she's involved.' That means you think I'm right and there was a heist."

"No, I didn't…I mean…what I said…" She moaned. "Ah, hell. And before you give me crap about hell, it's in the Bible, so no dollar."

I squeezed my eyes shut and did a fist pump. "Yes."

"All right, reel it in, wise-butt. I'm not convinced you're entirely right, but I'll give you this—something is going on. Why else would Majelski be up here? That's all I'm saying."

I pondered Zoe's question. "How'd she know about my suspicions?"

"Good question. Before she showed up, who'd you tell besides me and your parents?"

"Just Grant. I called him around lunchtime, and she showed up that evening."

Zoe's eyes bugged out. "*Grant*. Seriously?" She jumped off the bed, her arms waving in the air. "Lemme ask a question. Who told you about Majelski's role in that whole mess you got yourself into last year back in Tuscaloosa?"

My mind raced as a prickling sensation crawled across the back of my neck. I sucked in a breath. "Grant."

"And where is he now?"

"Out of town," I murmured.

"Where?"

"Don't know."

"Convenient."

"There's no way—"

"The guy is such a jackwagon. I'm warning you, be careful with those two. They're hiding something."

I slid down in the chair. "Oh my... Grant?"

Zoe sat back on the bed, a joyless smile on her pixie-like face. "Sorry, but it all fits. Hate to say it, but I think you're right. Somebody hit that vault, and it's obvious who. Problem is, how in the heck did they do it?"

Everything she said made sense, per usual, but no way Grant could be involved. Could he? After all, he was a federal agent. And we'd gone through so much together, he deserved the benefit of the doubt. Zoe couldn't be right about him. Could she? Uh-uh, no way. The more I thought about it, the more I liked Jake Barton for the inside man. Mrs. Majelski said the crew had to have advance knowledge of the Carlton's systems. What better inside man than the museum's facility maintenance manager? And if it turns out those keys and wad of money belong to him, then he'll have some explaining to do because he doesn't have access to the main vault. So how did he get in and why?

I pushed any suspicion about Grant out of my mind and sat up. "There's a theory I've been working on."

"Shocker."

"The vault is in the basement. I found out today from the facility maintenance guy its outer wall has dirt on the other side."

"Yeah, so? That's why it's called a basement."

"What if a crew tunneled to outside the vault and drilled into it?"

"From where? And what are they going to do with all the dirt?"

I turned my palms up. "Don't know. Still working on it."

We sat quietly for a minute, staring at the floor.

Zoe's fingers snapping shattered the silence. "Got it. I fricking got it."

"Yeah?"

"Did you know D.C. is built on all kinds of tunnels and stuff?"

"*Really?*"

She leaped off the bed, pacing around the room like a stalking tiger. "I remember reading an article about it when we were still living up here. It's like fricking Swiss cheese under the place. There are tunnels going back to before the Civil War."

"You think there's one connected to the Carlton?"

Her eyes twinkled as her wiry little body bounced around me to the point I was getting dizzy. "There's a website. Search on Washington tunnels."

"Zo, you gotta settle down. You're making me nauseous." I spun around and woke up my laptop. I was typing when my midsection got crushed into the desk's edge. "*Oof.* C'mon, quit shoving me into the desk. Give me some space here."

Zoe came around the side of the chair. "Sorry, I

was having a hard time seeing over your shoulder."

I scanned the search results. "Yeah, but you didn't have to climb up the back of the chair."

"You tall people don't get it. Try being five feet. You'll be climbing up things, too." She pointed to the screen. "Right there—www.WashingtonTunnels.com."

I clicked on the link. "Aptly named."

Zoe leaned in as we both read the home page of Washington Tunnels.

"Oh my gosh," I said, barely containing my excitement. "This has maps for all the tunnels running beneath the city."

"If this doesn't help, nothing will," Zoe muttered, her eyes fixed to the screen.

According to the website, it defined tunnels as "fully walkable passageways" in which adults could stand upright, which was exactly what I was after. I worked through each page of the website, ignoring the Metro subway tunnels because no way a heist crew would attempt traversing those due to the trains and pedestrian traffic. I started with the streetcar map and worked through every map, ending with the pedestrian map. Two showed promise. Sewers and steam tunnels.

I turned my head to Zoe, who was practically cheek to cheek with me. "You read all that?"

"Sure did."

"What'd you think? Sewers or steam?"

"Def steam. Too much water and crap in the sewers."

Letting her obvious comment pass, I clicked on the steam map and scrolled down the page. A map popped up showing three sets of steam tunnels, with one catching my immediate attention. I zoomed in. A long tunnel started at the West Heating Plant near Georgetown and ran south along Virginia Avenue, intersecting with one running along C Street.

With the cursor, I circled the area where the tunnel hit C Street, near the U.S. Department of State. "See this here?"

Zoe's nose was a foot from the screen. "Yeah, what am I looking at?"

"This"—I traced along the C Street tunnel—"is not far from the Carlton." I used the cursor to mark where the Carlton was located on Constitution Avenue with quick tight circles.

"Okay, but there's nothing running from it to the Carlton."

"Not that we know of."

I spun in the chair to face Zoe, my shoulder smacking her torso.

"Hey, thanks for the warning," she exclaimed, rubbing her elbow.

"Sorry. But I've got an idea."

"Not sure that's good or bad."

"What if there's an offshoot to the museum that the people who put this website together didn't know about?"

Zoe scratched the back of her head. "I don't get you."

"The home page said they put these maps together from publicly available maps and *other government sources*. That means they were only working with government documents. What if the Carlton cut a deal with the government to dig their own steam tunnel from the main trunk in exchange for something?"

"Like what?"

"Beats me. It's just an idea."

"A bad idea."

I eyeballed her. "Only one way to find out."

"I'm afraid to ask."

"Exactly. I'm going to ask. Tomorrow."

"Who?"

"Their inside man."

"*What?*"

"You heard me."

Zoe squeezed the sides of her head. "That doesn't sound like a good idea."

I flicked a dismissive hand. "No worries. Got it covered."

"Yeah, that's what's got me worried."

Chapter Eight

The inside man

I rapped lightly on the clear glass of the closed door.

A scruffy balding man glanced up from a gray metal desk strewn with papers and manila folders. "Yeah," he barked.

I opened the door and poked my head into a dingy office, the poster child for disorganization and how not to present a professional appearance. "Hi, Jake. I'm Sara Donovan. We spoke yesterday morning."

"Right."

"Can we talk?"

He smirked. "Depends. Common sense still chasin' after ya?"

One step inside the doorway, I straightened to my full, almost six feet. "Excuse me, but that wasn't funny yesterday and it still isn't today. May I come in?"

Barton stood, a bulging belly hanging over the desk, and waved me in with a chubby hand at the end of a muscular, hairy forearm. "Yeah."

I maneuvered around a tired gray guest chair, faded yellow foam protruding from a sizable tear on the side of the seat cushion. Taking a moment, I put my height to good use and towered over the troll of a man standing behind the desk.

He craned his neck upward, dark flinty eyes locking onto mine.

I held his glare before letting out a slow smile and sitting. "Thank you."

He sat, the elevation of his head barely dropping. "What's this about?"

"I'm curious, how's the museum heated?"

His head pulled back. "You ask strange questions. Still snooping around?"

"If you mean, am I still working on Archive's special project, the answer is yes. After you said there was no place to dig a tunnel from, I found a website on Washington tunnels and it got me thinking."

"Good for you." He finished with a triumphant smile.

We fixed on each other. I pressed my lips tight and dug into him, working my fierce look for all it was worth. All those hours of practice in front of the mirror instead of studying were paying off because I was making the little man uncomfortable. Seconds passed.

He broke eye contact and exhaled. "We use a boiler system. Here in the basement."

My shoulders slumped.

He glanced at me. "Wrong answer?"

"I thought maybe steam was used."

"It is."

I perked up. "Really?"

"The boilers generate steam which is used to heat the building."

"It isn't brought into the building?"

"Not no more."

"But at one time…"

"Years ago, the place was tied into the Fed's central heating system. But it got to be more trouble than it was worth. The guy before me sealed it off and installed boilers."

My pulse quickened. I fought to keep a calm demeanor. "How was steam brought into the building before the boilers?"

"Through a steam tunnel."

I knew it. That had to be how the thieves got outside the Carlton undetected. I just needed to confirm why the steam tunnel wasn't shown anywhere.

"Strange. I found a map of all the steam tunnels under the city," I said. "It didn't show anything connected to the Carlton."

He gave a half-hearted shrug. "Dunno why, 'cause we got one. 'Course, it's all sealed up, but it's there. Tied into a main line running along C Street."

"How did it work?"

"Brought four-hundred-degree superheated steam from a plant by Rock Creek Park. I think it's closed now."

"Where did this steam tunnel attach to the building?"

"Northeast corner."

Seriously, I can barely navigate a parking garage and he's giving me compass directions. I smiled politely. "Which is exactly where?"

Barton spun around in the chair so his back faced me and slid sideways, stopping in front of a dented, putty-colored flat file cabinet four feet high and at least three feet deep. He stood, the chair scooting back a few feet, his head clearing the top by maybe eighteen inches. His finger traced down the labels on each thin drawer, stopping on the fourth. He tugged it open, hauled out a thick three-foot-wide document, slammed the drawer closed, and dropped it onto the paper-covered desk. Thumbing through the pages, which the top page said were architectural drawings, he stopped on one, flipped the set open, and spun it around for me to see. A stubby finger jabbed the drawing. "Right there. Northeast corner."

Leaning over the desk, I studied the drawing where his grimy fingernail pointed to X-marks-the-spot. "And exactly what am I looking at?"

"Basement architecturals."

"Where's the vault?"

With his other index finger, he stabbed at the opposite end of the drawing.

"Pretty far apart, huh?" I asked.

"Can't get no farther. Satisfied?"

Still studying the drawing, I asked, "Does this show electrical wiring and stuff?"

"Nah, that's a different set."

I motioned with my head toward the file cabinet that held the drawings. "They in there, too?"

"Yeah. But they got nothing to do with the steam tunnel."

"Not directly."

"How's that?"

Standing to leave, I looked down at the jerk. "Who has access to those drawings?"

Barton stared up, a wary look on his unshaven face. "Just me and my crew."

"Has anybody else come down asking to review them?"

He scratched his head. "Nope, not really. Maybe

every once in a blue moon, but that's about it."

"What about the contractor doing the renovation work upstairs?"

His beady little eyes glanced off to the right before returning to me. "Yep, didn't think about them."

I fixed on his eyes. "One last thing. Did you lose your keys recently?"

His head snapped back, but he maintained eye contact. "Keys? What keys?"

"Car keys. Work keys. Both."

"There you go with them strange questions again."

"Did you?"

"Why you ask?"

"I found a set of keys in my cubicle."

He let out a short mocking laugh. "They sure ain't mine. I don't got no access to that place."

"Of course, you don't." I gave him a fake smile. "Thanks for your time."

After leaving facilities maintenance, I stopped by the security department and Mickey's office. I tapped once on the open door.

The ginormous security chief looked up from his newspaper. He yanked his feet off the desk and stowed the paper. "Hey, good morning."

"Got a minute?"

He waved me in. "Sure."

I entered the cramped office and settled into one of two ratty black-cushioned guest chairs. "Thank you. Hope I'm not disturbing you."

"Nah, just reading box scores." He read my reaction. "Baseball?"

I let out a nervous laugh. "Ah. Got it. Sports isn't really my thing."

He slurped from a white coffee mug. "Used to be my entire life."

"Really?"

"Yeah, played college football. Lived and breathed it."

"Wow. Where?"

"Rutgers. Played tight end."

A glorious vision of Grant's tight, rounded butt popped into my head. *Focus.*

"New Jersey?" I asked.

"Yeah," he said, a grimace coming over his wide, pocked face. "Could've gone pro. Until a cheap hit to the knee ended my career before it started." He stared with a rueful smile into the mug. Another slurp.

"Hey, you find out who those keys and money belonged to?"

He looked up. "Yeah. Tony Carlucci. Left them when he was closing the vault Wednesday night."

"Tony? How'd they get in my cubicle?"

"Said he was on his way out when the cell in his pocket rang. To get to it, had to take his car keys and cash out. He set them down, answered the call, then forgot about them and left. It was after he closed the vault that he realized he left them inside it. Had to take a cab home. Cost him over fifty bucks."

"And you believe him?"

"Of course, I do. No reason not to. Now, what can I do for you?"

I thought about pushing the issue, but a quick read of Mickey's face said that was a bad idea. "I was talking with Grant the other day—"

He threw a meaty hand out. "I'll tell you what I told him. That theory of yours, as he called it, is flat-out wrong. The exhibit remains one hundred percent secured."

I shifted in the chair. "I'm sure it is—now."

Mickey's eyes narrowed under unruly eyebrows. "Didn't he tell you I said it was best if you left it alone because nothing happened?"

"Um...yes, but I have an idea on how they might have done it."

"Steal the Star of Midnight?"

"Uh-huh."

"Who's they?"

"I don't know."

"How'd they get in the case?"

"Don't know."

An amused look came over Mickey's face. "But you know how the diamond was stolen."

"I have an idea."

The security chief leaned back, the chair groaning in protest. "Humor me."

"First, can you call Jake Barton down here? And ask him to bring the drawing he showed me."

Mickey studied me. "Drawing?"

"The one he showed me. Five minutes ago."

He crossed his arms on the desk and leaned forward. "Now why would he be showing you a drawing of..."

"The basement."

He squinted at me. "Our floor...the vault?"

"Mmmm, yes and no."

With his eyes still trained on me, he reached for the phone. "You know Grant told me how everything went down in Tuscaloosa last year. Everything."

I placed my hands in my lap. "Well, then I'm sure

you're aware my hunches are usually right."

Another amused smile spread across his face. "Yeah, not always. But I'm gonna hear you out because Grant believes in you." Mickey snatched up the handset and punched in an extension number. "Hey, Jake. Mickey. Can you come to my office and bring the drawing you showed to Sara Donovan?" He listened, his head nodding slightly. "Yep, understood. Just come on down. Thanks." He dropped the handset into the cradle. "He's not your biggest fan."

With a forced smile, I said, "He's a rude little man."

Mickey took a hit of coffee. "Sounds like the feeling is mutual."

A few uncomfortable minutes of silence later, the gnomish Jake Barton barged into the office, dumped the thick set of drawings on the desk, and plopped into the chair next to me. "I told her she was making a mistake getting up in your business."

The security chief raised a hand. "No worries." He gestured to me. "Okay, it's your show."

"As you know, I think the Star of Midnight was stolen while still in the vault before the exhibit moved to the Gem and Minerals Hall. I believe it—"

Barton interrupted. "Hold on. What's this all about? She told me she was working on a special project for Archives. Something about security soft spots."

Mickey gave me a questioning look. "Special project?"

I winced. "He put me on the spot."

"And that's the best you could come up with?" he asked in amusement.

That elicited a howl of laughter from Barton.

I wasn't about to give them more fodder for their entertainment, so I stayed silent and stared back at the grinning giant sitting across the desk from me.

After a few seconds, Mickey spoke up. "Okay, so you think the diamond was stolen when it was in the vault. That means a window of maybe three hours to get into the vault before the exhibit moved, then into the display case, and back out, all without setting off any alarms."

"Not if they already had a way into the vault," I countered.

"There's only one way in," Mickey said.

Barton groaned.

I sat up straight. "I believe they drilled into the vault from the back. From the outside."

Mickey shook his head. "Impossible. Besides, the sound and vibration sensors would have picked up any drilling."

"Not if they worked at night," I said.

"Come again?" Mickey asked.

"You've been keeping those sensors off because of the night renovation work," I replied.

The security man stared at me. "True. But not the motions and cameras."

"Are they powered from the electrical system?" I asked.

"Yeah," Barton chimed in. "But before you get going on that power outage thing, that's why we got them diesel generators as backup. The longest them motions and cameras would be out is one minute."

"He's right," added Mickey. "Besides, drilling through the three-foot wall won't get you anywhere.

Lining the interior behind the shelving are two three-inch steel plates sandwiching a copper alloy plate designed to disperse heat. That means you can't cut through it with an acetylene torch."

I turned to Barton. "Can you please find the basement drawing you showed me?"

He stood, combed through the drawings, stopped on one, and spun the set around for Mickey to see. "I s'pose you want me to explain about the steam tunnel?"

"Please," I said.

Barton sat and explained to Mickey the network of steam tunnels running beneath the city and how the Carlton was once connected to a main line. "But that was sealed off a long time ago," he concluded.

Mickey pored over the drawing. "The vault is at the opposite end of the building from the steam tunnel termination. Is there anything that connects it to outside the vault?" he asked Barton.

"Nope," came his clipped reply. "That's what I tried telling her. Just dirt all the way 'round."

"They entered the steam tunnel from somewhere," I said. "Probably the old heating plant by Rock Creek Park. From there they traveled through it to the museum, then tunneled from there to outside the vault."

"That's easily a three-hundred-foot tunnel," Mickey said, staring at the drawing. "That would take months to dig."

"They're determined thieves," I said. "After seeing that diamond, I can see why."

Mickey shook his head. "You're missing the point. We only found out two weeks ago that the exhibit was coming here."

I stuck a finger out. "*You're* missing the point.

What if the crew knew all along the exhibit was coming to the Carlton?"

"Impossible," Mickey retorted. "The plan was never for it to come here. It was supposed to go to the National Museum."

I gave him a sideways look. "Maybe that was Bancroft and Culpeper's plan." A beat. "But not the crew's plan."

Mickey furrowed his brow. "You're not making sense."

"Why was the decision made to bring the exhibit here?" I asked.

"Because the insurance company balked at it going to the National Museum."

"Why?" I prodded.

"Fire at an electrical junction box impacted some of its security systems," Mickey replied.

"You think that was a coincidence?" I asked.

He hesitated. "It's under investigation. Don't know what they've found."

"And why did the exhibit come here versus another local museum?"

Mickey rubbed his chin, his eyes scrutinizing me. "Because the Carlton was the backup site."

"When was the decision made to make it the backup?" I asked.

"Couple years ago, when Bancroft and Culpeper put together the tour. I wasn't here, but I believe it was their insurance company that selected the Carlton's proposal."

"So, it's been known for several years it would be the backup if something happened with the primary site?"

Mickey recoiled. "Hold on. Are you saying that fire was set on purpose?"

"I am."

He gripped the edge of the desk and stuck his neck out. "That is an *outlandish* suggestion. Do you realize your theory is implying it's an inside job?"

"I do."

I took a peek at Jake Barton. His eyes were flitting all around the room.

Chapter Nine

A curveball?

Danielle and I left the cafeteria following an early lunch since, for whatever reason, Fridays always drew a large crowd. And fortunately, after my little dustup with Mickey, the rest of this morning was uneventful, meaning he hadn't ratted me out to Boss Lady. Yet.

I pressed the call button for the elevator. "I can't believe it's Friday."

Danielle flashed a sly smile. "Somebody wishing it was Wednesday?"

"It's just not the same in the cafeteria."

She giggled. "Without what's-his-name?"

"I'll get his name next week."

"His *doctor's* name?"

"Ha-ha, very funny." The elevator arrived and we got into the car. "Let's hit the *Fire and Ice Exhibit* on the way back down to the vault."

"Sure. Hey, where did you go this morning?"

"Facilities maintenance and then security."

She screwed her face up. "Those are two strange departments for you to hit."

"I was following up on a few things."

The doors opened to the lobby and as we stepped out, a gorgeous, well-dressed guy from Human

Resources whom we refer to as Gentleman Hottie passed us and got in the elevator. As the doors closed, Danielle tossed him a wave, to which he responded with a smile of perfect white teeth.

"Man, he smelled so amazing," Danielle swooned.

"Haven't heard you talk about him lately."

"I've seen him around a few times. All I do is stare at his butt."

"Understandable," I said.

"Although I did swing by his cubicle last week."

"You didn't tell me. How'd it go?"

Danielle giggled. "I asked if he wanted any of my crackers."

"Way to put yourself out there."

"I got a little flustered."

"You think?"

"And he didn't take any."

Fanning myself, I said, "Oh my God, he's good-looking *and* wealthy."

Danielle grinned. "That's my read, too."

We entered the Gem and Minerals Hall and approached the exhibit. I put a hand on her arm. "Hold on. Let's wait until those people move away. I want to show you something."

She stopped. "I'm intrigued."

When the crowd cleared, I brought up on my phone the photos I took earlier of the diamond in the vault. "Let's go."

We got to the exhibit and took in the Star of Midnight.

"I can't believe how big it is," Danielle said. "It's so perfect and beautiful."

"No, it isn't," I said matter-of-factly.

She looked at me like I was a whack job. "What are you talking about? The other day, you were gushing over it when we were in the vault."

"Back then I thought it was perfect and beautiful, too."

"And three days later it suddenly isn't?"

I lowered my voice. "That's because that"—I pointed at the Star of Midnight—"isn't this." I showed her the photos on my phone.

She took the phone and stared at it. "What are you talking about?"

"Look at that pic, then look at the Star of Midnight in the case."

"What am I looking at?"

I leaned over and traced along the base of the diamond in the photo. "This is of the real diamond. I took this when we were inside the vault on Tuesday."

Danielle gasped. "You were told no pictures."

"Nobody saw. Now look, see how the bottom edges are both perfectly rounded. They're symmetric. A flawless pear shape."

"Got it."

"Now look at the one in the case. See how those edges aren't rounded enough compared to the pic? It's not quite pear-shaped."

Her eyes shifted back and forth between the photo and the display case. "They're the same. It's just some lighting thing."

"Nope, you're wrong. They're different."

She handed the phone back. "What are you saying?" she whispered.

"The Star of Midnight was stolen and replaced with a fake."

Danielle's eyes bulged. "Holy…have you told anybody?"

"Several people. That's part of what I was doing this morning at security."

"What'd they say?"

"That I'm crazy. Pssh. No biggie. I'm used to it."

"What are you going to do?"

"Get enough evidence to prove I'm right and get Mickey to do something." An elderly couple approached the exhibit. "C'mon, let's get outta here."

****

When we got back to the vault, I quickly finished up inventorying and categorizing Oliver Carlton's correspondence with Thomas Edison. Since both were inventors and scientists, their conversations were full of techno geek-speak. In fact, the museum's namesake and benefactor was a prolific writer of correspondence. A social influencer ahead of his time. No doubt if he were alive today, the man would spend his every waking minute texting and posting.

As I worked, I ran through this morning's conversations with Jake Barton and Mickey. They sure weren't impressed with my tunnel theory, but I know that's exactly how the thieves got into the vault. Because I know it was robbed. And since it was robbed, a tunnel was dug to do it. Obvious. And this weekend I was going to find that tunnel, show it to Mickey, and then vindication will be mine.

I returned the correspondence to the valuables vault and picked up the Last Will and Testament of Oliver G. Carlton. It was a single page framed in a protective glass that stated the Oliver G. Carlton Museum of the Arts and Sciences would receive the balance of his considerable estate and all his papers and journals, including his property in North Carolina. What fascinated me about the simple document was how it ended. There were no words but rather a series of different types of grids full of characters and symbols. According to Boss Lady, over the years, the Carlton spent considerable effort reaching out to cryptologists for assistance in determining the meaning, if any, of the odd markings. Nobody was successful, so it was unknown if there was a hidden message in the strange symbols, or if it was simply an eccentric rich genius who had an interest in cryptography having a little fun with his beneficiaries.

I glanced out the closed day gate to make sure nobody was watching. Satisfied the coast was clear, I whipped out my phone and snapped off several pics of the grids before setting the framed document back in its special place on one of the steel shelves at the back of the vault. Then I braced myself for the most mind-numbing part of my job. Conducting a monthly inventory of Carlton's journals, which numbered well over one thousand books, because the will stipulated such an inventory in no uncertain terms. Other than Carlton's directive, it made no sense because nobody could remove them from the vault. Not even in September, after construction of the reading room was completed as part of the main floor renovation. The will explicitly stated qualified researchers could have access to his papers *except* for his journals, which were to remain locked in the vault forever. As part of the inventory, there was also specific paperwork I completed for Boss Lady to sign and submit to the museum's Board of Trustees. Every dang month.

Tugging on white linen gloves and with a clipboard in hand, I stepped over to the far left of the shelves. Each three-foot shelf stuffed with leather-bound books had a number range in increments of thirty-six printed on white tape adhered to the front edge of the shelf. Taking the first journal off the shelf, I opened the cover and confirmed it was indeed—journal one. Replacing it, I marked it off on the paperwork and moved on to the next one. Yep, journal two confirmed. On to the next. Three. Four. Five. Seven?

I did a double take.

The gap between journals five and eight appeared too large, like somebody took number six. I replaced seven on the shelf and checked the next journal, hoping I misplaced six during last month's inventory. Nope, it was eight. A quick check of last month's inventory paperwork showed no journals missing. But not now. This was my third monthly inventory, and the first time a journal went missing. A fluttery feeling attacked my body as the air in the vault grew stale. My chest tightened. Was I going to get blamed for losing journal six? Of course, I was going to get blamed. And then fired.

You got this, Sara. Deep breaths. There's a logical explanation.

The breathing worked. With nerves sufficiently calmed, I forged ahead with the inventory, hoping it would turn up in the process.

Four hours and one thousand four hundred twenty-two journals later, it had not turned up. Worse yet, journals twenty-eight and four ninety-six were also missing. And for these other two missing ones, there was the same thin gap between the books, like each had been removed. I searched the entire vault. All the shelves. All the unlocked drawers. Nothing. I went back to the three gaps in the line of journals and rechecked the books on both sides of each gap. Nope. They were the correct ones.

Why does this crap always happen to me? The perspiration machine went into overdrive. What do I tell Boss Lady? I paced around the vault, running through my options. Should I even tell her? Maybe I submit the paperwork for her signature and see if she notices three books are missing? But if I keep quiet and she notices, I'm so fired. Or I can kick the can down the road and mark them as being present, and then quietly tear the place apart over the next month. Too many options. My brain hurt.

I blew out, tucked the clipboard under my arm, exited the vault, and plodded to Boss Lady's office. Ringing in my head was a fricking death knell, a clamorous sound I was all too familiar with, sadly. She was on the phone, but before I could make my escape, she saw me, signaling to come in and sit. My stomach lurched as today's tuna salad threatened to make a reappearance. I eased into the office and slipped into a chair.

"No, you listen to me," she growled into the phone. "That's your problem. I'm tired of the excuses. My reading room better be completed by September fifteenth or I'll see to it the Carlton takes every punitive action available to it, including assessing liquidated damages. Am I clear? Good." She slammed the phone down and regarded me. "Contractors are all alike. It's never their fault." She spotted the clipboard on my lap and extended a hand. "Is that my journal inventory?"

I gave her the clipboard with the paperwork. "It is…but…"

Her face tightened. "But what?"

"Um, well, there might be a *slight* problem."

Boss Lady drummed her fingers on the desk. "Problem?"

"Just a"—I pinched my thumb and index finger together—"slight one. Three journals *might* be missing."

She scanned the top page on the clipboard, then flipped to the next. "*Might* be missing?"

My shoulders sagged. "I looked everywhere in the vault, but they're not there."

"I see number six is unaccounted for. And twenty-eight." She flipped a few more pages. "I don't see the third."

"Four ninety-six."

"Ah, yes, I see it." She placed the clipboard on the desk and fixed a stare on me. "These are random numbers. Any thoughts?"

I shook my head.

She folded her hands on the clipboard. "This simply will not fly with the Board. Find those journals."

"I'll do my best."

"If that includes finding them, perfect."

I bit my lip. "That's the plan. When do you have to submit the paperwork?"

"In one week."

"Yes, ma'am."

She put the clipboard in a drawer and picked up the phone. "Keep me posted."

Back at my cubicle, I considered the situation. Boss Lady said the missing journals appeared random.

Fortunately, all the journals were digitized so I could go through the ones in question and see if there was a connection between the three. If there was, it might explain their disappearance and get me out of Boss Lady's crosshairs. If there wasn't, I would only be unemployed for one month before classes resumed.

I logged into the system and accessed the still-growing digital archives of the Oliver Carlton Papers. Although the journals could never be seen by researchers, the Board of Trustees made a decision some time ago to include them as part of the digitization process to ensure there was a duplicate set of the books in case of a disaster occurring in the vault.

I brought up journal six and attempted to read the first page, but quickly realized this was going to be harder than I thought. The man's handwriting was over-the-top flamboyant, with all kinds of loops and swirls and flourishes. As I struggled through the first few pages, it became painfully apparent Oliver Carlton was a man of infinite detail. He was also extremely boring. I clicked through the pages, searching for anything that appeared different. In other words, something not boring. After a mind-numbing read, following the very fricking last page, I found a smaller blue-lined page with four lines of block letters that spelled nothing, plus in three places an X or asterisk was placed above a letter.

It appeared he wrote the nonsensical lines of letters on a separate piece of paper he stuck at the back of the book. For someone as detailed and precise as Oliver Carlton, these lines of characters were the opposite of the man. There was nothing else on the page. I brought up journal twenty-eight. This time, before the journal's first page, the same type of lettering showed up on the same type of lined paper. Again, it appeared to have been placed there by Carlton.

To make sure that was the only strange page in the journal, I reluctantly continued through it, reading his stirring observations of birds and plants and other boring crap, until I hit the final page. Other than the first page, there was nothing else unusual. I brought up journal four ninety-six. Despite the incredibly dry subject matter, I found myself holding my breath with each click of the mouse. And in the middle of the book, I found it. Yet another smaller page of lined paper with the same type of lettering and nothing else.

I took a deep breath and combed through the rest of the book but found no more pages of cryptic nonsense. To confirm the three journals were somehow connected, I brought up ten other random ones and went through the same process of checking every page. None had anything remotely similar to the series of letters and characters I found in the three missing journals. I went back to the three strange pages, printed each, and shot back from the desk to—

Crash.

"*Hey.*"

"Sorry, Victoria," I called back over the cubicle as I hot-footed it for the printer to retrieve the copies before anybody saw them. Returning to my desk, I laid the pages out side by side and studied each. The characters were similar but different. This was not a coincidence. These bizarre pages proved the disappearance of the journals was not random. Somebody took them. Somebody—

Tingling exploded throughout my body.

Maybe the Star of Midnight wasn't what was stolen.

Chapter Ten

Something stinks

Last night was a restless one, and for once, it wasn't Mauzzy's fault. I tossed and turned because I couldn't get the missing journals out of my mind. And the strange writing on the papers I found in the digitized versions. That couldn't be a coincidence. Was it possible they were stolen instead of the diamond? Impossible. The Star of Midnight on display didn't match the pics on my phone. I knew the stone was stolen and replaced, but what if—both the journals *and* the diamond were stolen? And if so, why? What's the link between some old writings of an eccentric genius and one of the largest diamonds in the world? It made no sense. But was it a possibility?

After my conversations with Mickey and Jake Barton yesterday, and my mental gymnastics all night, Saturday morning couldn't get here soon enough because I had a full day planned. But the day started like every other one. A battle of wits.

"C'mon, Mauzzy. Just do it. My coffee is getting cold."

Sweet Handsome zig-zagged across the grass, his needle nose to the ground, sniffing up a storm. I read somewhere that dogs sniffing everything was their doggy newsfeed, so to Mauzzy he was out reading the morning newspaper. As I followed him across the lawn, I spied a battered red pickup parked across the street and two houses down. Somebody sat behind the wheel but ducked out of view before I could make the person out.

Mauz merrily worked his way back toward the street, pausing at a sapling. He sniffed and turned sideways in preparation to do the deed. Another sniff, followed by another sideways turn, followed by—him moving on.

"*Mauzzy*." I tugged at the retractable leash and clicked on the lock button, setting the line taut. "It's now or never."

He casually turned and sized me up. Then sat.

I hissed. "Seriously? You're pulling that move again?"

He scratched behind his ear and looked away toward the house. After a few seconds, he angled his head back and took a peek at me out of the corner of his eye.

"Fine," I huffed, turning to head inside. "You win."

The leash went slack. I glanced over my shoulder. Mauzzy trotted over to the sapling, his nose high in the air. Triumphant. He stopped at the wee tree, lifted a leg, and let it rip.

"You couldn't do that before? Now suddenly it's the right spot?"

Mauzzy didn't respond. He just pranced right past, leading *me* toward the front steps, a sly grin plastered on his mug.

I fell in line behind the devious dachshund. "Whatever."

We climbed the steps and entered the house as Zoe bounced down the stairs wearing black running shorts and a neon-green tank.

"Sure you don't wanna go on a run?" she asked, ending with a mischievous smile.

"Ha-ha. Very funny."

"Just asking."

I unleashed Mauzzy, who skedaddled upstairs, no doubt off for naptime on my pillow. "You only wanna see if this time I can make it to the end of the block before falling."

She snickered and jetted out the front door. "The thought crossed my mind," she called over her shoulder. "See ya."

I stuck my head out the door. The pickup blew past the house, but a ballcap pulled low over the driver's face kept me from making out any features. I filed it away in my head, proceeded into the kitchen, and retrieved my cold coffee from the kitchen table. Mom and Dad were in the family room each reading a section of the newspaper.

Mom looked over at me. "We'll be leaving soon for the beach."

"I hope you have good weather."

"Me, too," Mom said. "But if it rains, we can sit on the balcony and enjoy the ocean."

Leaning up against the island, I let out an envious sigh. "That's so cool you got an ocean suite. Hey, what about Zoe?"

"What about her?" Mom replied.

"She's been riding to work with Dad. She won't have a ride for next week."

Without putting his paper down, Dad said, "I told

her she can use my car since it has the base access sticker."

"Wow, Dad, you're letting her drive your prized jeep?"

"Of course not. I said my car. It has the sticker."

I took a gulp of ice coffee. "Oh. I was going to say. But still, pretty nice of you."

"No other option. I'm hoping she has better driving habits than my daughter."

A loud clunk sounded as my coffee mug hit the island a little harder than intended. "Hey. What do you mean by—"

Mom jumped in. "What do you have planned today?"

"Nothing much. Just a little research and maybe later I'll take Mauz to the park."

Dad snapped the paper into his lap and twisted around toward me. "Research? Sara, what's going on?" His tone, full of suspicion.

An apprehensive look crossed Mom's face.

"Pssh, nothing to worry about," I said.

"That's precisely what has me worried," Dad replied, eyeing me hard.

A brilliant idea popped into my head. I brought the photos of the strange grids from Carlton's will up on my phone. "Hey, Dad. You work with codes and stuff, right?"

"You might say that," he said warily.

I moseyed over to where he sat. "Look at these pics. What do you think it is?"

Dad took the phone and studied the photos before looking up. "Where'd you take these?"

"They're at the end of Oliver Carlton's will. My

boss says a number of cryptologists couldn't crack it and so the museum stopped trying, chalking it up to Carlton's famed eccentricity. So, what do you think?"

He enlarged a picture and squinted at it. "This is a type of pigpen cipher. Some call it a masonic cipher."

I wrinkled my nose. "Sounds disgusting. Why pigpen?"

He held the phone for me to see the pic and using his pinky, pointed to some of the symbols. "Notice how almost every symbol and dot has at least two lines around it?"

"Like a... Holy crap, I get it," I blurted. "It's like a fence is around the symbol. A pigpen."

"Exactly." He held the phone close to his face. "Its origins go back to at least the Knights Templar days during the Crusades. The Freemasons also used the method. Only, there's a level of sophistication with this one I've never seen before with pigpens. It's an extremely unusual variant using some symbols without any bordering lines. Like a key or something is needed to unlock the thing."

"Can you solve it?"

He stared at the phone. "Doubtful. I'll need a key or some additional information."

"Can you at least try?"

"If others have tried and couldn't, why do you think I can?"

I shrugged. "I don't know. Maybe because you're my dad?"

He cracked a smile. "Appreciate the confidence. I'll give it a try this week."

Mom frowned. "Thanks, Sara."

"Sorry, Mom. It can wait until you guys get back."

He handed me the phone. "Go ahead and send the photos to me. Now"—he trained his eyes on me—"tell me about this research."

With a casual brush of my hand, I downplayed it. "Like I said, nothing to worry about. Just some Oliver Carlton stuff."

I made a fast retreat for the hallway and flew up the stairs before the man commenced the interrogation. In my bedroom, I powered up the laptop and revisited the Washington tunnels website. Mickey made a valid point yesterday about the tunnel length if they started from the steam tunnel. In addition to the time required to dig a three-hundred-foot tunnel, that length raised many other issues, including where to put all the excavated dirt. There had to be another way in for the thieves.

If the steam tunnel wasn't it...I clicked on the sewer map button. A layout of the city appeared with teal-colored sewer lines traced on it. Scrolling through the page, I read the history of the sanitation network in D.C. going back to 1800 when Congress first moved to the city. It was fascinating, and more than a bit disgusting. Further down the page—score—was a picture of a huge brick-lined tunnel with raised walkways on both sides above a trench filled with water. A barrel ceiling easily fifteen feet at its apex lorded over the walkways and trench. The brick walls and ceiling were splotched with white plaster, apparent patches of prior leaks. The tunnel was called a sewer interceptor, and the city built a vast network of them between 1890 and 1910 to handle sewage and stormwater runoff. As I read, my excitement grew. These tunnels were anywhere from ten feet wide to over thirty feet and were so big a truck could navigate them during dry weather. If I could find an interceptor running by the Carlton, then this was it. I found their way in.

I focused on a long line cutting straight across the city, running along the northern edge of the Mall. "Look at that, Mauz. It sure seems like one of those things runs from the Potomac right along Constitution past the Carlton."

Mauzzy, stretched out on my pillow, raised his head and leered at me. Apparently, he took offense to my waking him. He laid his head back down, rolled over, and sighed. Seconds later, he was back to snoring.

Each interceptor ended with something called a sewer outfall. It was either a circle or semi-circle of the tunnel emptying into the Potomac River or other water sources like Rock Creek. The rest of the page addressed an ongoing project to modernize the sanitary system and reduce pollutants flowing into the Anacostia and Potomac rivers. Those new tunnels under construction wouldn't interest the thieves because too many people would be in them on a daily basis. But these old interceptors showed promise.

The thieves needed a remote entry into the network in order to move their equipment into the interceptor without being noticed. No way they could climb down through a manhole because to cut into the vault, they needed some kind of big drill with a power source, plus digging tools like shovels and pickaxes, and wheelbarrows. And probably wood or something for bracing. Way too much stuff to lower down through a manhole on a sidewalk or street.

I zeroed in on the outfalls. The ones emptying into the Potomac and Anacostia rivers required a boat to gain access, so I quickly ruled those out. According to the website, there were twenty-three throughout the sprawling Rock Creek Park, which raised some possibilities. I zoomed in on the map. A line ran through northwest D.C. along a portion of Piney Branch Creek, a short tributary of Rock Creek at the southernmost end of the park. It cut south through the city, eventually linking with the major line I found running along Constitution past the Carlton. After a little more digging, I discovered four outfalls along Piney Branch Creek.

As much as I hated the idea of investigating nasty sewer outfalls on a hot July day, it had to be done. But I wasn't about to walk into the belly of the beast unprepared. Rummaging through a dresser drawer, I snagged an old swimming nose clip and stuck it in my backpack. Since I was going into the field, taking a backpack was more appropriate than my purse. I transferred the contents of my purse to the backpack, including keys, pepper spray, latex gloves, first aid kit, small water bottle, four packs of crackers, external phone battery, and my OCD Tissue System (patent pending by Sara Donovan). The system consisted of a gallon-sized freezer bag for its heavy-duty construction and served as the "container of containers", holding two smaller sealable plastic bags. One was sandwich-sized, stuffed with clean tissues and a full travel-sized bottle of purple hand sanitizer. The second was a quart-sized freezer bag, again for its heavy-duty construction, to hold the grody used tissues. Proper Sara Donovan biohazard disposal procedures called for a replacement of this second bag in its entirety at the end of each day. Or worse, earlier, if it was full before the end of the day.

I checked the two travel-sized hand sanitizers attached to the backpack's strap and threw a third bottle into it. After all, I was investigating—ugh–sewer tunnels. I paused. Good lord, for this mission I was going to need an entire box of resealable bags to protect the backpack's contents for when I inevitably fall into the creek.

Hmmm. Fall into the creek.

After tossing in an extra pair of socks, I spent five minutes enclosing everything in sealable bags. Except for my phone. No choice but to risk it being unprotected so I could quickly make a call if trouble came knocking. Which was highly likely.

Unprotected phone around water?

I opened a small square box sitting on the desk's back corner with my handwriting scrawled across the top of the box. *Emergency Cell Phone Repair Protocol.* It contained several large medicine bottles full of gel silica packets and two one-pound bags of rice. I took one bottle and a bag of rice and shoved them into the backpack.

With the field kit fully assembled, I took my butterfly-embossed rain boots from the closet, slung the backpack over one shoulder, and roused Mauzzy. "Let's go to the park, Sweet Handsome."

Without lifting his head from the pillow, Mauzzy considered me out of one eye. He was having none of it. He knew something was up.

I scooped up my reluctant roomie. "Sorry, but no way I'm leaving you here to torment Dad before he heads out for his anniversary vacation."

At the bottom of the stairs, we were met by him.

"Research, huh? Where you off to with those boots? It's not supposed to rain."

"Thought we'd take a nice drive to Rock Creek Park. Aren't they calling for afternoon thunderstorms?"

His eyes narrowed. "Supposed to be clear all day. Why are you driving all the way there? Quiet Waters Park is five minutes away."

I played it cool. "Just something different."

"You're up to something. I smell it."

The man was good. *Real* good. If he only knew how close he was to the truth.

I gave him a warm smile and opened the door. "Nope. Just off to catch some sunshine and fresh air. Enjoy the beach."

As the door closed, Dad's voice raised. "That's my point. You don't—"

Before the man could come out and chase me down, I sailed across the front walk to the driveway. Jumping into the scarred hatchback, I nestled Mauzzy in his milk crate stuffed with pink blankets, dropped the backpack on the floor in front of him, fired up the engine, and blasted out onto the street. An hour later, we were cruising along Beach Drive through beautiful Rock Creek Park. I swung onto Park Road and parked at the tennis courts. Piney Branch Creek was less than a half-mile away.

Before getting out of the car, I replaced my shoes with the boots and opened the door. Immediately, I was walloped in the face by the oppressive heat and humidity. And it was only noon. The best was yet to come. I leaned over, grabbed the backpack from the floor, and turned back to the open door. As I got out of the car, the backpack briefly got caught on something behind me, but when I gave it a good yank, it broke free.

And so did the rearview mirror.

Apparently, a strap got hooked on it and my heave-ho ripped it off the windshield and onto the floorboard. But I wasn't upset. I've been there before, although the rearview mirror was a new casualty. Nothing a half roll of duct tape wouldn't fix when I get back home.

I circled around to the passenger door, leashed up an excited Mauzzy, and off we went. After a ten-minute sweaty march along Park Road, we arrived at Piney Branch Creek. We worked our way along the top of the creek's bank, fighting through unruly vegetation while searching for the outfalls. Mauzzy loved it, sniffing every dang tree and bush along the way. Me, not so much.

The creek itself was shallow, maybe four to five inches. The first outfall was easy to spot. And smell. An immense black wall extended out of the foliage, rising over the creek like a malignant spirit. In front of the wall, a crumbling concrete pad stretched between both banks with weeds growing out of cracks and muddy creek water dribbling over it. I put on the nose clip and we continued on. As we neared the outfall, the wall was a steel plate or panel covering the entrance to the tunnel. And running along the bank, down into the water, over the concrete pad, and up to the steel plate, were heavily rutted tire tracks. There were so many, they had to be from multiple vehicles.

I inched down the steep bank and into the water, grateful for the boots and praying there wasn't a hole in one of them. The leash went taut. I glanced to my right. Mauzzy's head was lowered as he fought to back up the hill. With a groan, I returned to the bank, reeled in a reluctant Mauzzy, and picked him up.

"Sorry about that, Handsome. I've got boots on and you don't."

His little pink tongue flicked across my chin, thanking me for considering his situation.

I eased back into the water, and after a few careful steps, stood on the concrete pad. With only an inch or so of water running across it, navigating toward the steel plate was much easier than sloshing through the creek. With my free arm, I brushed hanging branches out of the way and got up close to the black monstrosity. Painted across it in dancing white letters outlined with red and green was the word *AMORE*. The oversized letters were easily my height and had a raised line of some kind running up the *A*, across the top of the word, and then down the *E*. Like a door frame. I moved in closer. It appeared to be weld lines, like somebody cut a hole in the plate and then welded the cut piece back in place. Since the graffiti covered the weld lines, it told me the plate was welded first and later someone tagged it.

I took a few steps back, worked my phone out of the backpack's side pocket, and snapped some pics of the plate. Taking care not to dump Mauzzy into the mud and water, I bent and examined the tire tracks. Each was wide with a distinctive tread. Not like a car. More like from an ATV or something similar. I took more pictures and stood, my eyes following the tracks straight into the steel plate. They ran right up between the weld lines as if someone drove the vehicle—through an opening. Returning to the plate, I pushed in the middle of the two vertical weld lines with my shoulder. It didn't budge.

It was probably a repair job by the city's public works, but something seemed off. The tracks went right up to the plate. If maintenance people drove ATVs to this place to repair it, which was probable given the terrain, they wouldn't park them right up against the very thing they were going to work on. They would park away from it.

I surveyed the area. Other than the tire tracks, there was nothing except for some fallen leaves. And a candy wrapper. I picked it up. It was from a Shazam chocolate bar with hazelnuts. It's a popular candy bar, but the evening the vault was robbed, Tony Carlucci was eating a Shazam with hazelnuts somewhere in the main vault when the blackout occurred. And later, it was his keys and money in my cubicle. Now this wrapper outside the entrance to an interceptor tunnel leading right past the Carlton. Maybe that evening he was in *the* vault.

Chapter Eleven

The Carlton Secret

My discovery yesterday that three journals were missing from the Carlton Papers nagged at me all day, long after my return from Piney Branch Creek. Those cryptic pages had to be linked to their disappearance because the ten other books I checked had nothing remotely similar. Although, I only checked ten out of one-thousand-plus journals. Could there be additional ones with the same type of nonsensical pages? The idea of going back and checking every single page of every single book made me nauseous, like I was traipsing through Piney Branch Creek all over again.

I jumped on the Internet and searched on Oliver Carlton. All kinds of references popped up. I knew he was crazy rich, but didn't realize how rich. Right before his sudden death in 1888, he gave his longtime butler five twenty-pound gold bars and confided in him he was worth fifty million dollars. A quick check on the Internet said that was worth one-point-four *billion* dollars today. And his will required all land holdings, over two thousand acres, be sold except for Arcadia, his initial twenty-acre plot that included a mansion and chapel where Carlton, his wife, and infant child were interred. All proceeds plus the deed to Arcadia went to the Carlton Museum, with a stipulation the museum must never sell the property. However, the law firm handling the estate only transferred five million dollars to the Carlton plus the deed. This discrepancy created an uproar and was investigated by the museum's Board of Trustees, but nothing was found. The sale of the two thousand acres was handled properly and all the proceeds were included in the transfer.

There was also a mystery surrounding the source of his wealth. He was the son of a blacksmith with no formal education, yet in his early twenties, he started buying land throughout North Carolina's Brunswick County. Carlton always explained his wealth came from a gold discovery he made on Arcadia soon after he purchased the plot. He said he found an interesting twenty-pound rock in the creek running through his property. When he took it to a jeweler to examine, he was told it had gold in it and the jeweler bought it on the spot. Carlton went back to the creek, found more gold nuggets, and began digging out the creek's sediment, which resulted in a large amount of gold. Although this was the main story he told, other times he said he discovered emeralds in a limestone formation on his property.

Despite his explanations, things just didn't add up. I wasn't an expert on gold nuggets, but no way he dug up tens of millions of dollars in gold from a little creek. Presumably by himself, since I could find no corroborating accounts.

I looked up the price of gold in 1888. It sold for a little more than twenty dollars an ounce. If he was telling the truth and got his wealth from gold nuggets, that meant he found over seventy tons of gold. There had to be another explanation.

After more digging into Carlton's background, I

stumbled upon an obscure article theorizing his wealth was linked to the Legend of the *Nuestra Senora de Cadiz*, a Spanish treasure galleon that supposedly disappeared in November 1554 after being separated from its six-ship fleet during a hurricane off the coast of Florida. The overloaded ship was transporting to Spain seventy-five tons of gold and emeralds in seven hundred fifty chests. It was sailing from Cartagena, Colombia, via Havana, when the mainmast snapped and rudder broke off the ship, leaving it to the mercy of the ferocious winds. The last reported sighting from one of the ships in the fleet had it being driven north along the Florida coast. The ship was never found. Legend stated it drifted for days until running aground on the dangerous Frying Pan Shoals near Bald Head Island, after which the captain ordered the treasure be offloaded and hidden until a rescue ship arrived. Using its four dories, it took the crew a month to get the treasure off the ship and transported to the mainland. However, no rescue ship ever showed up and the entire crew inexplicably disappeared, leaving the location of the hidden treasure a mystery. Despite the legend, historians pointed to the fact the ship was never found and dismissed it as just that—a legend. A story. A myth.

I searched on the location of Bald Head Island. It was off the southernmost coast of North Carolina. In Brunswick County. The same county where Carlton bought all his land, including the original twenty-acre plot.

"Bingo, Mauz."

No response. He was too busy sleeping off dinner.

I jumped up and ran down the hall to Zoe's room. She was laying on the bed with headphones on and eyes closed, her fisted hands playing some fierce air drums.

"Zoe," I yelled.

Her right hand emphatically smashed what could only be a cymbal.

Leaning over the bed, I let it rip. "*Zoe*."

She cracked open an eye, hands frozen in midair, before jerking back and ripping off the headphones. "What the—cripes, girl. You scared the living shit outta me."

"Sorry, but you gotta hear what I found."

Zoe sat up, folded her arms, and leaned against the headboard. "I can only imagine."

I sat on the bed and told her everything, starting with the missing journals and finishing with the Legend of the *Nuestra Senora de Cadiz*.

She threw me a condescending smile. "You do realize you're getting carried away with this whole thing and blowing it up into something it isn't?"

I leaned back. "No."

"I thought this was about a diamond heist."

"It was. Still is."

"Then what's all this crap about missing money and treasure and shit?"

"Hey, that's a dollar for the jar."

"Your mom didn't hear me."

"But I did. I let the first one slide because I startled you."

She flicked her hand. "Whatever. Answer the question."

"I don't know what it all means, but I think there's more to the story of Oliver Carlton and his museum."

Zoe shook her head. "I'll give you credit, that interceptor thing might have some merit, but not to steal a bunch of dusty old books full of some geezer's ramblings about birds and trees and the weather. A big…as heck diamond, yes. But that other sh…stuff, no."

I grinned. "Know what I'm thinking?"

Zoe groaned. "Only God knows."

"We take a weekend trip to North Carolina."

Her hands slashed out sideways through the air. "Uh-uh. No way I'm getting dragged into one of your crazy ideas."

"But you said—"

"I know what I said, but if you think I'm wasting a precious weekend sitting in a car with you and Mauzzy for what, ten hours each way, chasing some legend, you're nuttier than I give you credit for."

"It's maybe six, six-and-a-half hours."

"Whatever. Still not going."

I crossed my arms. "What if I found more evidence?"

"Of what?"

"That Carlton found buried treasure from that ship."

Zoe got a smug look. "What happened to your diamond heist? It's like I always tell you, after two days you're on to the next crazy theory."

I chose to ignore her relatively accurate comment. "I haven't dropped that investigation. The Carlton treasure angle is another element of the same investigation. I think they're linked somehow."

Zoe snorted. "Only Sara Donovan can come up with someone going to great lengths, including digging a tunnel, to steal one of the world's largest diamonds and while in the vault on limited time, lifting a few crappy old books from a collection of what, a thousand of them."

"Sure, when you put it that way, it sounds crazy, but you gotta consider everything."

Her eyes grew wide. "Oh, believe me. I have. Everything." She finished with a smirk.

"Very funny."

"Just saying."

I stood, stepped to the door, stopped, and faced Zoe. "There's a connection. I know it."

She picked up the headphones and prepared to put them on. "Tell you what. You find something convincing and I'll go on that trip with you. But until you do, forget it."

"Deal."

Zoe slipped on the headphones and resumed air drumming.

I returned to my room and did a new search on Oliver Carlton, working through the results. Two hours later, I came across an interesting page from the Carlton Museum's website. It was a picture of Carlton's mansion in North Carolina. When Arcadia was transferred to the museum after his death, the Board of Trustees decided to make it available to the public, similar to Mount Vernon and Monticello. At the bottom of the page was a link for Arcadia. I clicked on it and up popped a website featuring aerial footage of the property. It was beautiful, full of lush trees, stone walkways, and colorful gardens. The mansion's architecture was exquisite, built from red brick with white trim, towering paned windows, and high arched doorways. A stone walkway wound through the gardens and past a small pavilion, ending at a chapel built of matching brick with similar arched windows and entryway. There was also an L-shaped white stone stable in the far corner of the property.

I took a virtual tour of the house before exploring the individual rooms' web pages. Each room had its own personality, from vibrant color palettes to rich tapestries and stylish drapes. All had elaborate fireplaces with ornate mantles, hardwood floors, soaring ceilings, and an abundance of light through stately windows. But Carlton's office at www.TheArcadiaMuseum.com/office really grabbed my attention. The expansive floor wasn't wood but pure-white marble with no rugs. In the center of some tiles were black diamond shapes arranged in a geometric pattern. The imposing walls were deep-red mahogany with an intricate sunburst carving within each panel, except for the wall behind the colossal desk, which was the only piece of furniture in the room. There was something strange about that wall's carvings. They were not sunbursts.

After enlarging a photo of the panel, I realized it was a grid comprised of fifteen rows and fifteen columns. When I zoomed in further, the carvings became numbers. According to the website, the strange set of random numbers remained a mystery, despite numerous attempts to unlock its meaning by cryptanalysts, numerologists, and mathematicians. There were no repeating numbers. No apparent patterns. The general consensus was it was some form of cipher.

I stared at the mind-numbing set of numbers.

A cipher?

Hiding a secret message?

I seized my tablet and dashed out of the room. "*Zoe*."

Chapter Twelve

Uncrackable?

I hurtled into Zoe's room, who was still reclined in bed but now reading on her phone. "I found it."

She rolled her head toward me. "Found what?"

"Something to convince you we need to go to North Carolina."

"Doubt it."

I sat on the end of the bed, flipped open my tablet, and brought up the Arcadia website. I clicked on the office page and handed the tablet to Zoe. "Check it out."

She sat up, took the tablet from me, and stared at it. "Nice office. Where's all the furniture?"

"Look closer."

She held the tablet up close and pored over the screen.

"Zoom in on the wall behind the desk."

She expanded the picture. "What the... Are those numbers?"

"Yep. A whole lot of 'em. Fifteen rows and columns."

She continued to scrutinize the tablet. "Is it a matrix?"

"People think it's a cipher."

Her eyes grew wide. "You mean this guy carved a huge coded message into the wall of his office? That's crazy."

"It's certainly weird."

"What's it say?"

"Nobody knows. Hasn't been solved."

"No kidding. How long has it been there?"

"He had it done a year before he died. So, 1887."

Zoe whistled softly. "That's a long effing time. Maybe there's no solution."

"What do you mean?"

"Maybe the old guy wanted to screw with everybody after he was gone. Used a bunch of random numbers to drive people like you all nuts and stuff."

I took the tablet back and looked over the numbers. "I don't know. That's a pretty big effort just for a joke."

"This is why you wanna go to North Carolina?"

"Uh-huh. What if this is the treasure map or leads to it?"

She chuckled. "Nobody has solved this thing for like way over a hundred years and you suddenly think you're going to solve it by going down there?"

"Didn't say I was going to solve it. But it tells me there's more to the Carlton story than people realize."

She pointed to the tablet. "Tell me how those numbers prove the diamond was stolen."

"I can't yet. All the more reason to get down there and see what we can find."

Zoe leaned over and stared down at the numbers on the screen, then slapped my arm. "Let's get the math geek in here. Maybe he can tell us something."

"Great idea."

I fired off a text to my brother.—*What you*

doing?—

    —*Watching a race.*—
    —*Come into Zoe's room.*—
    —*Now? It's Bristol.*—
    —*Kinda important.*—
    —*Sure.*—

"He'll be right in," I said.

Thirty seconds later, Matt appeared in the doorway, leaning up against the frame with his hands in the front pockets of worn jeans. "What's up?"

My brother was the runt of the family with unruly brown hair, pale skin, narrow face, and thin arms. In a word—skinny. Mom was my height, and Dad was well over six feet. Matt topped out at maybe five-nine, even though he insisted he was five ten. Mom said her grandfather was short, so he probably got his height from him. Or lack of it.

"Come over here," I said. "Look at this and tell me what you think."

With hands still stuffed in his pockets, he shuffled over to the bed.

I handed him the tablet. "See that wall carving I've zoomed in on?"

He studied the picture. "Mmmm hmmm. Looks like a bunch of numbers."

"Correct, and no two numbers are the same," I said. "The largest is nine-nine-nine-nine."

"Okay," Matt replied, still staring at the tablet.

"You think those are just random numbers?" I asked.

He shook his head. "Definitely not."

"You sound pretty certain," Zoe said.

He handed me the tablet. "That's because they're

not truly random. And I can prove it."

Zoe tilted her head. "How?"

He looked around the room. "You have a laptop with spreadsheet software?"

"Yeah, but it's not powered on."

I popped up off the bed and headed toward the door. "Mine is. I was just on it."

We tramped down the hall and into my room.

Matt sat at the desk, woke the laptop, and brought up a blank worksheet. He typed in a formula. "How many rows and columns are in that grid?"

"Fifteen by fifteen," I said, looking over his shoulder.

He copied the formula to create the same size grid. "These are properly generated random numbers from one to nine thousand nine hundred ninety-nine. Does anything stand out?"

Zoe and I leaned in toward the laptop.

"That's a whole lotta numbers," Zoe mumbled.

"They're mostly four digits," I said.

"Exactly," Matt said. "Now compare the numbers in the picture to the ones I generated."

I stared at the tablet then back at the laptop. "There are way less four-digit numbers on the wall."

"Bingo," Matt said.

Zoe took the tablet. "Son of a… You're right."

He eased around in the chair and faced us. "Think about it. If you're truly choosing random numbers from one to ten thousand, there are only going to be nine hundred ninety-nine numbers that are three digits or less, but *nine thousand* four-digit numbers. In other words, there's a ninety percent chance a four-digit number will be selected over a smaller one. And the more three-digit or smaller numbers are selected, the higher the improbability they were random. How many numbers less than one thousand are in that wall grid?"

"Seriously, you want me to count them?" I asked.

"Yep. Just proving my point."

"Zoe, count off each row and I'll keep track on my phone."

She worked through each row, calling out the count as I kept the tally on the calculator.

When we finished, Matt asked, "How many?"

"One thirty-three," I said.

"And that proves my point," he said, his voice laced with triumph. "In that fifteen-by-fifteen grid, there are a total of two hundred twenty-five numbers. Of that, one thirty-three are three digits or less. That's around sixty percent of the total numbers when it should be closer to ten percent or around twenty-two numbers. It's a statistical improbability."

"What are you saying?" Zoe asked Matt.

"That those numbers were deliberately chosen and I suspect each has a meaning or reference to something."

I stuck a finger out at Zoe. "There goes your joke theory."

She made a face. "Whatever."

"The website says some experts think it's some kind of cipher, but nobody has been able to solve it," I said.

Matt turned back to the laptop. "I assume you were looking at that website on here."

"Yep. It's minimized."

He brought up the website and stared at the wall picture that was still there from earlier. "No two numbers are alike?"

"That's what it says in the caption. I didn't check it," I replied.

Matt propped an elbow on the desk, chin resting in his palm. After a half-minute of studying the picture, he said, "You know, this could be a book cipher."

"What makes you say that?" I asked.

He spun around to face us. "Because there are no two numbers alike. That's significant. And it could greatly increase the level of security if it's a book cipher and an obscure book was used."

"What exactly is a book cipher?" Zoe asked.

"It's a message hidden in a set of numbers based upon a specific book or document."

"How do you do that?" I asked.

Matt rubbed the back of his neck. "The methods vary quite a bit, but what doesn't is a specific book or document that acts as the encryption key. For example, one of the infamous Beale Ciphers used the Declaration of Independence as the key, which in my opinion was a poor choice because it's a readily available document. The less available the book or document is to people, the stronger the security. The numbers in a book cipher can represent various things. They could be strung together to signify page number, line number, and word number. Or possibly a character number, such as the first or last character in a specified word or line. There are so many different ways to do it."

"What do you think the numbers in the grid mean?" I asked.

Matt grimaced. "If it's a book cipher, that's a tough question to answer without knowing the specific book used. And with those numbers going into four digits, it gets tougher. Ultimately, they would represent words or characters. The problem is not knowing the methodology used to encrypt the message. For example, maybe every other number is a decoy and is skipped. Or every third or fourth number. Or possibly you start at the first number, then the last number, then the second number, and keep rotating between the beginning and end of the cipher until you meet in the middle. There are so many ways to do it, but without knowing the book used, it's uncrackable."

Zoe raised her eyebrows. "Uncrackable?"

"Yup. And if this really is a book cipher, it's a very complicated one."

"Why's that?" I asked. "If you have the book, you have the key, right?"

"True, but like I said, you still have to figure out the system used. And once you do that, with some of those numbers reaching well into the nine thousand range, imagine counting nine thousand words in the key book to get a single word or character for the message, then start counting all over with the next number in the cipher."

"Holy… That would take forever to decode," Zoe said.

"Exactly," Matt said.

"If you're right and this is a book cipher, it would've taken Carlton forever to code his message," I said.

Matt grinned. "Yup, and decoding it would take much longer because you have to figure out the system first."

"You think this coded message is significant?" Zoe asked.

"Highly," he replied.

"Like directions to a buried treasure?" I blurted.

My brother shrugged. "Could be. Or some other secret. The thing I don't get is why carve it into the office wall?"

"Good question," Zoe said.

An idea popped into my head. "What if he wanted it to be found? The cipher. And by carving it into the wall, he's highlighting the significance of it."

"Found by who?" Matt asked.

"I don't know," I said. "Maybe his... Wait, maybe his heirs? The *museum*."

"How do we figure out which book he used?" Zoe asked.

Matt scratched his chin. "My hunch is it's a book in that office, although I don't see any books on the desk. But there could be some in the drawers. Or if he has a library, one of those. But figuring out which one is going to be exceedingly difficult. It could be something near and dear to him, like the Bible, or it could be a dictionary. No way of knowing. And if it's one of those, you also have to know the specific edition. It can't be any old Bible. But whatever is the key, it's gotta be in that house somewhere because that is presumably where he developed the cipher."

I gave Zoe a triumphant smile. "You know what that means?"

"What?"

"*Road trip.*"

Chapter Thirteen

Mickey Fraser

I spent all day Sunday and well into the night reading up on ciphers and codes. Matt was right. There were so many codes and ciphers and variants, I don't know how any ever got cracked. I gained a new appreciation for what Dad did over at the NSA, but no way will I ever admit it. That would be giving him the gift that never stops giving. And I mean—never.

Between me staying up so late, and Mauzzy constantly hogging the pillow throughout the night, I didn't get much sleep. Even after my shower this morning, I was beyond exhausted. Not a good way to start your Monday.

After a quick breakfast of coffee, I stumbled into my bedroom and plopped down at the dressing table. With the coffee not yet kicking in and me running late for work, I put on minimal makeup because I could already feel traffic building up on Route Fifty. But then I decided to make up for my minimalism with some nice perfume. I fished out from a side drawer one of the little samples I got from *Claudine's*. The card that went with it looked pretty earthy so I sprayed it twice onto my neck. And immediately, the fragrance slammed me in the face, which is so not what you want perfume doing. I read the card. *Undeniably the most masculine scent...*

Terrific.

I put on cologne instead of perfume.

Probably should have read the card first.

Ten minutes later, and three layers of skin scrubbed off my neck, I could still smell man musk. So, I got the brilliant idea of spraying perfume, actual perfume, over the remaining man smell. I hit it with dark vanilla and patchouli, thinking maybe the dark scent would meld well with the cologne and make it smell more feminine.

I breathed in.

Nope.

Now I smelled really, *really* weird. Like warm vanilla laced with meth being sold by a flamboyant drug dealer with slicked-back hair, a flowered silk shirt opened halfway to his navel, and bling on top of bling.

Yea, Monday.

I needed to get going or else Boss Lady was going to do her whole Boss Lady Thing on me. Again. Blaming my lateness on traffic clearly only works once with her. I dragged myself over to the bed and leaned down to kiss a lounging Mauzzy. He immediately started sneezing. Right in my face. I guess with my fragrance faux pas, I deserved it.

"Thanks, Mauz." I wiped my face with a forearm. "You have a good day, too."

He yawned, licked his lips, yawned again, and laid his head down on our pillow. The little dude had no conscience. None.

I grabbed my purse, stormed out the door, and down the stairs. Where I ran into Zoe.

"Oof," I grunted.

The accosted pixie shoved me off her. "Geez, girl, slow the eff down."

"Sorry. Late for work."

"I keep telling you to go to bed earlier."

"I meant to but got caught up reading about ciphers."

Zoe glanced up at the ceiling and shook her head. "Don't know why you gotta do that when you got the brainiac around."

"He hasn't agreed yet to go to North Carolina, so I have to get up to speed."

She chuckled. "Trust me. He'll go. He can't pass up exploring that wall of numbers."

"Hope you're right."

Zoe sniffed the air. "What the... What are you wearing? Musk?"

"Had a little mishap."

Another sniff. "No kidding."

I squeezed past. "Gotta get going. Can you take Mauzzy out? I ran out of time."

"Sure."

"Thanks."

"Go to bed earlier or get up earlier," she called after me.

I zipped out the front door and down the walk. Jumping into the hatchback, I fired up the engine and ripped out of the driveway and down the street, all the time praying the traffic gods were kind to me today. For once.

Thirty minutes later, I let loose a few choice words for the traffic gods as my car crept along Route Fifty just before it turned into New York Avenue. I checked the dash clock. Not good. While inching along, I called

115

Grant.

After the same series of strange clicks, he answered on the first ring. "Hey, everything okay?" His tone was one of concern. He knows me well.

"Yeah. Kinda. I guess."

"Uh-oh. I know that response. What have you done?"

"Nothing yet. That's why I'm calling."

I told Grant about my tunnel theory, the network of interceptor tunnels, and the strange black steel plate with the weld lines at the Piney Branch Creek outfall.

"I thought you were going to let this whole thing go?"

I slammed on the brakes. "Whoa, that was close."

"Close?"

"I'm stuck in traffic, and the car in front stopped suddenly."

Grant chuckled. "At least this time it was a near-miss."

I smiled to no one. "I have a history."

"Oh, I'm aware. Okay, back to my question. Why are you still pursuing this supposed heist when Mickey said nothing happened?"

"That's why I called. It's about Mickey."

"What about him?"

"You said I could trust him."

"You can."

"Are you sure, because I'm thinking about talking with him today about what I found at Piney Branch."

"I worked with him my first two years at DHS. I'm positive."

I sucked in a breath and blew out. "If he's involved and I tell him what I know, that'll put me in a bad

116

spot."

"He's no more involved than I am. Trust me."

"I do. That's why I called."

"Good. Talk with Mickey and let's see what he says."

"Okay." I paused. "I wish you were here."

"Me too. Big time."

"When you think you're coming home?"

"Unless we catch a break, which is highly unlikely, not for a few months," he complained. "But you never know."

"Well, be careful."

"Always."

"Thanks, Grant."

"Anytime. Let me know how it goes."

"I will. Bye."

"Bye."

Not long after ending the call, traffic eased, and twenty minutes later, I swiped into the main vault, keeping an eye out for a furious Boss Lady. I stowed my purse, made a cup of coffee, and slipped over to Danielle's cubicle.

She glanced up, relief washing over her face when she saw me. In a whisper, she said, "Where have you been?"

"Traffic. Was Evy looking for me?"

"Not that I know of."

"Guess I'll find out soon enough."

She wrinkled her nose and took two quick sniffs. "What's that smell?"

I raised a hand. "I was tired this morning."

"What'd you do? Smells like you just came out of the woods."

"Accidently sprayed on cologne, then attempted to cover it up with perfume."

"That fits."

My head dropped. "In so many ways."

"It's a Monday."

"Why are Mondays so hard?" I whined. "Like, today Friday is so far away. But on Friday, Monday is lurking so fricking close."

"Right?"

Just then my stomach spoke up, reminding me breakfast only consisted of coffee. The guy two cubicles over always had pistachios or cashews that he let me poach. "Nathan," I yelled. "You have any nuts?"

Nathan stood outside his cubicle talking with a guy I didn't recognize. For a brief moment, he paused, then slowly turned his head toward me.

Oh, God. Don't say it, Nathan. Please don't say anything. Forget I asked.

"I think that's a personal question," Nathan said softly, before turning back to the other guy.

Fricking Monday just kept on giving.

Danielle tipped her head toward the shared wall between our cubicles. "Better get over there before she shows up."

I gave a thumbs-up and darted around the end of the cubicle row to my desk. After a couple hits of coffee, I picked up the phone and called Mickey.

"Security, Mickey Fraser speaking."

"Good morning. This is Sara Donovan."

He let out a cry of pain. "Not how I wanted to start my week."

Rude, but it was something I was kinda used to with certain types of people. I flashed back to last year in Tuscaloosa. Primarily, security and law enforcement. And big Mickey here was starting to rank up there with Jake Barton for the biggest jerk at the Carlton.

"Sorry, but you *are* the chief of security. Would you rather me go to the FBI?" Even as I said it, I prayed that wasn't going to be my next move.

Another anguished cry. "Not necessary. What can I do for you?"

"You have time later in the day to meet?"

"Hang on." A few seconds later, "Eleven work for you?"

"Perfect. See you then."

I ended the call, scooted back, and crashed into the shelf on the cubicle's back wall.

"*C'mon*."

I stood and poked my head around the corner. "Sorry, Victoria."

A fuming Victoria Finkle fervently worked to contain a puddle of coffee spreading across her desk. "Can't you just stand like everybody else?" she said, her tone dripping with contempt.

"Said I was sorry."

Before she could reply, I took off for the valuables vault. I swiped my ID card through the reader, placed my right hand on the biometric scanner, and the day gate lock released. I crossed to the back of the vault where Oliver Carlton's journals were stored on the black steel shelves. My hopes for a miracle over the weekend were quickly crushed. The same three thin gaps in the line of journals stared back at me.

Crap.

Boss Lady said I had until this Friday to find those books. Or else.

I scoured the vault, and at the same time, looked for evidence of a tunnel entrance. Thirty minutes later, I found neither. After running through my options, I decided to conduct a second inventory on the off chance I screwed up and missed them last week, or misfiled them during last month's inventory. My fruitless hunt reached journal nine hundred when I realized it was just past eleven o'clock. I exited the vault, slammed the day gate closed, and legged it for Mickey's office.

When I got there, it was ten after eleven.

Mickey was typing furiously on a keyboard, his thick fingers showing surprising dexterity as he mashed away on the unfortunate keys. His gaze shifted over to me standing in the doorway and the assault on the keyboard stopped.

"Sorry I'm late."

"I was wondering." He gestured to one of the crappy guest chairs. "Grab a seat."

I entered the office, closed the door, and sat. "Thanks for taking the time to meet with me."

He folded his hands on the desk. "I don't think you gave me a choice, what with your threat to go to the FBI. That's something we can't afford over misplaced hunches."

"If I'm right, you're not going to have a choice."

"You still hung up on that supposed diamond heist?"

I ignored his cynical attitude. "I did some investigating over the weekend and think I found how they did it."

A quick rap on the door sounded behind me, followed by it being opened.

Mickey's gaze moved to the door. "Yeah, Jake?"

Jake Barton stepped inside. He threw me a nasty look before addressing Mickey. "Got them cameras and sensors hooked up in the readin' room. When you wanna calibrate 'em?"

"Give me ten or fifteen minutes to finish up here."

Barton scratched the side of his head. "Okay, I'll wait for ya over there."

"Sounds good."

The rude, grimy man gave me a snide look before turning and leaving.

Mickey focused back on me. "Who's they?"

"Excuse me?"

"You think you found out how *they* did it. Who's they?"

"Oh. Right. Yeah, I don't know. Yet. But pretty sure I discovered how the crew got to the museum undetected. Are you aware of the network of sewer interceptors beneath the city?"

He shook his head. "Nope."

I told him about the cavernous tunnels, how one ran right by the Carlton, and the Piney Branch Creek outfall with the steel plate and welded door.

All the while I talked, he sat with his beefy arms crossed, his eyes locked on me. His stare was intense. "That welding could've been from a maintenance team."

"I thought about that, but here's the thing. There are tire tracks everywhere outside the outfall. And some lead right to this welded door, as if somebody drove straight through it into the tunnel."

Mickey's bulging forearms crisscrossed on the desk as he leaned toward me. "What'd the tracks look like?"

I pulled up a photo and slid my phone across the desk to him. "Look how wide and very pronounced those treads are. And on the bank, they're really deep. But not from a car tire."

He picked up the phone and studied the pic, the phone dwarfed by his oversized hand. "Maybe an ATV?"

"That's my thought. And take a look at the photos I took of the plate and weld lines."

Mickey swiped through the photos, briefly studying each one before moving on to the next. "And one of these tunnels runs along Constitution?"

"Yup. If a crew got ATVs into the network from Piney Branch, they could navigate all the way to the museum. From there they could dig a tunnel to outside the vault and nobody would know."

He slid the phone back to me and stared off, mumbling, "Like an ATV." The giant man crushed his phone's speaker button and pounded the keypad.

"Jefferson Scott here."

"Jeff, Mickey. Something we need to look into. Quietly."

Chapter Fourteen

He's not hungry?

After my meeting with Mickey and the subsequent phone call with Jefferson Scott, the exhibit's security director, they told me to go back to the vault and tell nobody else about my suspicions. They would look into things and contact me if they had any questions.

I spent the afternoon back in the valuables vault finishing up the second inventory of the journals. And when I finished, the three missing ones were still missing. I had four days left before Evy submitted the inventory report to the Board of Trustees, after which all hell was going to rain down on me.

No sooner had I returned to my cubicle when the desk phone rang. The caller ID showed Evy Langston. Boss Lady calling me late in the afternoon? That can't bode well.

With my stomach tumbling, I picked up the handset. "Yes, ma'am?"

"My office. Now."

Before I could say anything, she slammed the phone down.

I replaced the handset, sat back, and closed my eyes. All kinds of scenarios ran through my mind. And none of them good. I took a cleansing breath and rolled away from the desk, taking care not to slam into the wall and get Victoria all fired up. I preferred to keep things simple and have only one person angry with me at a time.

I stood and dragged myself toward Boss Lady's office. With each step, I knew exactly how Marie Antoinette felt walking to the guillotine. When I got there, the door was open.

I stuck my head in. "Yes, Evy?"

She looked up, emphatically pointed to a guest chair, and motioned for me to close the door. Her face was hard. Complexion red. Eyes flaming.

Stepping inside, I closed the door, and slipped into a chair across from her.

Evy stared at me for several seconds, her lips pressed tight. When she spoke, her dispassionate tone belied the rage etched in her face. "Did you talk with Mr. Fraser today?"

My shoulders slumped. "Yes, ma'am," I mumbled.

"Did I not specifically tell you last week, Thursday I believe, to not take your absurd notion of a robbery in the vault any further?"

"Yes, ma'am, but—"

She jabbed a skinny finger at me. "No buts. I warned you. And now you have Mr. Fraser and Mr. Scott spun up. They want to inspect the vault."

"I'm sorry but—"

"Why on earth would you go to Mr. Fraser when I specifically told you to drop it?"

I straightened. "Because I uncovered evidence showing how the thieves were able to tunnel to outside the vault undetected and then drill it."

Evy's eyes narrowed. "How's that possible when

there's no evidence of the vault being breached?"

I explained about the Piney Branch outfall, the tire tracks outside it, and the interceptor network.

She flicked a hand through the air. "Utter nonsense."

"It's true," I insisted.

"I'm not questioning these interceptors or whatever it is you called them. It's absolute poppycock to think anybody could tunnel to outside the vault and drill it without any of our sensors or cameras picking it up and—"

"But don't forget—"

"—and leave no indication of the vault wall being drilled. It's simply not there."

"It just hasn't been found," I countered, holding her gaze. "They hid the opening. Somehow."

Her countenance grew harder. "Preposterous. Look, I told you I can't protect you if you took this further. As you have done today. Once they determine the vault is intact and there was no robbery, and they will, I won't be surprised if one or both demand I fire you for interfering in security operations."

I broke eye contact, my gaze dropping to the desk. "Understood. I was just looking out for the museum."

"That's Mr. Fraser's job," she snapped.

"Yes, ma'am. Just trying to be helpful."

Boss Lady softened. "If this blows up, I will fight for you. But you have put me in a very untenable position, making it appear I cannot control my staff. So, there are no guarantees. Understand?"

"Yes, ma'am. And thank you."

Her head pulled back. "For what? I haven't done anything."

"Just knowing you'll fight for me is enough."

A knock on the door followed by the sound of it opening briefly drew Evy's attention to behind me. "That's very likely all it will be. Now get back to work."

I stood and turned.

A hulking Mickey Fraser filled the doorway. Right behind him, Tony Carlucci.

Mickey stepped inside the office to allow me to pass. "You ready?" he asked Evy.

"Let's get this over with," came her terse reply.

I trudged back to my cubicle, sat, and put my face in my hands. After a minute, my jangled nerves calmed enough to allow me to focus on work. Barely.

Thirty minutes later, there was a rap on the cubicle's frame. Mickey stuck his head over the top of the partition.

My eyes pleaded with him.

He gave me a quick head shake. "We found nothing."

"Seriously?" I whispered.

Tony passed by. "You going to call Mr. Scott?"

Mickey looked over his shoulder. "Yeah, I'll let him know."

Tony nodded once and disappeared.

Mickey turned back to me. "I'm still gonna look into that Piney Branch outfall, but right now there remains zero evidence of a break-in."

My face scrunched up. "Am I in trouble?"

"Not with me. I know your heart is in the right place. Can't speak for Jeff. You heard him on the phone."

"He sounded pretty frustrated."

"That's being polite. I'll do what I can to handle him. But no more talk of a heist. Deal?"

"Deal."

Mickey double-tapped the top of the partition. "Okay, good. Have a nice evening."

As I contemplated my future at the Carlton, I glanced at my phone. It was quitting time. I made the no-brainer decision and hightailed it out of there before anything else happened.

When I arrived home, no cars were in the driveway. I unlocked the front door and shut off the alarm at the keypad. My gaze shifted around the hallway and up the stairs. Strange. No Mauzzy. He somehow always knew when I was outside the front door, waiting to greet me when I entered. From classes. From work. From anywhere.

"*Mauzzy.*"

Silence.

Although the alarm hadn't tripped, my scalp prickled. Something was very wrong. My stomach tightened as I slipped pepper spray out from my purse and crept through the hallway toward the back of the house. At the kitchen doorway, I stuck my head around the corner. Everything appeared normal. Edging into the room with the pepper spray out front, I did a quick check behind the kitchen's island before working toward the family room. As I tiptoed around the sectional, my pounding heart did its best to alert the intruder and simultaneously foretell my impending doom. But nobody lurked behind the furniture, or for that matter, anywhere else in the room.

That meant they were upstairs. With Mauz.

Either that or I was being overly paranoid, which

has happened on occasion, and the alarm wasn't tripped for a reason. Because nobody broke in, and Mauzzy was sleeping in our bed.

I spun back toward the kitchen when a flash of movement and a sound startled me so much, I took a quick reflexive step backward and flipped over the ottoman, my purse flying off into oblivion, the back of my head cracking into the hardwood floor. Bright white stars exploded in front of me, the brilliance beyond blinding. I fought to bring the pepper spray to bear, which miraculously was still in my hand, but couldn't move my arm. I tried to stand, but my lower legs were casually stretched across the ottoman.

Suddenly, I couldn't breathe. My chest was being compressed, something heavy holding me down. There I lay, torso pinned to the floor. Useless legs up on the ottoman. White light everywhere.

Oh, my God. The intruder was licking my face. What kind of perv—

As my head cleared, my eyes focused. "Mauz? Mauzzy. *You're safe.*"

The little guy was standing on my chest, going to town on my face. He stopped and considered me.

Easing his wee body off me, I dragged my legs down and worked up into a sitting position. "So, everything is okay, huh, Mauz?"

With eyes riveted on me, he sat.

"You want dinner?"

No reaction. Strange. Two words always sent the little guy into a tizzy. Breakfast and dinner.

I stood and bent toward him. In an excited voice, I said, "Mauz, *dinner?*"

Nothing. Like he forgot how to speak English.

I walked toward the laundry room where his food was stored, calling over my shoulder, "C'mon, Handsome. Dinner."

Mauzzy caught up and trotted alongside me. I picked up his bowl in the kitchen, stepped into the laundry room, and measured out his food. But the usual excited pitter-pattering of little feet was missing. I glanced down. He was sitting, watching me. The little guy appeared—bored.

Returning to the kitchen, with Mauzzy trailing behind me, I set the bowl down. "Dinner?"

No perked-up ears. No recognition of the word whatsoever. In fact, he wasn't bored, he looked sleepy, paying zero attention to the full bowl of food in front of him.

"Well, if you're not going to eat, I'm going upstairs to change."

I went upstairs, with Mauzzy right behind me. My concern was growing that he had a stomachache or got into something, which certainly wouldn't be the first time for the latter. Although even when he got into something, including the time he ate all my scented candles, he always had room for dinner. The dude had an iron stomach. But tonight, Mauzzy passed on a meal. That has never happened. I mean—never.

I entered my bedroom and froze. My pulse quickened as I stared at the desk with mouth agape. The laptop was open. I always closed it when not using it to keep dust and other crap from getting on the screen and keyboard. Always. And there was no reason for Zoe or Matt to get on it. They have their own. Somebody got past the house alarm and messed with my laptop. And if the intruder accessed it, that meant the person was a skilled hacker, would have checked my search history, and found my tunnel research. But why would...

Crap.

Somebody was onto my investigation.

Scooping up Mauzzy, I ran downstairs into the family room in search of my waylaid purse. It was behind the sectional where it landed after my flip over the ottoman. Digging into the purse, I pulled out my phone along with a folded slip of paper and called the number on it. After several seconds of clicking, the phone rang once. When a second ring never came, I quickly hung up.

"Now we wait, Mauz."

Chapter Fifteen

The big guns

Early the next morning, as I schlepped through the foul parking garage on my way to the Carlton, the heavily tinted passenger window of a parked SUV slid down.

A hushed voice called to me from inside the colossal vehicle. "Get in, dear."

Keeping my distance, I peered through the open window. Intense gray eyes beneath soft white curls stared back.

"Mrs. Majelski?"

A clunk came from the door. "Of course. Now get in."

I opened the door and climbed in. The elegant interior was outfitted in tan leather and ebony trim. It smelled of luxury. The opposite of the garage. "Where's your monster truck?"

The octogenarian's face wrinkled into a smile. "Tuscaloosa. Why do you ask?"

"Figured you'd drive it up here. You know, on account of it being all tricked out."

She chuckled and shook her head. "When in Rome, dear."

"Huh?"

"You're cute," she cackled. "That's why I like you." Her face grew serious. "That truck would stand out up here. This baby"—she patted the steering wheel—"lets me fit in without drawing attention."

"Fit in? Why do you need—"

"You called me yesterday. Something wrong?"

I told her about the Piney Branch outfall and my going to Mickey about it, the recent vault inspection, the open laptop, and Mauzzy missing a meal.

The entire time she never broke eye contact, throwing in an occasional nod or "mmmm hmmm" as I spoke. When I finished, she sat quietly for a moment.

"Anybody outside your family know the alarm code?"

"Just Zoe."

"I see." She tapped her lips several times with a gnarled finger. "Any sign of forced entry? Broken window, busted door, that kind of thing?"

"Nope. Front door was locked and all the windows are fine."

"Upstairs windows monitored?"

"Yes."

She gave me a sideways look. "You sure?"

"Absolutely. Dad added sensors to those windows after a bunch of neighborhood burglaries a few years ago. Crooks were finding ladders stored outside houses and climbing through second-floor windows."

"Back door?"

"Locked."

"Door from the house to the garage?"

My eyes widened. "Crap. That door is usually unlocked."

"There's your point of entry."

"But the garage doors were closed."

A crooked smile spread across her jowly face. "Dear, you can break into a garage in seconds with a metal coat hanger and a small block of wood."

"*Really?*"

She glanced in her side mirror before turning back to me. "Really. You should always keep that door locked. With a deadbolt."

"We will now."

"I'm curious, why bring up the dog in all this? Sounds like he just wasn't hungry."

"You don't know Mauzzy. He never misses a meal. Instead of begging to be fed, he acted sleepy."

She arched an eyebrow. "Meaning?"

"I think the intruder drugged him to keep him quiet. Maybe an antihistamine in a dog treat."

A finger shot out at me. "*Possible* intruder."

"You don't believe me?"

She shook her head. "Didn't say that. I believe you about the laptop. But could your brother or little friend have used it without your knowledge?"

"Uh-uh. I asked them when they got back home."

The geriatric wonder stared out her side window for a few seconds before checking the rearview, then the passenger side mirror. "Your instincts are fairly okay, so I'd say there's a possibility something's going on. Besides me, how many people have you told about this possible heist?"

In my mind, I ran through the past week. "My boss, Evy Langston. Mickey Fraser, the Carlton's chief of security. Jefferson Scott. He's the exhibit's security director. The Carlton's facility maintenance manager, Jake Barton. My work friend, Danielle. Grant. Zoe.

And my family."

A questioning look crossed her face. "Quite the list of people."

"I was trying to get somebody's attention. Nobody was listening to me."

"Sounds like someone might have been."

"Oh, and Tony Carlucci knows because he searched the vault yesterday with Mickey."

She eyed me. "Him, too?"

"Uh-huh."

Mrs. Majelski fell silent. Again, her gaze bounced from side mirror to side mirror, to the rearview mirror, before settling back on me. "Then I suspect the entire security department knows. Someone in there might have alarm skills, too. Is your home system wireless?"

"I think so."

"Makes sense. If there was an intruder, probably jammed the signal. Not hard to do if you know what you're doing. And that alarm company sign in your yard doesn't help."

My mouth flopped open. "How do you know about our sign?"

With a flick of the back of her hand, she replied, "Not important. Those signs work with the common criminal, but they also help someone who knows what they're doing."

"That sign is a bad idea? Never heard that before."

She stuck out a burly hand, clearly a byproduct of her iron-pumping routine. The old lady was a beast in the gym. "No, no. Don't get me wrong, dear. Those signs are an excellent idea since the overwhelming majority of break-ins are crimes of opportunity or brute-force entries. However"—she raised a forefinger—"if someone with the technical means is targeting a place, the sign identifies the alarm company, which points that person in the right direction for figuring out the frequency a wireless system is broadcasting on. After that, it's just finding the right equipment and the alarm system can be jammed."

"Dad would have a cow if he heard this."

"Keep it to yourself." Another quick check of the mirrors. "This has all the earmarks of a highly targeted, highly sophisticated operation."

"Like by a crew that can break into a museum vault without anybody knowing about it?"

"Precisely."

I glanced at the clock on the dash. "I need to get going before I'm late for work. That won't go well with Boss Lady."

"What time do you get off?"

"Five."

"Can you meet me tomorrow after work at the outfall?"

"Sure, but you don't know where it is."

She gave me a knowing smile. "I'll see you there, dear. Bring rubber boots and a flashlight."

I opened the door to leave when the ancient wonder latched onto my upper arm. The old lady had quite the grip, too.

"Don't be followed."

Chapter Sixteen

Sometimes even a nose clip is not enough

The next day, I turned into the lot at the Rock Creek tennis courts and parked beside Mrs. Majelski's SUV. Before exiting, taking care not to rip off my duct-taped rearview mirror, I dragged up a loaded backpack from the passenger side floor still packed with gear from my last trek to the outfall, including my rain boots. The only thing I added was a flashlight.

The SUV's door opened and the old lady climbed down from the driver's seat. She wore blue jeans, a denim shirt, and boots. Slung low over her eyes, a black ball cap emblazoned with a swirling *W*, white hair spilling out from underneath it. "You're a half-hour late," she growled. Gone was her grandmotherly tone.

"Sorry, but there was an accident on Nineteenth and another big one had Sixteenth down to one lane. It was a zoo."

"Should've called."

"Thought I would make it on time."

She said nothing and instead focused her gaze on the tennis courts before shifting to Park Road. After several seconds, she sprang to the rear of the SUV, opened it, and unloaded a red contraption of some kind. She set it on the pavement and leaned back into the vehicle.

While Mrs. Majelski rummaged around, I studied the piece of equipment. It had a handle at the top and held two tanks, one red and the other green. At the top of each tank were two round meters and a strange-looking brass device with what appeared to be nozzles sticking out from it. A coiled double-hose, one red and the other green, rested on the contraption in front of the tanks. At the end of the hose, a two-foot-long brass tube with a pointy thing coming off the end at a ninety-degree angle. As I stared at the thing, it dawned on me. Mrs. Majelski had brought a cutting torch.

She reappeared from the back of the SUV holding an oversized military-style backpack that she wiggled into. A blue metal flashlight protruded from one of its side pockets. Hefting the cutting equipment, she flashed me a cheerful smile. My tardiness was forgiven.

"Ready, dear?"

"What'd you do, trade in your walker for a cutting torch?"

With a short laugh, she replied, "Let's get going. It'll be getting dark in three hours."

I slung my backpack over a shoulder and fell in behind the geriatric paradox as she rambled along Park Road toward the outfall. With her leading the way, we arrived at Piney Branch Creek in no time. While I pulled my boots from the backpack and put them on, she scanned Park Road and the creek below.

"All set?" she asked.

I hoisted my backpack. "Yep."

She picked up the cutting torch carrier. "Let's go."

We descended from the road to the creek and marched along the bank, the stench growing as we neared the outfall. Before we climbed down the bank to the steel wall, I fished out the nose clip from my backpack and put it on.

Mrs. Majelski caught sight of the pink nose clip and grinned. She set the cutting torch on the bank, wriggled out of her backpack, and took from it a welder's mask, dark heavy-duty goggles, a folded brown leather apron, and long heavy gloves, all of which she set on the ground.

With a wink and a smile, she said, "Safety first."

"You're really going to cut a hole in the wall?"

She gave me her backpack, slipped the apron over her head, and tied it in back. Motioning with her head toward the cutting torch, she said, "Why else would I lug that thing all the way here?"

"But we can get in trouble. Isn't that vandalism?"

"You worry too much." She removed the ballcap and handed it to me. "Store this, dear."

I took the hat and crammed it into her backpack.

"Hey, hey, careful with that," she scolded. "Got that after doing a favor for their star third baseman."

"Star who?"

"Just fix it."

I retrieved the hat, made some room in the backpack, and carefully returned it to a newfound place of honor in the bag.

With me sufficiently reprimanded and the transgression against the hat rectified, she put the goggles on, slid the lenses up to her forehead, and chugged over to a good-sized bush. With a sweep of her arms, the bush vanished and a dark-green two-seat ATV appeared, camouflaged netting crumpled on the ground in front of the vehicle.

"Where'd that ATV come from?" I asked.

"Actually, it's called a UTV, short for utility task vehicle. And let's just say I had a colleague pre-position this for me." With another wink, she scampered back to the cutting torch, hefted the carrier, and placed it in a small cargo bed behind the vehicle's seats. Then she did the same with the gloves and mask. "You'll have to walk down. Too dangerous to have you riding with me down that steep bank."

Without waiting for an answer, Mrs. Majelski nimbly scrambled into the driver's seat and started the engine. It made no sound.

"It's so quiet," I said.

"Electric, dear. Can't be making noise driving through those tunnels."

She eased the vehicle forward and expertly maneuvered it down into the creek and onto the concrete pad in front of the steel wall.

I chased after her, not-so-expertly crashing down the bank, juggling her oversized backpack as I slipped toward disaster. Fortunately, I regained my balance right before hitting the water. The thought of taking a bath in the grody liquid almost made me vom.

With a thin smile on her wizened face, Mrs. Majelski climbed out of the UTV and geared up. She pointed to the steel plate. "Was that there when you were here last?"

"The plate?"

"No, that graffiti. *AMORE*."

"Oh. Yeah, it was there."

She studied the colorful graffiti. "Interesting."

"Really?"

"Remember that Antwerp heist I told you about

last week?"

"Uh-huh."

"The crew was Italian. And that graffiti is Italian for love."

"You think they pulled the heist?"

"*If* there was a heist, that graffiti puts them at the top of the list." She fixed the goggles over her eyes, put the mask on over the goggles, lowered the face shield, and fired up the cutting torch. "Step back, dear."

I inched away, keeping an eye on the edge of the concrete pad. The last thing I needed was to back right off the pad and end up sitting in Piney Branch Creek.

Sparks flew as Mrs. Majelski went to work, cutting inside the existing weld lines. Soon, a rectangle slightly taller than her, so maybe four foot ten inches, and wide enough to accommodate the UTV, appeared in the wall. Mrs. M pushed in on the plate as she finished the final cut and the piece fell inward with a loud bang. She stowed the cutting torch and protective gear in the cargo bed, took her backpack from me, and pulled out a headlamp and several sheets of paper.

I glanced around. "That was loud. Think somebody heard?"

She threw the backpack in the cargo bed, put the headlamp on, and climbed into the driver's seat. "We'll know soon enough. Saddle up."

Not exactly the answer I wanted to hear.

With another look around, I got in, set my backpack on the floor, and produced the flashlight.

Mrs. Majelski handed me the papers. "You're the navigator."

I looked at the pages. When put together, they made up the interceptor map from the Washington tunnels website.

"Why can't we use my phone?" I asked.

She chuckled lightly. "Because it won't work. No line of sight to the GPS satellites. We'll be fine with that map. We have five miles to cover but don't have to turn into another tunnel until we get near the river."

Mrs. Majelski switched on the headlamp, turned on the headlights, eased the UTV through the opening, and drove onto the left walkway. "We'll be making all left turns, just like a stock car race."

I did a double take.

She glanced at me with an amused smile. "My great-nephew got me hooked on racing. Remember Billy?"

Coincidentally, I met him last year after I made a nine-one-one call. He's a Tuscaloosa cop. Go figure.

"Of course, I do."

"He's a good boy. We do Talladega every year."

I wasn't about to ask what in the heck was a Talladega. Or a stock car race. With this lady, it could be anything.

For forty minutes we rolled along in silence. Inside the tunnel, it was exactly as the website's pictures portrayed. High arching ceiling, a wide passageway with footpaths on each side, and a trough in the middle containing some amount of water. The walls were brick but white splotches easily covered half the walls and ceiling. The farther we drove, the more thankful I became for my nose clip because even with it, the stench was borderline unbearable. If the crew traveled through this network to dig their tunnel, which would have taken weeks if not months, either they had nose clips, too, or the power of greed overcame the power of the stench.

"See that light up ahead?" Mrs. Majelski said. "That's an outfall into the Potomac. Right before it, we're going to hang a left."

I shined my flashlight on the map. "I see the turn. After that, we'll continue until it empties into another tunnel. Then hang another left. That will take us to under Constitution."

"Right. Once we're in that tunnel, we'll slow down and start looking for where they broke through the wall."

I studied the map. "There's an offshoot going to the left away from the Constitution tunnel and connecting with another running along C Street. The museum will be just past that offshoot on Constitution."

Mrs. Majelski steered the UTV to the left into the tunnel before the Potomac outfall. "We're now running along the river."

After ten minutes, we slowed as our tunnel emptied into the Constitution tunnel. To our right, light signaled another outfall opening into the river. The UTV cut to the left, and we continued at a reduced speed.

Minutes later, a surge of adrenaline hit me when I aimed my flashlight down into the trough. "Look at all the dirt and mud in there."

Mrs. Majelski eased the vehicle to a crawl and peered past me. "Mmmm hmmm. Didn't see anything close to that on the way in."

"Their tunnel entrance has to be here somewhere," I said, fighting to control my growing excitement.

"Put your light on the left wall. That's where it would be. To the right leads to the Mall and Lincoln Memorial."

As we crept along, I examined the wall. It was all just brick and white patches.

"There's the C Street offshoot," Mrs. Majelski said.

"The amount of dirt keeps increasing."

"Mmmm hmmm. But not enough to be from a tunnel. Should be at least five hundred cubic yards. That's around forty dump trucks. There's nothing close to that."

"But why here and no place else?"

Mrs. Majelski said nothing as we inched through the tunnel. Every few seconds she leaned toward me to check the trough. "You know, this crew was clever dumping the dirt down there. With every rain, the water carried away some of it."

"That's brilliant."

She stopped the UTV and got out. "We should be pretty close to the museum. Careful when you step out. Don't want you falling into the trough."

I stuck my head out and looked down. It was a good thing Mrs. Majelski warned me because there was less than three feet to the edge. With my balance, as in minimal, it might as well have been three inches. And falling into that nasty mud teeming with—I can't even. After yet another successful vom suppression, I slid across the seat and exited from the driver's side.

When I climbed out and realized she only had three feet of space to the wall, it hit me. "Oh my God. How are we going to turn around?"

Mrs. Majelski looked over her shoulder at me and let out a brief, husky laugh. "I'm going to back up and into that C Street offshoot, dear. Then it's all right turns back to the outfall."

My cheeks grew warm. "And I'm your navigator?"

She ran her hands along the brick wall. "In title only. I know how difficult it is for you to be in a sewer."

Ugh. I've been in a *sewer* for an hour. Calling it an interceptor made it *soooo* much better. Now I really needed to vom.

"You gave me that job to keep my mind occupied?"

"Sure did."

We spent the next hour working our way up and down the wall but found nothing. No entrance. No digging tools. Nothing except dirt in the trough.

"Sorry, dear, but there doesn't seem to be anything here."

"But there's got to be. Why all the dirt?"

Mrs. Majelski checked her watch and signaled for me to get into the UTV. "I don't disagree, but we're not going to find it today. There's only about an hour of daylight and I still have to reweld that plate back in place."

I got in on the driver's side and scooched over into my seat. "It sounded heavy when it hit the ground. How are you gonna weld it back?"

She climbed in and gave me a wink. "I have some friends waiting for me."

I stared back, openmouthed.

Chapter Seventeen

The moment of truth

The following day as I enjoyed the morning's first cup of coffee, Danielle stopped by my cubicle.

"Good morning," she sang.

"Hey, good morning. Sounds like you're feeling better."

"For sure. I think it was a twenty-four-hour thing. More importantly, did you get it?"

I cocked my head. "Uh, no, I feel fine."

Danielle giggled. "Not the stomach bug. Did you get his name yesterday? You know, Wednesday?"

"Ah, Hot Lunch Guy."

Her eyes grew large. "Yeah, so?"

I raised my chin and smiled broadly. "As a matter of fact, I got two names."

"Two?"

"Yep. His—and his doctor's."

Danielle busted out laughing.

"Almost blew it again. He first gave me his doctor's name."

In between laughs, she spit out, "Seriously?"

"Oh, yeah. Pretty eventful day yesterday. Also drowned my phone along with Dad's jeep Tuesday night."

Her laughing changed to instant concern. "*What?*"

"My parents are at the beach so I took his jeep to run an errand for Mom. The top was down when a monsoon blew through while I was inside an express mail place. Some crazy guy at the front of the line couldn't seem to understand when sending a fax, the paper doesn't actually travel through the phone line. The dude kept arguing with the clerk, saying he couldn't have sent the fax because he was holding it in his hand. Even called him a simpleton."

"Are you serious? Somebody really thought that?"

I raised a hand. "Wouldn't have believed it if I hadn't seen it myself. Because of that whacko, I drove home with water sloshing around my feet. The fricking car mats were even floating. And when I hit the brakes to keep from running a red light, my phone slid off the seat into the lake. Almost wrecked trying to save it."

"Is the jeep ruined?"

"My brother took care of it. Apparently, the thing has drain plugs. He said Dad will never know."

"Whew, you're so lucky."

"For once."

Danielle glanced at the phone on my desk. "Looks like you dried the phone out okay, too."

"Nope. Replaced it yesterday *after* Hot Lunch Guy."

"Priorities, right?"

"Obvis."

My desk phone rang. It was Mickey Fraser.

"Sorry, gotta take this," I said.

"Tell me more over lunch."

I gave her a thumbs-up and answered the phone. "Good morning, Mickey."

"Morning. Hey, on the way in today I checked out that Piney Branch outfall. Thought you said there were weld lines like a door was cut out and then welded back in place."

"I did. You saw the pics."

"Well, now there's a smaller set of weld lines inside the ones you saw."

"Yeah…about that."

Silence.

"Hello? Mickey? You there?"

"Yeah, I'm here. You know something about it?"

"How about if I come down to your office?"

"Fine," he snarled.

Click.

Five minutes later, I stood in the doorway of Mickey's office. He was on the phone.

"Yeah, I don't know what's going on," he fumed. "But I'm damn sure gonna find out. I'll call you after I'm done with her. Right. I understand. Okay, stand by. Don't call Dana until you hear from me." He hung up and stared at me, his piercing brown eyes digging into me. It wasn't even eight-thirty, yet his tie was already askew and white shirt badly wrinkled. A hand gestured to a guest chair. "Shut the door."

I closed the door behind me and settled into the chair.

He rested his elbows on the desk, steepled his fingers in front of his mouth, and exhaled. "That was Jeff. He's beyond pissed. And so am I. Despite the lack of evidence, somehow all this talk of a heist got back to Dana Wainwright."

I bit my lip but said nothing.

"Tell me what you know about that second set of

weld lines," he said, his tone controlled.

I shifted in the chair. "Um, I was there when it was cut."

A good five seconds passed before he spoke, his eyes fixed on me the entire time. "Who did the cutting?"

My chest tightened. "I...um...can't tell you."

"Why not?"

My body melted into the chair as my mouth went dry. "I don't want to get the person in trouble."

His face darkened as a vein in his temple bulged. "I see. Who welded it back in place?"

"I don't know. Wasn't there. She told me to go home because she needed to get several people to help."

"She?"

I didn't respond.

He clenched his jaw. "Look, I don't give a damn if you and your friend vandalized public property. What I do care about is that you keep perpetuating this heist myth despite being told several times to drop it." He stopped his rant to consider me for several seconds. "The fact you didn't call this morning tells me you found nothing inside those tunnels. Correct?"

I hesitated. "Mmmm, not exactly."

His head jerked back. "Come again?"

"We drove through the sewer interceptors and were able to navigate to where we thought the Carlton was located. When we—"

"Drove?"

"With a UTV."

His eyes bored into me, the vein becoming more pronounced. "Who's helping you?"

"Like I said. Can't tell you."

"Fine," he growled. "But if you made it to the Carlton, sounds like you found no tunnel dug. Meaning, no heist."

"True, we couldn't find their tunnel. But we found evidence of one being dug."

"What'd you find? Tools?"

"Dirt."

"Where?"

"In the ditch running between the two walkways."

Mickey waved a dismissive hand at me. "That's not evidence. It's probably been collecting down there for years. It's a damn sewer."

"I don't think so."

He angled his head, his anger ebbing. "Why?"

"Because there was too much of it. We didn't see close to that amount of dirt anywhere else in the network. Everywhere else it was pretty much just water."

"But no tunnel. No tools. No nothing, except some dirt."

I was getting nowhere with the man. His mind was closed tighter than Dad's wallet. He refused to accept the possibility I'd been right all along. I decided on a longshot approach.

"That's right," I replied evenly. "But that doesn't mean it isn't there. And it's been done before."

His lips curled up into a cynical smile, like he knew exactly where I was going with my approach. "By who?"

"I found an article last night about a crew out in L.A. that dug tunnels to right beneath two bank vaults. They drilled both over a weekend and made off with millions in cash and valuables from safety deposit boxes. They were called The Burrowing Burglars. And they were never caught."

Mickey wasn't impressed. "Mmmm hmmm. And when was this?"

Oh yeah, he knew all about them. The man playing with me.

"Mid-eighties," I replied.

With a fake look of surprise, he said, "That long ago? No relevance here."

I scrunched up my face. "Yeah, I'm not so sure. They dug their tunnels from storm drains and used ATVs to get away in those same drains. And they also used those storm drains to wash away the excavated dirt. It's *exactly* how our vault was robbed."

Mickey forced a smile. "Sounds like you have an overactive imagination. You seriously saying this crew hit the museum after laying low for decades?"

"I only brought them up to show my theory is not implausible."

Mickey let out a short, derisive laugh. "Listen, I know about that case. They left plenty of evidence behind. Thieves usually do. But not yours. *That's* implausible."

I gritted my teeth but said nothing because it would have gotten me nowhere. His mind was made up.

"I'm curious, how'd you know you were near the Carlton?" he asked. "GPS won't work down there."

"Printed up a map of the interceptor network from washingtontunnels.com."

Mickey scrutinized me. "You're not going to let this go, are you?"

"I'm more convinced than ever a crew stole the Star of Midnight. All that dirt I saw didn't just wash into the sewer from the street."

He crossed his arms and leaned back in the chair. "So, the answer is no?"

"Correct. You'll thank me later."

"Doubtful." His eyes narrowed. "There's a big problem with your story."

"What's that?"

"Why only the Star of Midnight? Why not take the Heart of Fire, too, or even all the stones?"

"I have two theories."

Amusement was splashed across his face. "Do tell."

"To avoid detection when they sell it, the crew's plan is to recut the Star of Midnight into several smaller stones. It's big enough to do that. All the other stones are way too small, making them too risky to move as is."

He continued to grin. "Possibly. And your other theory?"

"They replaced the Star with a fake. Making fakes for all the rest would be too much effort. That would be twenty-nine more."

Mickey's amusement vanished. He rested an elbow on the desk, put a fist over his mouth, and stared at me. He briefly closed his eyes, let out a long exhale, and picked up the phone. "Hey, Jeff. It's Mickey. She's adamant the diamond was stolen." He stared at me as he listened to Jefferson Scott go off, his voice booming from the handset. "Believe me, I know. I know. The best way to put this to bed and calm Dana down is to get somebody in here to check out the stones." He listened with closed eyes. "I understand. I'll sign off on the cost. When? The sooner the better, but for security reasons, it's gotta be when the museum is closed. Right." He hung up and stared at me. "He'll contact the exhibit's gemologist. Thinks he can get him here tonight if he can catch the shuttle from New York. Happy?"

"Can I watch?"

"You're pressing your luck."

"Can I?"

"Sure," he replied, his tone mocking. "It'll give me great pleasure to see your face when you're proved wrong once and for all. I'll let you know when."

I stood to leave. "Thank you. And I'm not wrong."

****

The same day, Mickey called me at four-thirty to say the gemologist was coming that night and would begin the examination at eight. With all the traffic issues at rush hour, it wasn't worth the risk to go home, feed Mauzzy, and immediately drive back to D.C. So, I ate dinner at a little bistro around the corner with a killer vegetarian menu and then passed the time strolling around the Mall people-watching. When I arrived back at the Carlton, it was eight-fifteen. Standing around the exhibit's empty display case were Mickey, Jefferson, Tony Carlucci, and four armed security guards. Next to the display case stood a folding table covered by black velvet fabric. In the center of it sat a microscope and a lit gooseneck table lamp. Spread out in a glittering array on the left side of the table were the exhibit's stones. Sitting and hunched over the table, a fat man in his mid-sixties with black hair plastered to his head. Unfortunately for him, the hair was an obvious home dye job. Like he used a bottle of shoe polish. A heavy gold bracelet dangled from a plump wrist protruding from the sleeve of a brightly colored silk shirt. In a word, the dude was slimy. His stubby fingers held a diamond under the lamp as he peered at the stone through one eye using one of those magnifying gizmos.

"That her?" Jefferson asked Mickey.

"Yeah," he replied.

"This baby here is the real deal," the gemologist said in a heavy New York accent. He set a small diamond off to the right and picked up another stone.

Jefferson took the diamond, set it back in the display case, then approached me. "You're the young lady with the lil' pup."

"Yes, sir."

"You've made things quite difficult for me, what with all your yammering on about a heist and tunnels."

"I'm sorry, sir, but I can't let something go just because someone tells me to."

"You're like a dang 'ole bulldog, I'll give you that. But I'm gonna tell this, young lady. When Merv over there"—he hooked a thumb toward the skeezy gemologist—"gets through and finds all them stones are genuine, you're gonna stop all this nonsense talk. Got it?"

"Yes, sir."

Merv set another stone on the right side of the fabric. "Real. Quite a beauty, too."

Jefferson eyeballed me. "Good. Now stand right there and stay outta my hair." He strode over to the table, picked up the stone Merv set down, and returned it to the display case.

A smirking Tony whispered something to Mickey, who looked over at me and cracked a smile. My face burned hot, but I remained in place and said nothing. Soon they will see I'm right. Then we'll see who's smirking.

For the next hour, Merv methodically worked through the stones on the left side of the table, with him grunting "real" each time he set a stone to the right. He appeared to be saving the Star of Midnight and Heart of Fire for last. When he finally picked up the heart-shaped ruby, I held my breath and waited.

"Excellent color," Merv mumbled as he peered through his lens. "Mmmm hmmm. Rutile silk inclusions." He placed the ruby under the microscope. "Proper structure." Maneuvering the stone around as he continued to stare into the eyepiece, he said, "Not lab-grown." Merv picked up a silver instrument with a hook on the end similar to a dentist's tool. Taking the ruby from the microscope, he turned it over and scraped it with the tool. "Can't scratch it. Proper hardness." He set the ruby to his right. "I've always loved this rock. Real."

Jefferson shot me a smug look before he took the ruby and placed it back in the case.

I crossed my arms and gave him my fierce look.

Merv picked up the Star of Midnight.

My stomach somersaulted and heart pounded. This was it. The moment of truth.

He raised the diamond to his eyeglass. "D color. Fantastic." Rotating the dazzling stone while still studying it through his gizmo, he mumbled, "Mmmm hmmm."

A weird shakiness attacked my limbs, forcing me to concentrate on remaining upright. Something was very wrong. This examination wasn't going as expected. It's an obvious fake. *C'mon, Merv. This shouldn't take that long.*

He placed the diamond under the microscope and manipulated it around as he stared through the eyepiece. After several minutes of examining the rock, he removed it and gave a thumbs-up to Jefferson. "Absolutely flawless," he announced. "This baby here is most certainly not a fake."

I gasped. "That's impossible."

Merv twisted around to face me. "What?"

"I'm sorry, but that can't be," I said. "Can you please examine it again?"

He snorted, then let out a hoarse laugh that turned into a hacking cough. "No reason to do that, sweetheart. It's clearly the Star of Midnight. I'll stake my reputation on it."

Jefferson took the huge diamond, set it in the display case, and closed the top. He wheeled around and jabbed a finger at me. "That's enough outta you. No more trouble." He turned to Mickey. "Let's lock it up."

They each took out their black fob and two loud clunks came from the case.

"I'll call Ms. Wainwright and tell her this fuss was all about nothing," Jefferson said to Mickey.

"Please give her my apologies," he replied, shooting me a stony stare.

My shoulders slumped as I pushed back the tears.

Chapter Eighteen

Road trip

After leaving the Carlton following my complete and total embarrassment in front of Mickey, Jefferson, and smirking Tony, I sat in my car and ran through the situation. How did this happen? Mauzzy was never wrong. I know he heard something in the vault during the blackout. And what about all the dirt in the sewer interceptor? It was right next to the Carlton, exactly where excavated dirt from a tunnel should be. Plus, after our ride through the tunnels, Mrs. Majelski was convinced I'm onto something. So why was I feeling like such a failure?

Maybe I needed to approach the situation from a different angle. What would Mauzzy do? I pictured the little guy in his recliner working out his schemes. The one thing consistent about him was he refused to take no for an answer. If he really wanted something, like getting into the bag of treats in the cabinet, he kept at it until he achieved success. If one plan didn't work, he hatched a new one. And if that didn't work, he went back to the drawing board. He was all about perseverance.

Perseverance?

That was it. I won't accept defeat. I'm going to

channel Mauzzy and come up with a plan.

Leaning my head back, I closed my eyes, blew out tonight's humiliation, and calmly thought things through. All the exhibit's stones are real. That's been confirmed by skeezy old Merv. But no way was the power going out a coincidence. It had nothing to do with the storm. And dogs hear way better than humans. Mauzzy was onto the crew in the vault. No doubt about it. So, if they didn't steal the diamond...

My eyes popped open.

I started the engine and sped out of the parking garage. As the car tore down Constitution toward Sixth Street, I called Zoe.

"Sara, where are you? It's way past nine-thirty."

"On my way home. I was watching the exhibit's gemologist examine the stones."

"Yeah, and?"

"They're all real."

"So, all this crap about secret tunnels has been just that. Crap."

"Nope. I'm not sure why, but it's about those missing journals."

Zoe groaned. "We've already been through this. No way thieves are going to dig a tunnel for some dead guy's whacko writings and experiments."

I tugged on the wheel and the hatchback responded, careening through the intersection onto Sixth Street. "Only one way to find out."

"You're scaring me, girl."

"Tomorrow's Friday. Can you call in sick?"

"Depends. Why?"

"Start packing. We're driving to North Carolina tomorrow."

****

When I got home, Mauzzy sat inside the front door. Only this time, he wasn't happy to see me. For sure he was happy to see me home, but not happy to see me. I bent to pet him, but he jumped up, sidestepped my hand, and scowled at me. I knew that look all too well.

"I'm so sorry, Handsome. I forgot to ask Zoe to feed you."

He gave me one sharp bark and scurried for the kitchen, his squat legs working double-time.

I followed the miffed Mauzzy into the kitchen and filled his bowl, throwing in a little extra for his inconvenience. Not that it will convince the guy to forget this egregious act I committed against him. Even while I hung around downtown waiting for the museum to close, something I was forgetting nagged at me. Now I know.

The sound of Mauzzy inhaling his food filled the room. Yeah, I'm going to be paying for this transgression for a long time.

Over in the family room, my brother lay sprawled on the sectional, watching TV.

"Hey, Matt. Whatcha watching?"

Without taking his eyes off the screen, my talkative brother said, "Baseball."

I sauntered over. "We winning?"

"Uh-huh."

I sat on the ottoman and faced him. "Cool beans. So, whatcha got going on this weekend?"

"Nothing much."

"Wanna go with Zoe and me to North Carolina?"

His eyes remained glued to the screen. "Why?"

"We're going to that mansion with the huge cipher

on the wall."

"Yeah?"

"Yep. So, how about it?"

Matt glanced sideways at me and hesitated before waving a hand. "Nah."

"Why not? You seemed pretty excited about that cipher the other day."

"Yeah, it's intriguing. Just not into long drives. Not my thing."

I leaned toward him. "You were about to say something before you said no. What was it?"

"Nothing. You'd never go for it."

"Try me."

He sat up. "Okay. I'll go if you agree we go see the Stock Car Hall of Fame in Charlotte while we're down there."

I pulled back. "I keep hearing about stock cars from you and Mrs. Majelski. What in the heck is a stock car?"

He glanced briefly at the ceiling and shook his head. "It's a regular car that's been souped up for racing. The largest race organization in the country puts on stock car races all over the country. Millions watch 'em on TV every weekend. There are even stock car fantasy leagues."

"*Fantasy?* What the heck type of—"

"Knew I shouldn't have mentioned fantasy leagues."

"Yeah, because it sounds pervy."

Matt closed his eyes briefly. "That's my sister." He considered me. "So, we got a deal?"

"How far is Charlotte from Brunswick, North Carolina?"

"Couple hundred miles?"

I checked the distance between the two places on my phone. "Charlotte is two hundred miles from Brunswick. Uh-uh. No way we're going there."

My brother focused back on the TV. "Then I'm not going."

"C'mon, Matt. I need you down there with me. I need your help with that cipher."

He crossed his arms and took a peek at me. "Only if a visit to a stock car track is part of the trip."

"How about if I find a stock car thingy near Brunswick? Will that work?"

"Depends on what this *thingy* is."

I gave him an exaggerated smile. "Ha-ha. Go back to your game while I work my magic."

"Good luck with that."

I searched for stock car racing and found the race organization Matt was talking about and also a list of the tracks they used. Charlotte was the only one in North Carolina and a track in Darlington the only one in South Carolina. The distance from Brunswick to Darlington was around one hundred thirty miles. That might be doable. Then I noticed the route. More than fifty miles of it ran along I-95, with the Darlington track only eight miles off it. I-95 is what we'll take from Annapolis until we exit onto I-40 for Brunswick, and I-95 is what we would take all the way home if we left from Darlington. And the distance from Darlington back to Annapolis was only twenty miles more than the return trip leaving from Brunswick. Very doable.

When I looked up from the phone, the kitchen was silent. And Mauzzy wasn't in his recliner, the place he always went to sleep off dinner. That told me he retreated to our bedroom to sulk. Not good. Or worse, to plot his revenge.

"Hey, Matt."

"Huh?"

"How does Darlington sound?"

He tore away from the screen and perked up. "Seriously?"

"Yep. This says they also have some kind of museum there."

"Yeah, they do. It's called the—"

"OMG, you're *such* a dork. So, are you in?"

"Hell yeah, I'm in."

"Awesome sauce. Start packing. We leave first thing tomorrow morning."

Matt switched off the TV and ran out of the room, shouting, "Holy crap. I'm going to Darlington."

I smiled to myself. That was way easier than expected. I girded myself for the next battle waiting upstairs. And it wasn't Mauzzy. Yet.

I found Zoe in her room sitting in bed watching a show on her tablet.

"Hey, Zo, you got—*whoa*, when did you ditch the red streaks?"

She glanced up and paused the show. "Today after work. I needed a change." Turning her head side to side, she said, "You like?"

"Looks great. Only you can pull off neon green."

She beamed. "My hair guy said it complemented my eyes."

As if her eyes needed any help. They were a stunning, mesmerizing green that always twinkled, even when she was in a huff. And yet her fierce look still put mine to shame. If she had dark brown eyes, yeah, that look would be too scary to imagine.

"Hey, Zo, whatcha—"

Her effervescent smile evaporated. "I'm not sitting in a car for half the day just so you can hunt for some old books."

I sat at the foot of the bed. "We're not hunting for the missing journals."

"Then why are *you* going?"

"I see what you did there. *We* are going. Matt, too."

"The hell I am." She stuck a finger out. "And don't even. No effing way I'm paying for that one."

I let her comment on the curse jar pass. "You said last Saturday you'd go with me if I found something convincing. Then I showed you the wall grid Matt says is significant. Followed by a ton of dirt we found in the sewer interceptor right by the museum. And now the diamond is real. How is all that not convincing?"

She stuck her chin out. "How's the diamond being *real* considered convincing evidence for a frigging trip to Podunk, North Carolina?"

"It means the thieves broke into the vault to steal the journals. It's obvious."

"Only to you."

"What about all that dirt I found?"

Zoe snickered. "Who knows how long that crap has been there. It could've come from when the museum was built."

"No way. It would've washed away a long time ago."

That comment got a laugh out of Zoe. "Good one. Now you're a sewer expert."

"C'mon, you promised. I need you on the trip. It's going to take the three of us to crack that cipher and figure out what's going on."

Zoe studied me. "You're convinced something's going on? Even with the diamond being real?"

"More so than ever before. I think that wall cipher might tell us what's so significant about those journals. Like scattered through them are bits and pieces of directions to a treasure, but you have to crack the cipher to know how to find these pieces and put them together."

"You know your track record isn't the best with your hunches."

"I'm aware, but in the end, I'm usually right."

Zoe lost it. When her laughter subsided, she said, "Yeah, but you're *always* wrong."

I twisted my face up. "Ha-ha. So?"

"I hate long car rides. Got a bladder the size of a peanut."

"Don't worry. We'll be taking plenty of pee breaks with Mauzzy."

"Comforting." After several seconds of silence, she piped up. "You said Matt's going?"

"Yep. Promised him a trip to a race track in Darlington."

"Okay, I'll go. But you owe me. Big time."

I pumped my fist. "Awesome. Thanks, Zo. First thing in the morning call in sick and then we'll hit the road."

"You realize none of us have a clue what we're doing. This trip of yours is gonna be the blind leading the blind."

"Which is no big deal if the lead person has a guide dog."

That got another laugh out of her. "Mauzzy is no

guide dog."

"We could do worse." I jumped up from the bed. "Gotta go pack."

I returned to my bedroom, opened the door, and stopped. Resealable plastic bags were strewn across the floor, along with a multitude of perfume sample cards. In the middle of the room, joyously flopping around on his back like a fish out of water, was Mauzzy. Beneath him lay an *Allons* perfume card, his favorite fragrance.

"*Mauzzy*."

He stopped mid-roll and assessed me.

"Is this payback?"

He lay on his back for a few seconds, unblinking hazel eyes staring at me. Clearly, he was mulling over a response. Then he rolled over, stood, twisted his head around, and slid his neck and back over the *Allons* card, ending up over by the bed.

"I'll take that as a yes."

I exhaled. This was going to be a *very* long car ride.

Chapter Nineteen

It's stupid brilliant

Other than multiple pee stops for Mauzzy and Zoe, the trip to Brunswick was uneventful. And took forever. Between the pee stops and perpetual beltway traffic around D.C., we lost so much time that a quick recon trip to Arcadia Friday afternoon was not possible. Instead, we grabbed dinner and spent the evening complaining about the crappy Wi-Fi. A service the motel boasted as complimentary. That's what we get for twenty-dollar-a-night rooms.

The following morning, after the motel's complimentary breakfast of weak coffee, stale bagels, and watery powdered eggs, we were in the car on the way to Arcadia. Since dogs were not allowed in any of the buildings, Mauzzy gladly stayed behind, luxuriating on our bed's pillows while watching *Puppies and Things* on TV. At least somebody enjoyed the motel.

Ten minutes later, we were nearing Arcadia. Rolling along the two-lane road, I lowered the window to throw my stale gum out. As I cocked my wrist to make the toss, a finger caught the edge of my sunglasses and they followed the gum out the window and onto the road.

"Crap."

"Smooth," floated up from the back seat. "That's my sis."

As Zoe belly laughed, I spied the forlorn sunglasses laying near the center line, veered onto the shoulder, and stopped. "Maybe I can—"

"No way you're running out there for cheap sunglasses," she barked.

I eased the car forward along the shoulder, watching my side mirror. "Never mind."

"Good decision," Zoe said. "You're finally listening to me."

A dump truck roared past, the wind buffeting our car.

"Wasn't my decision," I said, pulling back onto the road and punching it. "That dump truck rolled right over them."

"Better them than you," she advised, pointing down the road to the right. "See those stone columns. That must be the entrance."

"Got it," I said.

We turned off the road and passed through the columns onto a long, tree-lined drive, the heavy canopy giving the illusion of a leafy tunnel. The mansion appeared in the distance. As we neared, the elegant red brick house with soaring windows, white trim, and arched doorways came into full view. To the right away from the main building was a sprawling visitors parking lot built by the Carlton when it converted Arcadia into a museum. A few cars dotted the lot.

"Holy crap, this place is awesome," Zoe gushed.

"Wait 'til we get inside," I replied.

Her glittering eyes took in the majesty of the place. "This Carlton dude was stinking rich."

This was a first for me with Zoe. We've been friends since the seventh grade, and I've never seen her flat-out awestruck.

"Yep, that's partly why we're here," I said.

"Because he was rich?" Matt asked from the back seat. "I thought we were trying to solve the office cipher."

I parked the car and we got out. Despite it being only ten-thirty in the morning, the heat and oppressive humidity brought out the perspiration as soon as my feet hit the pavement. "We are," I said, slamming the door. "But I think this whole thing is somehow tied to Oliver Carlton's wealth. And that office cipher is the key."

By the time we tramped through the parking lot and entered the mansion through arched twin glass doors, I was glistening. Zoe and Matt, not so much.

Zoe whistled softly. "Whoa."

We stopped and glanced around the great entrance hall.

The ceiling soared two stories above a white marble floor, ringed at the top by one-foot-thick carved cream-colored crown molding. A wide curved balcony ran along the back half of the hall's two side walls and the entire rear wall. Heavy red-brown wood doors flanked both sides of the room, two midway and two in the back corners. In the center of the rear wall were paned-glass French doors that reached up and touched the underside of the commanding balcony. Beneath a tapestry of rich reds, blues, and golds on the front half of a side wall was a glass display case containing an architect's model of Arcadia. A stack of brochures sat on the front left corner of the case. Next to it, an information desk and an empty chair.

Matt shuffled over to the case and picked up three brochures. "Let's get moving and find the office."

I took a brochure from my brother and opened it. Inside were layouts for three floors. "Looks like the first floor is the living area. Bedrooms are on the second floor. Third is some kind of observatory." I glanced up at the doors, then back at the layout. "That door on the back right leads to a big suite including a library and his office."

We exited the main hall through the rear door, passed through a small sitting room with blue walls and a fireplace, and into a library with ten-foot ceilings, gray walls, and heavy cream-colored molding. Dark-brown hardwood floors spanned the space, which was segmented into two sections. The first contained an oversized secretary's desk and chair, a grandfather's clock, and a bureau. We entered into the second section through a wide arched passageway framed by a two-foot-thick curved beam matching the molding, its two side walls lined by ten-shelf bookcases stuffed with old books of various sizes and colors. In front of both rows of bookcases was a wheeled wooden ladder, the top attached to some kind of rail system.

"There's gotta be thousands of books in here," Zoe said as she slowly spun around. The towering bookcases were twice her size, making the wee pixie appear insignificant.

"If that's a book cipher in the office, the key could be any one of these," Matt muttered. "We'll never find it."

"No sh...kidding," Zoe added.

"Way to stay positive, guys," I said.

"Just being honest," he replied.

I stepped past them toward a smaller arched opening leading to the office. "We'll find it."

We entered the office and stopped. It was exactly like the pictures on the website. A pure-white marble floor like the one in the entrance hall stretched in front of us, only this one had the black diamond geometric pattern in the tiles. Imposing walls of deep-red mahogany with floor-to-ceiling arched windows encircled the room. At the far end sat an oversized mahogany desk in front of the wall with the carved numbers.

"It's more impressive in person," I said under my breath.

"Sure is," Zoe said in amazement.

Matt crossed the floor, stopping at the desk. He craned his neck as he stared at the incredible carvings.

We came up behind him.

"What do you think?" I asked.

"It's remarkable," he replied, his attention captivated by the wall.

"That's all you got?" Zoe grumbled.

"Don't mess with him, Zo. We just got here."

She crossed her arms. "I'm just sayin', he's the brainiac and all."

Matt glanced back. "I'm looking for a clue to what book might be the key."

"Where? In the numbers?" I asked.

He refocused on the wall. "Uh-uh. Between them. In the grid. Looks like there's some small markings."

"That's more like it," Zoe retorted. "Brainiac sh…" She caught a glimpse of me.

I put out a finger. "Careful or I'm gonna charge

you."

"Brainiac *crap*." She gave me an over-the-top smile.

"C'mon," I said. "Let's leave Matt to it in here. I wanna check out all those books."

We left my brother staring upward and returned to the library.

"What are we looking for?" Zoe asked.

I stopped in front of one bookcase section and examined a shelf of old books. "Don't know. Maybe they're numbered."

Zoe positioned herself in front of another section. "Not on this shelf." She bent. "Not on this one, either. Man, this dude read some effed-up crap."

"From what I've read, some considered him an intellectual eccentric. Others said he was a true renaissance man. And you're right, no numbered books on these lower shelves."

Zoe sidestepped to another set of shelves. "Reading this crap is probably why he was whacko."

I took in the long row of bookcases and scanned one section from top to bottom. "Maybe they're virtually numbered."

Zoe spun around and stared at me. "See what I mean? Reading these titles is making you whacko, too."

"What are you talking about?"

She jammed her hands on her hips. "What are *you* talking about? They didn't have virtual crap back then."

I closed my eyes briefly and shook my head.

She stuck her neck out. "What? This guy lived in the eighteen hundreds."

"What if he numbered all these books without numbering them?"

Zoe's index finger drew little circles in the air around her ear. "You're losing it, girl."

"Listen to me. There are roughly three hundred books on that one section. Count how many sections are on that wall and I'll count them on this one."

Zoe counted the other wall's bookcase sections and I did the same with mine.

"I got eighteen," I said.

She turned back to me. "Same here."

"Okay, so there are thirty-six sections." I pulled my phone out from a front pocket and brought up the calculator. "That, times three hundred books per section, is a total of ten thousand eight hundred books. More or less."

"I thought your brother was here to do the math?"

"What was the highest number on that grid?"

"Beats the sh—crap outta me."

"Nine-nine-nine-nine."

"You remembered that?"

I gave her a proud smile. "Why are you so surprised? You know my superpower of observation."

"Yeah, it's right up there with your superpower of BS."

"My point is, there are enough books in here to match all those numbers in the grid."

Her brow furrowed. "I don't get you."

"What if Carlton assigned a number to each book in here, starting with the number one for the top left book in the first section? Then the next book was two. And so on. Right through to the very last book on the bottom end of the thirty-sixth section."

Zoe's eyes widened. "So, each number in the grid corresponds to a book in here?"

"Maybe. Or like Matt was saying the other day. The first number in the grid could be the book, the second is the page number of that book, and the third is the actual word or character in the book that's part of the secret message. And then the pattern repeats itself as you work through the grid until you have the message."

"Holy... That's *stupid* brilliant."

"*Matt.*"

Chapter Twenty

On the hunt

Matt ran into the library, concern etched on his narrow face. "Everything okay?"

"Tell him," Zoe urged.

I took him through my theory of how the books in the library fit with the cipher's numbers.

He scratched the back of his head and grimaced. "I don't know, that sounds too difficult to put together. Almost to the point of an improbability."

I leaned back and folded my arms "Why?"

"Think about the numbers in the cipher," Matt said calmly. "They're all different and all over the place. They're not even close to being sequential. The guy would be going up and down those ladders to grab and return books as he developed the thing. Continually up and down."

As usual, my brother made sense. But this whole thing was crazy for a reason. "Maybe, but if that cipher is a treasure map, or leads to piecing together directions in the journals for finding a treasure, wouldn't you make it really hard to solve? Legend says the ship was carrying seventy-five tons of gold and emeralds. What's that worth today?"

Matt looked off as he ran through the calculations.

"Setting aside the emeralds and assuming the tonnage is all gold, and the price of gold today is maybe seventeen or eighteen hundred bucks per ounce, that's a little over four billion."

"*Dollars?*" Zoe blurted.

"Yep," Matt replied.

Her eyes bugged out. "You did that in your frigging head?"

He stuffed his hands in his pockets. "Just simple math."

Zoe exchanged a glance with me, her mouth wide open. I couldn't tell if she was shocked at the treasure's value or my brother's human calculator trick.

"And *that's* my point," I said. "This treasure's value was and is redonk. So, the map or directions to it is going to be uber difficult to solve without the key."

He pulled his hands out and took a step back. "Hey, I don't deny the logic. The thing I'm still having a hard time grasping is why put how to find your fortune on a huge wall for anybody to see?"

I screwed my face up. "Who knows? The guy was quite eccentric. But I swear it's the key to something big."

"I'm not denying the cipher might lead to something incredibly valuable," my brother said. "I just don't think all these books relate back to it."

"You still think it's only one from these thousands?" I asked.

"Afraid so."

"We'll never find it," Zoe complained.

"Find anything in the grid lines?" I asked Matt, ignoring the piqued pixie.

He gave me a quick head shake. "Nope. But I still

think there's a clue in there identifying which one of these books is the key."

"Okay, before the place starts to fill up, let's take a ton of pictures," I said.

"Just in here?" Zoe asked.

"No," I replied. "The entire office suite."

"You're by far the tallest," Zoe said. "You do the library and I'll work with Matt in the office."

I gave her a thumbs-up. "That's a plan. But don't touch anything."

We spent the next hour creating a photographic record of every inch of Oliver Carlton's office suite. When we finished, Zoe and I left Matt in the office to see if he could uncover a clue to finding the book key while we returned to the entrance hall to study the architectural layout in the display case. In addition to the mansion, Arcadia included a chapel, stable, greenhouse, gardens complete with statues and stone walkways, and a small pavilion.

"We gotta split up," I said. "There's a ton to cover."

The sprite-sized Zoe was on her tip-toes leaning on the case, her cute little button nose inches from the glass. "Where you want me to start?"

"Go through the rest of the mansion while Matt works the office. I'll check out the other buildings, starting with the chapel."

"What am I looking for?"

"Anything unusual. More sets of numbers. Or one particular number."

She pushed away from the case. "There's more numbers carved here?"

"Not like what's in the office. But there may be

smaller sets. Or possibly one number, the same number, appearing in various places throughout the house. You know, maybe carved in some decorative stuff or in the wall art or something."

Zoe picked up a brochure and opened it to the floor layouts. "Got it. I'll hit his bedroom suite first." Without waiting for a reply, she bopped across the entrance hall toward a door on the other side.

I proceeded to the French doors at the rear of the hall, passed through a spacious parlor, and exited through exterior French doors onto what the brochure called the south portico. From there, I followed a winding stone path through colorful gardens that ended at the chapel's door. When I stepped inside it, the place blew me away.

The interior was breathtaking. Floor, ceiling, and walls were all golden oak. Crisscrossing beams created a grid effect in the ceiling with intricate designs carved into the sides facing the floor. Thick crosses cut deep into the wall panels created a three-dimensional effect, with each panel outlined by fleurs-de-lis. An aisle separated four short rows of pews and led to three white marble tombs dominating the far end of the chapel.

I crossed the floor to the tombs. All together, they were easily six feet high because I couldn't see over the top. In front of them, a series of words were carved into the floor.

In death all is revealed and then all will make perfect sense.

Oliver Carlton's tomb was flanked by the tombs of his wife and infant son, who both died during the baby's birth. An incredible sadness hit me. I closed my eyes, bowed my head, and said a silent prayer.

Opening my eyes, I noticed something on the side of Oliver Carlton's tomb. I dashed over to it, my heart quickening. Chiseled into the marble was a grid of strange—symbols. Not numbers. I counted the columns and rows. It matched the cipher's grid, fifteen by fifteen. There had to be a connection. A quick check of the other sides of the tombs revealed none had strange carvings.

After taking a picture of the words and also the strange grid of symbols, I spent several hours going over every inch of the chapel, but nothing else stood out. I returned to Carlton's tomb and studied the grid. Unlike the office grid, some symbols were repeated in various places, although never side by side. By far, the most used symbol was a diamond. As I pored over the strange symbols, a pattern emerged. Not only was a diamond the most used symbol, every sixth one was a diamond. All the way until the end. A total of thirty-seven.

I took several steps back and immediately noticed how the diamonds lined up in five columns with two columns between each having just symbols. Within each column of diamonds, every other row was a symbol. Stepping back to the grid, I carefully inspected every symbol to see if any could remotely resemble a number. None came close.

Then it hit me.

There was an implied number within the grid. The thirty-seven diamonds. Were they signifying the thirty-seventh book in the library was the key? Was it that simple?

I dashed out of the chapel and raced through the gardens toward the mansion. At the south portico, I stopped at the bottom of the steps and bent over, trying to catch my breath. Two months of not going to the gym was catching up with me. And so was the high humidity. My shirt was plastered to my back. So gross. I had to get back into air conditioning. Thank God somebody at the Carlton had the good sense to upgrade Arcadia with AC.

I pounded up the steps and barged through the exterior French doors into the parlor. All the people scattered around the room stopped what they were doing and stared at me. One old lady sporting a schoolmarm's gray bun gave me the eye while another relic held a hand to her chest and gaped at me, open-mouthed. I smiled politely at the leering lady and beelined it for the doors leading to the entrance hall. Nobody talked as a roomful of judging eyes followed me through the parlor and out the French doors.

Hanging a left through the door leading to the office suite, I blew through the two outer rooms and charged into the section with the books. Thankfully, the place was empty. "Matt," I called out. "I think I've got it."

Zoe popped into the room from the office, followed by Matt.

She brought a finger to her lips. "What the eff are you doing?" she whispered harshly.

I squinted back and mouthed, "What?"

She yanked a thumb back toward the office. "People."

"Crap."

Zoe sized me up. "You're a mess. What have you been doing?"

A bead of sweat dripped into my eye. I wiped it

away and brushed damp hair off my brow. "Running."

She glanced at my bare knees. "Looks like you didn't fall. That's progress."

"What'd you find?" an impatient Matt asked.

I brought up the picture of the grid from Carlton's tomb and handed the phone to my brother. "Check it out."

He took the phone and enlarged the pic. "Same number of rows and columns. Pretty funky symbols. No numbers." He looked up at me. "There could be a correlation to the cipher. But it's not obvious."

Zoe stuck her hand out for the phone. "Lemme see that."

Matt relinquished the phone and stood behind Zoe, staring over her shoulder at the pic.

Her eyes bulged. "What the eff. This was some weird dude."

"Take a look at all those diamonds," I said.

Matt's chin practically rested on Zoe's shoulder. "Hey, there's a pattern. Every sixth square has a diamond."

Zoe recoiled and rubbed the side of her head. "Hey, dude, quit whispering in my ear."

He straightened and looked down. "Sorry, didn't mean—"

She handed him the phone and flashed a warm smile. "Just screwing with you. You're good."

Matt smiled awkwardly but said nothing.

I walked to the first section of bookcases and stared straight up at the top shelf. It seemed miles away. "Exactly. There's thirty-seven of them."

My brother studied the phone. "Every sixth square," he muttered.

Zoe called over to me. "What are you doing over there?"

Pointing to the top shelf, I said, "The book key might be the thirty-seventh book."

Her mouth flopped open. "For real?"

Matt raised his head. "You could be right, but how are you getting up there with people walking around?"

"I don't know yet."

Zoe's arms slashed through the air. "No way you're climbing that ladder. That's a disaster waiting to happen. I'll go up."

She had a point. If I climbed the ladder, it would probably roll away and I'd end up crashing through the wall. Or worse.

"Deal," I said. "Let's hang around and hope people clear out. Then I can be the lookout while you make the grab."

"Works for me," Zoe said.

Matt stuck a hand out. "Whoa, whoa, whoa. Hold on. Are we *stealing* that book?"

"Of course not," I said. "Just borrowing it. We'll return it when we're done."

He shook his head. "I don't know, Sara."

"Got a better idea?" I asked.

"Not at the moment." Matt stepped past and gazed through the arched opening into the office as he muttered to himself. "Diamonds in the tomb grid. Every sixth square. Diamonds on the office floor." He spun around to face us, his brown eyes gleaming. "The diamonds on the floor are every sixth tile."

I stared at the wide-eyed Matt. "You think the number of the book key is six, not thirty-seven?"

A tour group exited the office and meandered

through the library toward the blue sitting room. "Okay, now we'll cross the grand hall to the majestic dining room," the guide announced. "Since all of Arcadia's staff were paid employees, to save money, Mr. Carlton developed some ingenious inventions that allowed him to minimize the number of domestic staff required." Her voice trailed off as the group filed through the library's outer room and into the sitting room. Soon we were by ourselves.

Zoe passed through the small arched opening leading to the office and poked her head into the space. She turned back toward us with a thumbs-up. "All clear."

Matt furrowed his brow as he addressed my earlier question. "Not sure. Both numbers could be involved somehow. He could've used two books. Or maybe you skip every sixth number in the cipher and the thirty-seventh book is the key. Or—" He breathed out. "—the guy liked using that diamond shape in his decorative work and there's no connection."

Zoe skipped over to us. "C'mon, what are we doing? Am I going up that ladder or what?"

I considered Matt. "What do you think?"

He winced. "If we get caught, I could lose my scholarship."

"We're not getting caught," I insisted. "Zoe will be up and down in no time."

Matt opened his mouth but then hesitated.

Zoe positioned herself at the base of the ladder, her diminutive hands wrapped around two rungs with a foot resting on the first rung. "C'mon, guys. We're wasting time."

My brother closed his eyes. "Get both books," he

croaked.

"Don't mix them up," I cautioned. "I'll go see if—"

Zoe sprang up the ladder, not waiting for me to check if the sitting room was clear. Seconds later, she jumped off the ladder, handing me a thin red book and a thicker green one. "The green one is thirty-seven."

I took a step back from her, refusing to take the books. "I don't have any place to hide those. Tuck one in the back of your shorts and cover it up with your shirt. Give the other to Matt."

Zoe gave me a look. "Why me? Why can't you tuck one in your shorts?"

Now it was my turn to give her a look before doing a brief half-turn to show her the back of my shirt. "Look at me. I'm a sweaty mess. Running. Remember?"

"Fine." She stuffed the red book halfway down the back of her shorts and handed the green one to Matt.

I faced my brother. "Do the same thing. Then let's get outta here."

He shoved the book in the back of his shorts and pulled his shirt over it. "Please tell me you can't see it."

I gave him a once-over. "Nope, you're good. Same with you, Zo. Let's go, but don't walk too fast. Don't wanna raise any suspicion."

"I can't believe I'm doing this," he whined as we exited the library.

"Just be cool, Matt," Zoe said gently.

I did a double take. "Where's that reassuring tone been for me?"

We exited the sitting room into the main hall and headed for the doors.

"Reassuring you has never been an issue," she said

in a low voice. "Try the opposite."

A college-age girl with straight blonde hair falling past her shoulders sat behind the information desk and observed us as we approached.

My heart beat faster. *What the frick were we doing?* I caught a glimpse of my brother out of the corner of my eye. The kid was staring at the girl and looked petrified.

I had to distract her before Matt got busted. "Don't stop," I said under my breath before slipping behind Matt and Zoe and moseying over to the desk. "Excuse me, are you open tomorrow?"

The girl slapped on a courteous smile. "Yes, we are. Between ten and five."

"Perfect. We way underestimated how long it would take to go through Arcadia," I gushed, laying it on thick to buy my fleeing cohorts more time. "There's so much to see."

"Everybody says that. I don't work tomorrow, but feel free to stop here at the desk and ask for a docent to take your group around."

The entrance doors opened, the hall sucking in outside air. "Thank you. I think we'll do that very thing. Have a wonderful day."

"Thanks. You, too."

I exited through the doors for the parking lot. Zoe and Matt were already in the lot hustling to the car. Keeping an even gait in case the girl was watching me, I took out the car's key fob and unlocked the doors for Zoe and Matt. Ten seconds later, I joined them.

Dropping into the driver's seat, I hit the locks, fired the engine up, and we rocketed out of the parking lot. "Piece of cake, guys."

"Easy for you to say," Matt groused.

I looked in the rearview mirror. Sweat dripped down his face.

"Thanks for doing this, little brother. When we get to the motel, we've got some work to do."

"First we're getting something to eat," Zoe added. "Stealing from a museum always makes me hungry."

Chapter Twenty-One

Can nothing mean something?

We worked well into the night trying to crack the cipher using both books and many different methodologies. All it got us was gibberish, both in garbled messages and eventually, our conversations. The tedious work left us exhausted, frustrated, and no further along than when we started. After a search on the Internet, we found where both books could be downloaded, but Matt still made us take pictures of every page because he discovered one book had several reprints and editions, which would do us no good. We needed the correct edition Carlton used to develop the cipher, otherwise, it was a waste of time. When I suggested we take the books with us and I could return them through the Carlton at a later date, Matt paled and insisted we return the books to Arcadia. And for some reason, Zoe supported him. Fervently.

The next morning, the plan was to get to Arcadia right after ten. With it being a Sunday, we figured few patrons would be arriving immediately after opening, presenting us the best opportunity to return the books unnoticed. As Zoe and I packed up, Mauzzy monitored us out of one eye from a pillow on my bed.

When we were ready to leave, I called Matt's

room, then turned toward the bed. "Okay, Mauz, we'll be back in a couple hours to check out."

He raised his head, studied me, and farted. Then he laid back on the pillow, sighed, and rolled over.

"Love you, too, Handsome."

Outside, the sun was already hot and the humidity high. I so missed autumn.

Zoe met Matt with a dazzling smile as he exited his room. "Good morning. Sleep well?"

He rubbed his eyes as he stumbled to the car. "Yeah, just not enough."

"You can sleep on the way back home," Zoe offered, her tone one of comfort and understanding.

Matt opened the back door. "Count on it."

Comforting tone? Zoe? I narrowed my eyes. Something was up. She answered my questioning stare with a sly smile.

We climbed into the car and blasted off for Arcadia. When we arrived, it was five after ten and there were only three cars in the parking lot. That bode well for the immediate mission.

As we exited the car, I said, "Okay, guys, we only have two hours before we have to get Mauz, check out, and head home."

Matt piped up. "Hold on. What about going to Darlington?"

I held up a hand in apology. "Right. Totally forgot. That means we only have one hour if we want to get home at a reasonable time."

He pumped a fist. "Yes."

Zoe cast a playful eye at Matt before addressing me. "Only one hour? What's the plan?"

I pointed to the books she was carrying. "First,

we'll smuggle those in the same way we took them out."

"Wait a sec," Zoe countered. "Why don't *you* put a book down your pants? You're not sweaty today."

"Because I'm way bigger than you two, so I'm going to walk between you and the desk. You know, to block the vision of anybody sitting there."

Zoe huffed, handed Matt the green book, and stuck the red one halfway down the back of her shorts. "I hate these rare occasions when you actually make sense."

I gave her an exaggerated smile. "We're going straight to the library so you can do your thing on the ladder. Then Matt needs to see the chapel."

As we hurried through the parking lot, Matt's Darlington exuberance disappeared, replaced by the same petrified look he wore yesterday when we smuggled the books out. "Matt, make sure you walk normal and don't stare down the person at the desk."

My brother barely acknowledged me.

Zoe put a hand on his arm. "Don't worry. I'll talk with you as we walk through the hall."

He shared a quick look with her. "Thanks."

With a gentle smile, she said, "Sure thing."

When we hit the entrance hall, a gorgeous guy of maybe twenty with black hair and the bluest of eyes sat behind the information desk. As we entered the hall, I positioned myself between the Adonis and the smugglers, who were chatting up a storm. Okay, mostly Zoe was chatting up a storm. My brother was either tongue-tied from Zoe laying it on thick and heavy, or he was beyond terrified of getting caught. Or both.

Giving the docent a head toss, I said, "Hey."

His incandescent smile rivaled Zoe's in its splendor

and wattage. "Good morning. Welcome to Arcadia."

I returned his smile, but no way mine could compete with the magnificence of his. "Thanks."

"Anything I can do for you?" he asked.

Now there's a loaded question.

I stopped in front of the desk as the chattering Zoe and unnerved Matt continued through the hall toward the door at the far end leading to the library. "I don't think so. We're finishing up what we couldn't get to yesterday."

"Totally understand. We get that response quite a bit." Another heartwarming smile. "I'll be here all day if you have a question."

I threw a quick glance at Zoe and Matt. From a distance, the books' outlines were visible underneath their clothes. I needed to close the gap fast.

One more big, loving smile for Adonis. "Okay, thanks. I need to catch up with my friends. Have a nice day."

"You, too."

I barreled through the hall, catching up with them as they passed through the blue sitting room. "Hang on, guys."

Both stopped and whipped around toward me.

"We good?" Zoe asked.

"Yep. I'll hang here as a lookout. Matt, stay on the phone with me so if I see someone coming, I can warn you. Zo, make it quick."

As the pair disappeared into the outer room of the library, I called Matt's phone and positioned myself so I could see through the door leading into the hall.

After a nerve-wracking minute, Matt and Zoe reappeared. He was a picture of relief as she gave me a thumbs-up.

"Awesome," I said. "Let's hit the chapel."

We made our way back into the hall, through the parlor, and out into the gardens. When we entered the chapel, Zoe and Matt stopped abruptly, which in turn caused me to stop.

"Whoa," Zoe said in a hushed tone.

Matt took in the gleaming golden wood walls and ceiling, his mouth open.

"I know it's amazing, but c'mon, we don't have much time," I implored. "Matt needs to see the markings on the tomb." I pushed past them and headed down the aisle. A quick look over my shoulder caused me to stop and turn. "Guys, let's go."

That snapped them out of it, and they followed me toward the mammoth tombs, stopping in front of the floor carving with the saying, *In death all is revealed and then all will make perfect sense.*

"What the heck is that?" Zoe asked.

"Don't know," I replied. "Probably some old biblical reference Carlton liked."

She shook her head slowly. "Mmmm, pretty sure that's not in the Bible."

"We'll search on it when we get home," I said.

With his gaze still lowered, Matt asked, "You find any other sayings like this?"

"Nope," I replied.

He glanced up at the tombs. "Nothing on any of those?"

"Not that I could find," I said. "Just the grid."

Matt took a big step over the floor carving and approached Oliver Carlton's tomb. He eased around to the right side and placed his hands on the grid, fingers probing along the outer and interior lines. His face was inches from the marble.

Zoe slipped alongside him and leaned in, her shoulder brushing up against his. "Whatcha doing?" she whispered.

In that instant, my suspicions were confirmed. My best friend had her sights set on my clueless brother. Made me want to vom.

"Looking for hidden words, numbers, or symbols," he whispered back, his attention fully on the carvings.

"Any luck?" she asked.

"Not yet."

While Matt worked on the grid, and Zoe worked on Matt, I circled the tombs, searching for anything that didn't look right. But everything appeared normal. I returned to the front of Oliver Carlton's tomb. Matt continued to examine the grid, and Zoe continued whispering in his ear.

"I'm going to check out the stable and pavilion," I said to the pair. "Call me if you find anything."

Zoe looked over her shoulder at me. "Sounds good."

With a quick glance at my phone, I said, "We have about forty-five minutes before we gotta get going. Anything yet?"

She shook her head. "Nope."

"Okay, maybe I'll get lucky."

A picture of Adonis popped into my head. Mmmm.

I left the chapel and strolled through the gardens to the nearby pavilion situated in the middle of the main garden. It was a square brick structure matching the mansion and chapel's red brick and white woodwork. Each side had a high arched opening with a gabled roof topping the structure. I circled it looking for clues but found nothing. Sitting inside on the flagstone floor were two wicker chairs with red cushions separated by a small wicker table with a glass top. I stomped around on the floor checking for any hollow spots, but all that did was get my ankles and feet upset with me. After snapping off pictures of the interior and exterior, I headed for the stable in the far corner of the main grounds.

After a ten-minute hike along a dirt road, I found an L-shaped whitewashed stone structure with a dirt floor. Inside were twelve stalls, six on each side of the long portion of the "L." Carved above a rear corner stall was a small pair of angel wings over praying hands, presumably for a favored horse of Carlton's that passed on. Above the opposite corner stall, a carved sunburst matching the ones in the office on the wall panels. Stored in the stable's short end were two carriages plus a small room with various gear for outfitting horses.

I wandered through the place, searching for something, anything, that could be linked back to the chapel and office carvings. But like the pavilion, I found nothing. And with the dirt floor, I didn't bother looking for anyplace hollow because of it being—dirt. However, the exterior stone walls were a foot thick, which easily could have a hidden space within them that held a treasure map or something, like those phony rocks people used to hide keys in their yard. I spent most of my time working around the structure, rapping the walls every few feet. But that brilliant exercise only resulted in skinned knuckles. I finished up by taking a sufficient number of pictures before heading out.

As I made the slog back to the chapel, I rubbed my

stinging knuckles. Why the heck did I knock on those dang stone walls? What did I expect was going to happen? Rocks are hard. Just like—

A revelation slammed into my head, bringing me to a stop.

Just like diamonds.

Skeezy Merv performed a scratch test on every stone except one. The very last one he examined. The Star of Midnight. Did he simply forget? Or was there another reason? I filed that away for future investigation and started back up.

When I entered the chapel, Zoe and Matt were sitting close to each other in a front pew talking quietly. "Time to go," I called out.

Both startled before jumping up and spinning around. Zoe's hands shot up in the air. "Cripes, Sara, you scared the living crap out of us."

I matched her glare with one of my own. "We gotta go. Why'd you stop investigating?"

They walked down the aisle toward me, Matt with his head down and hands stuffed in his shorts pockets. "Because we were done," he said. "Didn't find anything."

My shoulders sagged. "Nothing?"

Matt stopped in front of me, Zoe right by his side. And I mean, *right by his side*. "Nothing might be a good thing," he said.

I jerked my head back. "How's finding nothing a good thing?"

He grinned. "After we finished with the tomb, we checked the decorative carvings in the wood walls and ceiling and didn't find what we were hoping to find."

"And again, that's a good thing?"

Matt exchanged a knowing glance with Zoe. "We think so."

"What were you looking for?" I asked.

"Diamond shapes," Matt replied.

"And you found none?"

"Yep," he replied. "That tells me the diamond symbols in the tomb grid and on the office floor mean something. I think they're signifying the number six is key to solving the puzzle."

I furrowed my brow. "How'd you come up with that?"

"The ones in the tomb grid are spaced exactly six apart throughout the entire thing. And it's the same on the office floor. That's no coincidence."

Chapter Twenty-Two

Dad

When we got home from our North Carolina trip, it was past ten in the evening. Mauzzy and I were first through the front door, followed by Matt and Zoe.

Waiting for us in the front hall was the formidable figure of—Dad. "It's about time. Your note said you'd be home by eight."

I put Mauzzy down, and he wisely scampered up the stairs. "Matt wanted to see some racing stuff in Darlington. Ended up staying longer than planned."

"It was really cool," Matt said. "The stock car museum was awesome."

"And it's why we're late getting home," I added.

Zoe pushed past carrying her overnight bag. "Hey, Mr. D. How was the beach?"

"Hot."

She bounded up the stairs. "So was NC."

Dad turned his attention to me. "About that."

Matt rushed up the stairs after Zoe, taking them two at a time.

And just like that, I was one-on-one with The Man. "About what?"

"North Carolina. Why did you kids up and leave for there?"

"We wanted to see Arcadia."

"Which is what?"

"Oliver Carlton's estate. It's pretty amazing."

Dad studied me. "So amazing it's why the three of you decided on a whim to drive seven hours to see it?"

I swallowed. "Um, yes."

His eyes remained riveted on me. "This is about that whole vault robbery thing, right?"

Unbelievable. The dude always sees right through me. He's a really cool dad, always willing to help. It's just that, over the years, he's seen me get in a few—situations—entirely of my own making. So, with me, he's extra vigilant. And even more suspicious.

This was going to require some finesse. And luck. "Mmmm, sorta."

"The thing I told you to leave alone a couple of weeks back?"

"Kinda."

"Let me guess. You told the museum's security chief you thought the vault was robbed. He checked it out and found nothing. But you knew he was obviously wrong, so you kept pushing him, to no avail. That's when you decided to take things into your own hands, and that's how you ended up in North Carolina. How am I doing?"

I grimaced. "Pretty darn good."

Dad exhaled. "I've seen this movie more than a few times. I'm going to regret this, but did you find anything at this Arcadia?"

I straightened. "As a matter of fact, maybe."

That loosened him up because he chuckled and shook his head. "Now that's definitive."

"Let me take my stuff upstairs. Then I'll get Zoe

and Matt and we can tell you everything."

"I'll be in the family room."

Five minutes later, we were all together. Except Mauzzy. I didn't know where he disappeared to, and that worried me. Matt and Zoe sat on the ottoman, with Dad next to me on the long side of the sectional so I could show him pictures from my phone. Mom worked on the computer on a small desk up against the back of the sectional, so she could see everyone. I brought him up to speed on the diamond being real and what we found at Arcadia.

"Speaking of ciphers," Dad said. "I worked on that pigpen cipher last week."

I brightened. "Any luck?"

He shook his head. "Like I said before, there's such a level of sophistication it's simply impossible to crack without more information. I've never seen anything like it." He paused, a perplexed look coming across his face. "You have any pictures of those strange symbols from the tomb?"

I brought up a pic of the grid and handed my phone to Dad. "While Matt drooled over old race cars at Darlington, I researched the carving. Cryptanalysts think it's related to the office wall grid since they're both fifteen by fifteen, but nobody can make the connection."

Dad took the phone from me and stared at the picture. "My first reaction. This ties back to the pigpen cipher. Not the wall grid."

"No shi—kidding," Zoe exclaimed, her attention shifting to an attentive Mom, who stopped typing.

"What makes you think that?" Matt asked.

Dad pointed to several symbols in the grid for me

to see. "What do those look like?"

"The symbols in the will," I gushed. "Holy crap, Dad, you did it."

He chuckled lightly. "Far from it. There's still work to do if you have any hope of sorting all this out." He tapped the picture. "But I'll bet this is integral to cracking the will's code. This might be that missing piece of data I mentioned earlier." A beat. "Or not."

"What about the number six?" Matt asked, his voice cracking with excitement. "Could that be the missing link between the tomb grid and the pigpen cipher?"

Dad focused on my brother. "Depends. Why that number?"

Matt explained about the spacing of the diamonds in both places as I showed Dad a pic of the office floor.

His forehead wrinkled. "It appears the number six could somehow be the key to solving the wall grid. And if I'm right about the tomb grid being connected to the will's message, that, too."

"Oh, and Dad, the first number in the wall grid is six," I added.

"Really?" he said. "Show me that wall grid again."

I found the pic and handed him the phone.

"Son of a gun," he said under his breath before looking up at us. "I'd say the number six fits in this whole puzzle somehow."

"I knew it," Matt burst out.

Zoe beamed at my elated brother and gave him an affectionate shoulder bump.

Casting a glance at Zoe before looking at me, Dad asked, "What else you got?"

"That's about it," I replied.

"Well, sounds like you had a productive trip," he said. "Although after hearing the diamond wasn't stolen, I don't see how all this is tied to your now debunked vault robbery theory."

I glanced at Zoe, who watched me closely. Dad, too. "I don't know. Something's still telling me the Star of Midnight is a fake."

Concern crossed Dad's face. "I thought you said the museum brought in an expert to examine it?"

"They did. He examined the stones in the exhibit and said they were all real. No fakes."

"Yet you don't believe him," Dad said slowly. "Why?"

"During his examination of each stone, he scratched at it with a small metal pick, kinda like a dentist's tool. But he didn't do that with the Star of Midnight, which he examined last."

"Sure you didn't miss it?" Mom asked.

I shook my head. "Positive. He was very deliberate. Went through the same series of steps with each stone, like he's done it a gazillion times before. But with the very last stone, the most valuable one in the exhibit, he skipped that last step. Why?"

Dad leveled his gaze on me. It was piercing. "Sara, sounds like you're doing it again."

I pulled my head back. "What?"

Zoe jumped in. "Taking something that has a logical explanation, like somebody making an innocent mistake forgetting to scratch a stone, and turning it upside down into some crazy sinister idea and in the end, you end up stepping in—" A quick look at Mom. "—crap."

"I wouldn't have exactly put it like that," Dad said.

"But, yes, what Zoe said."

"I've been right a lot of times, too."

Zoe scrunched up her face and wiggled a hand in the air. "Mmmm, maybe. But you never get it quite right."

My face burned. "Sometimes I do."

Dad put out a hand. "Forget about the diamond. They checked and it's real. Leave it alone. But what you found on your trip to North Carolina has merit. Focus on that. And since your old man happens to be a cryptanalyst, tell me what I can do to help?"

"Really?"

"Sure, but again, given your history, I'm not making any promises we'll find anything."

Chapter Twenty-Three

Skeezy Merv

The following morning when I arrived at work, a voicemail awaited me. From Boss Lady. Asking me to see her as soon as I got in. Not good. I debated whether it was a good idea to first grab some coffee to calm my nerves, but realized if Evy caught me sipping coffee at my desk before seeing her, things could go from bad to worse real fast.

I tapped on Boss Lady's open door. "Good morning, Evy. You wanted to see me?"

She looked up. "Come in. And shut the door."

That sent my stomach tumbling, my chest tightening as I sat and waited.

"I got your voicemail Friday morning." She gave me the once-over. "Feeling any better?"

"Yes, ma'am."

"Very well. You find those missing journals?"

I slumped into the chair. "No, and I looked everywhere."

"I see. Do you realize by not coming in on Friday, you put me in a bad position? I had to make a decision regarding your incomplete inventory paperwork for those missing journals."

"I'm sorry. I'll finish it up for you this morning and

show them as missing. I don't know what else to do."

"Too late. The report was due to the Board by noon last Friday."

I winced. "Did I get you in trouble?"

Boss Lady took two sips of tea before setting the teacup gently on its saucer, her eyes remaining on me the entire time. "I submitted it Friday."

"What did they say about the missing journals?"

Her eyes stayed on me. "Nothing."

I gave a little head shake. "Nothing?"

"That's right."

"Nobody noticed?"

"There was nothing for anybody to notice."

"I don't understand."

She straightened, slid the cup-and-saucer to the side, and folded her hands on the desk. "It's quite simple, really. I didn't identify those journals as missing."

"But they *are* missing."

Boss Lady forced a smile. "Apparently, from what you just told me. However, on Friday, with you not in the office and my report due, I had to make an assumption, which was you found them. Because otherwise"—her face hardened—"you would have told me in your voicemail Friday morning. In the absence of that information, I assumed you found them." A harsh coldness permeated her words.

I swallowed hard. "But I didn't."

She pointed toward the door. "But you will. I bought you one month. Find them."

I stood to leave. "Yes, ma'am."

Boss Lady held out a thin knobby finger, her pale blue eyes digging into me. "And not a word of this to anyone. Understand?"

"Uh-huh."

I returned to my desk a bit confused and plenty worried. Evy Langston, chief curator of the Carlton Museum, falsified a report to the Board of Trustees. A document with my name on it as the person who conducted the inventory and prepared the report. And she pretty much threatened me if I told anybody.

As my head spun, I realized my body was lacking morning's most essential element—coffee. I hit the coffee station, made a mug of blonde roast for the added caffeine, and sat in my cubicle pondering my latest situation. As the caffeine worked its magic, the obvious solution became clear. Find those fricking journals.

With that problem sorted out, for now, it was time to focus on the Star of Midnight and Skeezy Merv. I picked up the phone.

"Security. Mickey Fraser speaking."

"Hey, Mickey. Sara Donovan."

"Yeah, I was expecting your call."

Last night I asked Grant to call Mickey this morning to bolster my sagging credibility after Thursday night's humiliating disaster, courtesy of Skeezy Merv. It appeared Grant already followed through on my request.

I feigned ignorance. "Oh?"

"Nice try. I talked to Grant earlier this morning. He said you'd be dropping by."

Sufficiently busted, I dropped the act. "You have time now?"

"Come on down."

Minutes later, I stood outside Mickey's office. He

was reading the newspaper, feet up on the desk, a mug of steaming aromatic coffee on the desk.

I knocked and entered the office, closing the door behind me.

He lowered the paper, saw me, and put his feet down. "I hesitate to ask, but what's on your mind?"

Taking a seat, I said, "I still believe the Star of Midnight on display is a fake."

That statement produced a disparaging laugh at my expense. "Grant told me to keep an open mind about you. That your instincts are usually pretty good. But you're pushing it. Now I see why he didn't want to say what you were going to talk to me about."

"And will you keep an open mind?"

"Grant and I are buddies. I promised him I would, so yeah, I'll keep an open mind." He stuck out a brawny hand like a traffic cop. "Up to a point. What makes you think the diamond is a fake? You were there when it was examined last week."

"What do you know about this guy Merv?"

He leaned back in the chair. "The gemologist guy?"

"Uh-huh."

His forehead wrinkled. "Not much. Works for Bancroft and Culpeper at their New York location."

"How long has he been with them?"

"Not a clue. Why?"

"He didn't do a full examination of the diamond."

"Sure, he did. He went through the exact same steps as he did with the other stones."

I shook my head. "Not all the steps."

Mickey leaned forward, his eyes narrowing under bushy salt-and-pepper eyebrows. "I didn't realize you were a gemologist."

"It was subtle, so I can see how you might have missed it."

"Missed what?"

"He didn't scrape at the surface with his pick like he did with the other ones."

He pulled his head back. "He did, too. I saw him."

My eyes stayed locked on Mickey. "Sorry, but you didn't. You may think you did, but you didn't."

"Even if he didn't, so what? He's a professional. He knows what he's doing."

I scoffed at him. "Oh, I'm sure he knows exactly what he's doing. He knew if he scraped at that diamond, he'd scratch the surface. Because it's a fake. You can't scratch a diamond."

"I don't believe it."

"It's true."

Mickey took a slurp of coffee, his eyes studying me over the edge of the white mug. He set it down and leaned forward, elbows propped on the desk, one hand folded over the other in front of his mouth. Seconds ticked by before he spoke. "Why pull such an audacious stunt right in front of everybody plus the security cameras?"

"Isn't it obvious?"

"Humor me."

"He's either part of the crew, or someone bribed him."

He pressed his lips together tight and considered me for several seconds. "That's some accusation to make against somebody you don't know and only saw for maybe an hour."

"Did you see the guy? He's the poster child of

slimy."

"You *do* realize just because somebody looks shady doesn't mean he's a crook?" His tone was scornful, like I hit a nerve.

I brushed off the giant man's judgmental attitude. "It's not because of his appearance, although, that doesn't help. It's no coincidence the one examination that differed from the others was on the Star."

Mickey shook his head emphatically. "No way. I'm not about to impugn a man's professional reputation based on a hunch from a kid who knows nothing about him."

I crossed my arms. "Pull the security footage from that night. You'll see I'm right."

The chief of security scrutinized me. With a dismissive shake of his head, he mashed the desk phone's speaker button and pounded four numbers on the keypad.

"Yes, sir?"

"Pull the footage of the *Fire and Ice Exhibit* from last Thursday night between eight and nine-thirty and send it to my computer."

"Roger. Give me ten minutes."

"Thanks." Mickey ended the call and regarded me. "You can wait or I can let you know what I find."

"I'll be back in ten minutes."

"Sure."

I left his office, went upstairs to the *Fire and Ice Exhibit*, and stared at the Star of Midnight. Since it was early on a Monday morning, no patrons were crowding around the display case, which allowed me to really give it a close inspection. As I studied the stone, a sudden dizziness swept over me.

Something wasn't right about the fake diamond.

I brought up the real diamond's pictures on my phone. The ones I wasn't supposed to take inside the valuables vault. My attention bounced back and forth between the phone and the display case. The shape of the diamond in the display appeared more rounded at the bottom, like the actual Star. I found the pic of the fake on my phone and compared it to the one in the case.

Crap.

They sure didn't look the same. Was I losing my superpower of observation?

I brought back up the picture of the real one and worked my way around the display case, stopping every couple of feet to compare the diamond in the case to the one on my phone. My lungs battled the boa constrictor squeezing my chest, breaths coming in short gasps. Midway around the display, my fingers and toes went numb.

Could it be I was looking at the Star of Midnight? Has it been there all along? Or did their inside man replace the fake with the real one when I was in North Carolina because they knew I was zeroing in on them?

After inching around the case, I ended up back in front of the sparkling diamond, focused on the lighting. Could it be different, and that's why the fake appeared real? Did someone tweak the lighting? I brought back up the picture of the fake and stared at it, then the case. The current lighting seemed brighter, whiter, more brilliant. And the stone appeared more lustrous. That might be it. The stone was still a fake. They just covered the flaw with a blanket of brilliant light, the resulting reflection blinding viewers from the flaw.

Or could it be something else?

Like, I was wrong.

I looked at my phone and realized it had been over fifteen minutes since I left Mickey's office. Five minutes later, I stood in his doorway. "You get the footage?"

With eyes focused on the computer screen, his humongous hand manipulated an invisible mouse. "Yeah."

I stepped around the desk and looked over his shoulder at the screen. Mickey zoomed in on Merv, who was peering through his microscope, looking as skeezy as I remembered him.

"What's he examining?" I asked.

"One of the smaller diamonds. His methodology has been consistent with every rock, ending with him scratching at the surface."

"How come no sound?"

His eyes remained fixed on the screen. "In D.C. it's illegal to record people's conversations without a warrant unless one of the people in the recording consents."

"Oh, good to know."

Mickey gave me a sidelong glance but said nothing.

Over the next hour, Skeezy Merv worked his way through the stones. After each examination, he set the stone to his right on the black velvet fabric spread out on the table, after which Jefferson Scott returned it to the display case.

I pointed at the screen. "He has the Heart of Fire."

"Mmmm hmmm."

Merv worked through his process, ending with him

scratching at the ruby's surface with his dental tool. By his reaction, he was clearly satisfied with its authenticity as he set the magnificent ruby to the right and picked up the Star of Midnight.

I leaned closer to the screen, absorbed in the gemologist's every move. "Here we go," I muttered.

Merv squinted at the diamond through his eye gizmo, turning it around while studying the enormous stone. Eventually, he placed it under his microscope and moved the rock around as he stared through the eyepiece. Several minutes later, he removed the Star from under the microscope, set it to the right, and gave a thumbs-up to Jefferson. Then he spun around in his chair to say something to me. The look on my face, one of total shock. Jefferson took the Star, returned it to the display case, and pointed angrily at me as he said something.

Mickey paused the recording and I took a seat in one of his crappy guest chairs. On his face, muted surprise. "Looks like you were right. He didn't perform his scratch test on the big one."

"Now you believe it's a fake?"

"Not yet. I wanna see what Merv has to say." He picked out a business card from a pile on the desk, briefly studied it, then placed a call. "Yes, hello. This is Mickey Fraser, the chief of security at the Carlton Museum. Is Merv Glickman available?" Mickey listened for a few seconds, his eyes watching me. "Uh-huh. You know when he'll be back? I see. If you happen to hear from him, can you have him call either me or Jefferson Scott?" Mickey gave both their phone numbers, then hung up.

"That sounded interesting," I said.

Mickey's eyes widened. "Sure was. Nobody has seen or heard from Glickman since he left New York to come here last Thursday."

"You mean he's missing?"

"Appears so."

Chapter Twenty-Four

The moment of truth–part two

The next day, I was finishing things up to go home when Mickey called.

"Hey, Sara. You busy tonight?"

"Depends. I was getting ready to head out for the day."

"Thought you might wanna stick around. Got a local gemologist coming in to examine the stones."

"Really? What's happened?"

"Asked a buddy of mine over at DHS to check if Glickman ever got on his return flight to New York. He didn't. Cameras over at Reagan didn't pick him up. So, he checked with Dulles and footage showed the guy Thursday night passing through security to the gates. Problem is, he didn't show up on any passenger manifests for that night."

"How's that possible?"

"My buddy thinks he's got a phony passport and fled the country."

"Which is why he didn't show up on any manifests."

"Exactly."

"You think he stole the diamond when he was examining it? You know, palmed it and made a switch."

"Only if he did it before the exhibit got here. We

checked the footage frame by frame. He didn't swipe any of the stones."

"Any idea where he disappeared to?"

"Right now, he's in the wind. Could be anywhere. We're gonna check the stones starting around eight, once we confirm the museum is cleared of patrons."

"I'll be there."

"Okay. See you then."

I hung up, sat back, and smiled triumphantly. Tonight, vindication was going to be mine. Finally. 'Ole Skeezy Merv was on the lam. And Mickey and Jefferson were going to soon find out I've been right all along. The Star of Midnight was a fake.

The time was just past five. It was going to be tight getting home and then—a disturbing vision popped into my head. I needed to call Zoe.

"What's up, Sara."

"Where you at?"

"We're on Ninety-Seven."

"Listen, I'm staying late at work. They're bringing in another person to examine the diamond."

"No shit."

In the background, Dad's deep voice said something to Zoe.

"Sorry, Mr. D. Let's keep that one between us, okay? You're the best. So, girl, you've been right the whole time?"

"Appears that way. Hey, can you feed Mauzzy when you get home?"

"What's the matter? Don't want him getting into your perfume samples again?"

"Aargh. Or worse."

"Sure. A half scoop, right?"

"Mmmm, let's give him a little more tonight."

"A little bribery never hurt, huh."

"With him, definitely. That's speaking his language."

"I gotcha covered. Good luck."

"Thanks." I tapped off and closed my eyes. One crisis averted. Hopefully.

****

A band of thunderstorms that rolled through last night resulted in today being a rare beautiful day, with the humidity and temperature more akin to April. Since I had several hours to kill before they examined the exhibit, I strolled up past K Street and ate dinner at an awesome little German place Danielle raved about that specialized in vegetarian dishes. Everything was so delicious, it was with great regret when I tore myself away from gastronomic heaven to get to the Gem and Minerals Hall a little early. I had a suspicion Mickey was going to have the Star of Midnight examined first, as opposed to last like Skeezy Merv did, and I didn't want to be late. Like, adult late. Not Sara late, which provides a fifteen-minute window for me to be on time.

They had set up the same small table with the black velvet fabric along with the gooseneck lamp. Four armed guards, Tony Carlucci, and Jefferson stood around the exhibit's closed display case.

Jefferson was talking to Tony, and the exhibit security director did not look happy. He glanced over at me walking across the floor and scowled. "Young lady, you're a dadgum thorn in my side. Didn't I say no more trouble from you?"

I stopped in front of the white-haired man with the bad comb-over and smiled politely. "You did. But this isn't my doing."

"Yeah, that dog won't hunt," he growled.

"Sounds to me like you have a lazy dog," I said sweetly.

He jabbed a finger at me. "You're mixed up in this somehow. I was fixin' to have a nice supper when I got a call from security to come open that dadgum case."

"Sorry to hear that, but I really don't have anything to do with this. You need to talk to—"

"Me," boomed Mickey's voice from behind me.

I whirled around to see the daunting frame of Mickey Fraser closing fast, a lady of about fifty in a gray business suit trailing behind him wheeling a black hard-shell suitcase. She was as wee as Zoe with a dark brown pixie cut, further dwarfed by the gigantic security chief.

Mickey stopped in front of Jefferson and stared down at the man. "Sorry I didn't call you myself but"— he motioned to the lady now standing beside him—"I was busy tracking down Ms. Cara Twigg here."

The exhibit security director acknowledged the lady with a quick head bow and polished smile. "Ma'am, a pleasure. Jefferson Scott."

She tipped her head.

He regarded Mickey. "What's this all about?"

Tingling tore through my body as a sensation of weightlessness hit me. This was it. My moment. After two weeks of being disregarded and blown off, everybody was going to see I'd been right all along. Me. Sara Donovan. A hero. If I was a thorn in Jefferson's side before, what was he going to think in about ten seconds?

Mickey briefly looked at me before answering. "I

received some information today that's given me reason to believe at least one of those stones is a fake."

Jefferson took a quick step backward as his mouth fell open. "What? Fake? That's… That's…" He rattled his head. "Impossible."

As I witnessed from my lofty perch the possibility of the diamond being a fake wash over the man, something tugged at my heart. I couldn't place the emotion, but it was there.

Mickey looked over at Cara Twigg. "Why don't you go ahead and get set up and when you're ready, we'll open the case."

"It'll only take me a few minutes."

Mickey turned back to the befuddled Jefferson Scott. "Best we can tell, Merv Glickman never flew back to New York. Looks like he's traveling on a false passport."

Jefferson's eyes bugged out. "What? False passport? Merv?"

"Appears so."

"That don't figure. You sure there ain't some misunderstanding?"

"Always a possibility. That's why I asked Ms. Twigg to help us out. If those stones are legit, then we'll let Glickman be. For all we know, he's running from a divorce or something. But if any of them are fake, then he's culpable and I've gotta get the FBI involved."

Jefferson squeezed the sides of his head. "This thing here is gettin' all cattywampus. You call in the feds and Ms. Wainwright will be fit to be tied."

"They'll only be called if any of those stones are fake. And if so, I'd think she'd want the FBI investigating."

"Mr. Fraser," called Cara Twigg. "I'm ready."

Mickey extended an arm toward the display case. "Shall we?"

I followed the two men as they walked over to the exhibit, each reaching into their pocket and taking out their black key fob. Seconds later, two electronic clunks sounded in rapid succession. Jefferson raised the glass top and picked up a small yellow diamond.

"Jeff, let's start with the big one," Mickey said.

Jefferson looked back over his shoulder. "Don't reckon it matters, but sure." He replaced the yellow diamond, picked up the Star of Midnight, and handed it to the gemologist.

"Thank you," she said, taking the diamond and examining it through the same kind of eye gizmo Skeezy Merv used last week. Seconds later, she took the eyeglass down and addressed the two security bosses. "This is a fake."

Yes. *Vindication.*

Jefferson sucked in deep, his eyes blinking rapidly. "*What?* That can't be."

"That was fast," Mickey said. "You sure?"

"Positive." She held up the fake diamond. "Gentlemen, this is leaded glass."

Jefferson clasped his hands behind his head. "That just can't be. It just can't."

My vindication was short-lived, a heaviness settling into my limbs, as the man's reality crashed down on him. Pangs of guilt tore at my tightening chest. What have I done?

Mickey glanced over at the shocked Jefferson Scott, then turned to the gemologist. "Can you do a full examination of it?"

"I can if you want, but it's really not necessary. I can easily show you it's glass." She picked up a pointy metal tool from the table. "Come on over and see this."

The two men stepped over to the table.

She held the fake diamond underneath the lamp and placed the sharp point of the tool up against the stone. "If this is a diamond—" She made several sharp motions with the tool across the surface of the glass bauble. "—I won't be able to scratch it." She leaned back, still holding the stone under the lamp. "See for yourself."

Mickey and Jefferson leaned in close.

Using the tool, she directed their attention to an area on the fake stone. "See those marks?"

Mickey peered at the piece of glass. "Son of a…"

Jefferson said nothing as he stared at where Cara Twigg was pointing.

"Let's get the rest of the stones checked out before I call the FBI," Mickey said.

"Absolutely," she said. "Are you satisfied, Mr. Scott?"

Jefferson straightened. "Yes, ma'am." His tone was subdued. His face, ashen.

"Jeff," Mickey said quietly.

"Hmmm?"

"You gotta get the stones from the case for Ms. Twigg. Exhibit requirements don't allow me to touch them."

Jefferson jerked his head. "Right. Right. Apologies." He puttered over to the display case, his arrogant confidence replaced by profound desolation. "You want the big ruby next?"

"Yes, thanks," Mickey replied.

Ninety minutes later, Cara Twigg finished her examination of the other stones. "Well, that's it. The only fake was the first one."

A disheveled Jefferson Scott wore a tired smile. "Thank the good Lord for that."

The man had aged a good ten years. His career was over, and he knew it. In less than two hours, Jefferson Scott disintegrated before my eyes to now just a shell of a man. I was staring at rock bottom.

Mickey stepped over to the open display case, crouched, and examined beneath it with his hands. "Don't see any indications of tampering."

Jefferson joined him and examined the inside edges. "Don't see nothing here either." He bent and checked the underside. "Yep, nothing here, too." He stood and regarded Mickey. The exhibit's man was trembling, his eyes two blue dinner plates. "How'd this happen?"

"Gonna have to go through the chain of custody papers," Mickey replied. "Since we checked the vault and it was secure, and so is the case, somebody had to switch it out before the exhibit arrived here. Any thoughts on how somebody made the switch?"

He shook his head slowly. "Don't know how I'm gonna tell Ms. Wainwright."

Mickey called over to Cara Twigg, who was packing up her microscope and tools. "Will you be available tomorrow? Going to need you to confirm to the FBI the Star of Midnight there is glass."

"Not a problem. I'll also have a certified report prepared for you and Bancroft and Culpeper tomorrow."

"Thanks." Mickey pointed to Tony. "I wanna see the footage from both vaults when the exhibit was stored there, and start going through all the footage from here after the exhibit was moved upstairs. Keep two guards posted here until we can sort things out."

"You got it, chief."

Mickey faced Jefferson, who had a blank stare. "Jeff, you need to close the case," he said quietly.

The exhibit security director gave a slight nod and slowly lowered the lid. He took the black key fob from his pocket and a clunk came from the display case.

Mickey did the same with his fob, and a second clunk sounded. He approached me with a contrite smile. "Looks like you were right. Sorry for not listening to you."

"It's okay. I'm used to it."

There was my long-awaited vindication, my triumph, yet I felt awful. Nauseous. I glanced over at the dazed Jefferson Scott. That earlier emotion I couldn't label now had a name. Sadness.

Chapter Twenty-Five

The FBI

I was sitting at my cubicle sipping coffee and mulling over last night's pronouncement by Cara Twigg when a commotion of voices erupted at the main vault's day gate. Rolling to the edge of my cubicle, I saw Mickey leading four dour-looking men into the vault. Two were in business casual and two were wearing jeans and carrying black cases. Bringing up the rear was Jefferson. He appeared much calmer than last night when the poor guy was about to have a heart attack or something.

Mickey spotted me and mouthed "FBI" as Boss Lady's voice rang out from behind. "Gentlemen. Good morning."

To my left, Evy marched toward the group. Everyone stopped right outside my cubicle.

Mickey nodded toward Boss Lady. "Moss, this is Evy Langston, chief curator and the person responsible for all that goes on in the vault." Turning to Boss Lady, he said, "Evy, as I mentioned to you earlier, the FBI here is investigating the theft of the Star of Midnight."

Boss Lady clasped then unclasped her hands. "Yes, dreadful news. Simply dreadful. Let me know what I can do to help."

Moss, the lead fed, spoke up. "Ma'am. Moss Bailey. My team is going to need access to the vault that held the exhibit."

"Certainly," she replied. "This way, gentlemen."

The group followed Boss Lady to the locked day gate of the valuables vault. After she opened it, the men entered, but when Evy attempted to follow them in, somebody from inside stopped her. She said something before storming away.

Twenty minutes later, Mickey, two of the agents, including Moss Bailey, and Jefferson, showed up outside my cubicle.

Mickey rested a hand on top of the front partition and leaned inside, his burly body blocking the view of the rest of his party. "Sara," he said softly, "we're gonna need to talk with you."

Although I was sitting, a sudden faintness hit me. "Why me?" I mouthed, working hard to hold it together.

He gave me a slight head shake. "Not here." He tipped his head toward the entrance day gate. "Come on. I'll be with you."

I gathered my phone and purse, insides quivering like a bowl of disgusting green gelatin salad that for some reason Mom loved to make every Thanksgiving. I followed the men out of the vault, eventually ending up in Mickey's office. Agent Bailey sat in Mickey's chair and the other agent turned the second guest chair toward me before sitting in it. Mickey and Jefferson leaned up against a work table behind the desk.

Agent Bailey produced a thin wallet from his blazer's inner pocket, flipped it open, and slid it across the desk toward me. "Sara, I'm Moss Bailey with the

FBI." He gestured to the agent sitting next to me. "That's Special Agent Mike Mahoney."

Agent Mahoney handed me a similar wallet with a picture ID and a small gold badge.

As a chill ran down my spine, I inspected both before handing them back to each agent. "Not sure why you want to talk to me. I don't know anything."

"There's nothing to worry about," Agent Bailey reassured me. "We're trying to determine when the diamond was stolen. Right now, an evidence response team is examining the valuables vault to see if it was penetrated. That's why we wanted to talk with you."

My body inadvertently stiffened. "I didn't break into the vault."

Agent Bailey smiled evenly. "Nobody said you did. We reviewed the security footage for the exhibit from the time it arrived at the vault to the moment the Star of Midnight was confirmed a fake. Several unusual things popped out to us, each involving you."

It's never good when a G-man wants to talk to you, let alone when he mentions unusual things popping out to him regarding you. I exchanged a glance with Mickey, who gave me a slight nod of encouragement.

"Unusual?" I asked casually.

"We found a one-minute lapse in the footage due to a power outage," Agent Bailey explained. "You and a museum security guard were the only two people in the main vault. Immediately before the outage, you were running around looking in cubicles and under desks. You were in Evy Langston's office when the power went out. All that running around looked like you were making sure nobody was in the vault. Then, after the exhibit moved upstairs, you kept showing up around the display case. Almost every time, you took pictures from all angles around the display and constantly looked over your shoulder and up at the cameras. Can you explain what you were doing?"

I struggled to keep it together and appear calm to my inquisitors. "The power outage occurred right around closing time. Everybody already left. I was last out because I was…well…searching for my dog."

"Yes, we saw you catch him by the valuables vault door," Agent Bailey said. "But here's the thing. Immediately after the lights came on, you were at the side wall of that vault. You were no longer in the office."

"That's because my dog pitched a fit when the lights went out. I needed to find him."

"Did you hear anything coming from inside the vault immediately before or after the power outage?" Agent Mahoney asked.

I shook my head. "No, sir, but Mauzzy sure did."

"Your dog?" he asked.

"Yes, sir. He was in the back corner along that side wall barking and scratching at it."

The two G-men exchanged a glance.

Agent Bailey produced a phone from his jacket and placed a call. "Jerry, check the lower left back corner." A pause. "I understand there's shelving. Check it anyway. Right. Thanks." He slipped the phone back into his pocket.

Jefferson piped up. "You thinking the vault was breached there?"

Agent Bailey rotated around in the chair to face him. "Could be. Dogs have a keen sense of hearing. Sounds like he may have heard something in that area."

My heart swelled with pride. Mauzzy was never wrong. Never.

Agent Bailey swiveled back to me. "Can you explain your suspicious activities in the Gem Hall around the display case?"

Suspicious? Crap. I couldn't tell him about the pics I took in the valuables vault. That would make me look really bad, and I was told to put my phone away, too. "I was a patron. I love the exhibit."

"Why the interest in the cameras?" Agent Bailey asked.

"And the constant picture taking?" added his partner. "A few photos should have been sufficient."

"Not for me. I take tons of pictures."

"And the interest in the cameras?" prodded Agent Mahoney.

A trickle of perspiration slid down the small of my back. These guys were taking too much of an interest in me. I've been here before, and this time I didn't have Mauzzy to run interference.

I threw him an easy smile, hoping to disarm the suspicious G-man. "Didn't realize I was doing that. Maybe it was just me being highly observant. You know, being aware of your surroundings and all."

Jefferson tapped his lips with a forefinger. "Mmmm hmmm. You know, when I was with INTERPOL, I was tracking a pretty dang sophisticated crew. Y'all ever hear of the Pink Panthers?"

I focused on him. This was the second time in two weeks somebody brought up the Pink Panthers, Mrs. Majelski being the first.

"Of course," Agent Bailey said. "Why?"

"Well, seems to me, if somebody surreptitiously

busted into that vault, they needed a level of expertise you don't find with typical crews."

"I don't disagree," Agent Baily said. "If we find a breach, it will be an angle worth exploring."

Jefferson glanced over at Mickey, then back to Agent Bailey. "I'm real familiar with their methods. Clever as all get out. Audacious and precise. Expert planning leaving nothing unaccounted for. Military discipline in execution. In and out in minutes. Sometimes seconds. High-value targets. And—" He focused on me. "—they use well-dressed pretty young gals to conduct their surveillance and later act as lookouts when they pull their jobs."

Why was he looking at me like that? Wait, he thinks I'm good-looking? I mean, that's flattering and all, but what a perv. He's old enough to be my grandpa.

Jefferson crossed his arms, tilted his head, and drilled into me. "Seems to me, if someone is gonna bust into that vault during the daytime, they gotta be dadgum sure ain't nobody's hanging around outside it. So, they have someone check all around to make sure the coast is clear right before they execute. That what you were doing there, young lady? Acting as the lookout? Using your lil' pooch as a decoy?" He looked off to the right before turning his attention back on me. "And you know, maybe the vault wasn't robbed. Maybe they tried but couldn't pull it off so they sent this young lady to conduct surveillance up in the Gem Hall, and that was where they made the switch. Don't know how, but like I said, these fellas are real sophisticated. So, young lady, that what you've been doing? Acting as their surveillance and lookout gal?"

Everybody stared at me.

My head pulled back. "*What?*"

Jefferson stuck his neck out. "You heard me."

I glanced over to Agent Bailey, who signaled to answer the question. I stared down the white-haired perv. "You can't be serious. I've been the one saying all along the diamond was a fake. Mickey, tell them."

"It's true," Mickey said. "Her boyfriend called me the day after the blackout to run her theory of a robbery by me."

Boyfriend? My cheeks burned hot.

"And what'd you do?" Agent Bailey asked.

"Nothing," Mickey replied. "I told him, and later Sara when she confronted me directly about it, that without evidence I wasn't doing anything."

"See?" I exclaimed. "I've got nothing to do with it. Why would I say the vault was robbed if I was a part of it?"

Jefferson scrutinized me. "Like I said, these rascals are clever. By having some young gal raise the alarm over nothing, they knew nobody was gonna believe her with no evidence. And if their fake diamond ruse was ever discovered, she was protected by her saying something right from the git-go." He paused. "And if she's protected, they're protected 'cause she's got no reason to squeal on 'em."

I appealed to Mickey. "You believe me, right?"

His gaze shifted to Jefferson, then back to me where he considered me for several seconds. "I did."

A stoic Agent Bailey scrutinized me, as did his sidekick.

I jumped up and spun around to behind the chair, gripping its back as I leaned in toward the skeptical group of Y-chromosomes. "Guys, listen. This is nuts.

I'm a college kid on summer break. The first I heard about the Pink Panthers was…" Mrs. Majelski popped into my head. "Was just now. Besides, like you said, there's no evidence of the vault being broken into."

"How long have you been working here?" Agent Bailey asked.

"A couple months," I said.

"Ever work here before?" Agent Mahoney asked.

"No."

"Her boyfriend helped get her the job," Mickey added.

Agent Bailey's head whipped around toward Mickey. "Who's he?"

"Grant Doherty," Mickey replied. "He's okay. He's an agent over at DHS. I worked with him for a few years."

"HSI?" Agent Mahoney asked.

"Yeah."

"Where's he now?" he asked.

Mickey flipped his hands open. "Dunno. He's undercover."

That got Agent Bailey's attention. "Really. For how long?"

"Since the end of May," I said.

Agent Bailey focused back on me. "Have you had contact with him?"

Relaxing my death grip on the chair, I straightened. "A couple times. On the phone."

He eyed me. "Know where we can find him?"

I shook my head.

Agent Bailey's phone rang. "Yeah, Jerry." As he listened to the caller, his gaze jumped to Agent Mahoney, then back to me. "Okay. Either of you go back in there? Uh-huh. Right. Well planned. Ingenious. Give us a few minutes to finish up here, then we'll be down. Right. Good work." He tapped off and looked over at the two security men.

"Y'all find something?" Jefferson asked.

"We did," Agent Bailey replied, before turning his attention back on me. "The vault was drilled. There's a tunnel on the other side."

I smiled nervously. At this point, I didn't know if that was good news or bad.

Chapter Twenty-Six

Shazam

The room fell quiet as Agent Bailey's news of the tunnel sunk in. I slipped around to the front of my chair and sat. A sinking feeling slithered up from the pit of my stomach. Things were about to become even worse.

Mickey didn't disappoint. He stuck an accusing finger out at me and shattered the silence. "How'd you know they dug a tunnel and drilled the vault?"

I stayed silent and stared back, praying they couldn't hear my pounding heart.

Agent Bailey's head snapped around toward Mickey. "Say that again?"

"She came to me a few weeks back with what I thought was a cockamamie theory about how the vault was robbed, including digging some crazy long tunnel." Mickey fixed a hard stare on me. "Everything Moss just said, she already told me. Two weeks ago."

Jefferson propelled himself off the table and took a step toward me. "I'm telling y'all, this young lady sounding the alarm back then was part of the plan. It puts her in the clear if things went all sideways. Which it appears, is happening." He returned to the work table and leaned against it, finishing with a sneer.

Mickey looked over at Agent Bailey. "Where does

the tunnel originate from?"

"Don't know yet," the G-man replied. "It went several hundred feet but ended at a boarded-up entrance. They're processing it before taking the boarding down."

Mickey went back to staring hard at me. "Well, I'd be willing to bet on the other side of the entrance is a large sewer interceptor running underneath Constitution. And inside it you'll find tire tracks leading back to an outfall in Piney Branch Creek."

"She tell you all that?" Agent Mahoney asked Mickey.

"Yeah," he replied.

Agent Bailey cast a wary look at me. "That would fit. Jerry said it was the work of pros. The tunnel is elaborate. About eight feet wide and six feet high. Wood beams for bracing. The way it was constructed, somebody had an engineering or construction background including soil composition training. They knew exactly what they were doing, and where they were going, to be able to dig that kind of shaft two hundred feet to a precise location outside the vault."

"Sounds like they had the museum's blueprints," Agent Mahoney said with a quick look at me.

Mickey studied me. "Or access to them."

"Maybe even built models," Agent Bailey added as his phone rang. "Yeah, Jerry? Sewer?" He looked back to Mickey as he listened. "Right. Okay. Get a couple of guys to follow the tracks. Thanks." He tapped off. "The entrance led to a huge sewer tunnel. They hid it by boarding the hole up and spreading mortar over the wood. It blended in with the white patches on the sewer's walls."

Jefferson crossed his arms, an obvious gleam in his eyes. "Sounding more 'n more like the Pink Panthers. Your fellas see how they got into the vault?"

"They left their equipment behind," Agent Bailey replied. "Used a commercial diamond core drill to cut through the reinforced concrete until they hit a steel-plate sandwich."

"That plating is over six inches thick," Mickey said. "How'd they cut through it? An acetylene torch won't do it because of the copper alloy center."

"Plasma cutter," Agent Bailey replied. "Both for the plating and the steel shelving up against the inside wall."

Mickey furrowed his brow. "Something's wrong. We searched the vault. There was no hole cut in the shelving or anywhere else for that matter. Not even the floor."

"There was, your guys just missed it," Agent Bailey said. "They cut an opening in the far lower left portion of the corner shelving unit. When they exited the vault into the tunnel, they covered the opening and the entire shelf's back with a matching piece of steel and duct-taped it into place from the tunnel side. Those specific shelving units are readily available at commercial storage supply stores. They probably bought a matching unit and cut out the back of one shelf. Jerry said unless you knew *exactly* where to check, the hole was impossible to find."

Jefferson gently scratched his head, taking care not to ruin his pitiful comb-over. "How'd they know to bring a plasma cutter? That ain't something a crew carries around with 'em."

"And also knew the exact type of shelving unit?"

Mickey added.

The lead fed turned to me. "Both good questions. Going by the precision of the tunneling, the plasma cutter, and the replacement shelf panel, sounds to me like they had someone on the inside with knowledge of the vault, its location, and its security systems."

I shifted in the chair. "Why are you looking at me like that? I don't know anything about that stuff."

"I disagree," Agent Bailey replied. "You work there."

"You know," Mickey said, "she told me it was an inside job."

"Of course, she did," Jefferson retorted. "It was part of her backup plan to deflect suspicion if things went south."

"Hey, Moss," Mickey said, "did the Bureau finish its investigation of that junction box fire over by the National Museum?"

"Not that I've heard," Agent Bailey said. He glanced over to his partner. "You hear anything, Mike?"

He shook his head.

Agent Bailey turned back to Mickey. "Why?"

"Because she said the fire was set to get the exhibit moved to the Carlton. That the crew knew the Carlton was the backup site. Said they were digging the tunnel for months despite us only having two weeks' notice that the exhibit was coming to the museum."

The agent's head swiveled toward me. "That true?"

"Yes, sir," I said quietly.

He studied me, his face stern. "How is it someone your age second-guessed seasoned security professionals and been right about so much that has happened?"

"Beats me. I usually get something wrong along the way."

"When you get back to the office, Moss, pull her file," Mickey said. "I'm sure it will be an enlightening read."

"You see," Jefferson crowed. "She's had prior run-ins with y'all. I'm telling you, she's their surveillance and lookout gal."

Agent Bailey gauged me. "We have a file on you?"

"Probably," I replied matter-of-factly.

His eyes narrowed. "Why?"

I screwed my face up. "Kinda got into a little situation. In Alabama."

"From what I understand," Mickey said, "she had her own little investigation going over something until it blew up on her."

Agent Bailey's eyes remained trained on me. "Interesting. Is that what you've been doing on this? Investigating?"

"Yes, sir."

"Why?" he asked.

"Because nobody would listen to me," I said, shooting an annoyed look at Mickey.

A thin smile crossed Agent Bailey's face. "Not sure I entirely believe you, but rest assured I'm going to read your file. If I find you've not been completely forthcoming with us, that you've been giving misleading answers, it won't be good."

"Trust me, I'm well aware of the penalties for lying to a federal agent," I replied.

"I bet you are," Jefferson interjected.

Agent Bailey paid no attention to the outburst

behind him, his unwavering gaze remaining on me. "Humor me. If you're not the inside person like Mr. Scott alleges, who do you think is, because it's becoming pretty clear they had someone on the inside."

I broke eye contact with the agent, my gaze flicking over to Mickey. "I don't know."

Agent Bailey looked over at Mickey, then back to me. "But I'm sure you have some ideas."

Still leaning up against the work table, Mickey cocked his head to the side.

I sized Agent Bailey up. He wasn't going to let it go without getting some names. "Maybe somebody from the contractor doing the lobby renovations."

The agent raised his eyebrows. "Why do you think that?"

"Some of their workers have access to the building's blueprints," I replied. "Like you said, that would help the crew target the specific location of the vault so they could dig to the right spot. And avoid any underground utilities and stuff."

Agent Mahoney took out a small spiral notebook and jotted something in it.

"Anybody else?" Agent Bailey asked.

"Jake Barton, the Carlton's facility maintenance manager," I said.

"Because he has access to the blueprints?" Agent Bailey asked.

"Yes, sir. And he would know how to build a tunnel. Plus, he acted super nervous when I told Mickey this was an inside job."

"He was in the same room when you laid your case out to Mr. Fraser?" Agent Bailey asked.

"Yes, sir."

The agent looked over to Mickey. "That true?"

"Yeah."

"You notice the same thing with this Jake Barton?" Agent Bailey asked him.

Mickey shrugged. "Not really, but I wasn't focused on him. I was watching her."

"Have any issues with him?" Agent Bailey asked Mickey.

"I've only been here a year," he responded. "But during that time, nah, no problems. He's rough around the edges, but seems okay."

"You've only been here a year?" Agent Mahoney asked.

"Yeah," Mickey replied. "Before that, I was over at DHS."

"Who was your predecessor here?" Agent Bailey asked.

"Buck Bivens. He'd been here about ten years."

Agent Mahoney scribbled some more in his notebook.

"Know anything about him? And why did he leave?" Agent Bailey asked.

Mickey's heavy brows knit together. "All I know is from when I transitioned in. We had a two-week overlap. He was a retired Montgomery County cop and left the museum to retire to Florida."

"I knew the fella," Jefferson offered. "Dealt with him a couple years back when we were vetting backup sites."

"Anything stand out?" Agent Bailey asked.

Jefferson cracked a smile. "Yeah. He couldn't stay married."

"Multiple divorces?" Agent Mahoney asked.

"Got that right. Three of 'em. Every time we spoke, he bitched about all the alimony he was paying out."

More scribbling in Agent Mahoney's little notebook.

"Could he have sold information?" Agent Bailey asked.

That question brought a good laugh out of Jefferson. "A fella paying out to three ex-wives? Yeah, he could've sold intel for sure. He was pretty bitter about working for his exes."

"He ever complain to you about money?" Agent Bailey asked Mickey.

"Nope."

Agent Mahoney looked up from his notebook. "If he was having money problems, how could he retire to Florida?"

The two security men exchanged glances.

"On his cop pension?" Jefferson suggested.

"That wouldn't be near enough to support himself and three ex-wives," Agent Mahoney said. "We'll check him out."

Agent Bailey focused back on me. "Anybody else?"

Crap. I did have another suspect, but if I said his name, Mickey wasn't going to like it. My gaze jumped to him before settling back on the G-man. The giant security man was eyeing me, his burly arms crossed.

I twisted my face up. "Somebody in security."

"How's that?" Jefferson roared.

"In security where?" Mickey asked cautiously.

I swallowed. "Um, here."

Mickey's eyes about popped out of his head.

"Here?"

"Uh-huh."

"Impossible," he said firmly.

Agent Bailey glanced quickly at Mickey, then back at me. "Who?"

"Tony Carlucci," I said.

In a flash, Mickey was at the desk, leaning over it on both fists. "*Impossible*. I know Tony. He's a decorated Marine who served his country with honor. What evidence you got?"

"He was in the main vault when the power went out. Said he was going to hang around until five so he could clear and close the vault. And he was—"

"Doing his job," Mickey countered, leaning forward until his head hung over the front of the desk. "*How's that evidence?*"

I wasn't about to let the man use his size to intrude into my space in an obvious attempt to intimidate me. I sat forward in the chair, stuck my head out, and stared him down. "Like Mr. Scott said, if a crew is going to drill into the vault during daytime, they needed to make sure nobody was outside the vault who could hear them. Since I'm not involved, and Tony was in the main vault, *there's* your lookout."

I threw a triumphant smile at Jefferson, who responded with a malevolent scowl.

Mickey straightened and angled toward Agent Bailey. "Moss, she's ridiculous. Tony's as straight as they come. We don't even know if they drilled the vault during the daytime. She said"—he pointed at me—"they drilled the vault at night when the sound and vibration sensors were off because of the night renovations."

Agent Bailey turned to me. "He's right, you know. If that's your basis for naming Carlucci as a possible suspect, it's a nonstarter."

"I didn't say that was everything," I said, glancing at the steaming Mickey Fraser. "I was interrupted."

"Okay, go on," Agent Bailey prodded. "What else?"

I shot a look at Mickey. "First, Tony is the *evening* security supervisor. So, he still could have been the lookout if they were drilling at night."

He glared back at me, the veins in his thick neck pulsing, but he stayed silent.

I continued. "When Tony was in the vault right before the power outage, he was eating a Shazam candy bar. The one with hazelnuts."

Mickey went off. "That's it? Eating one of the most popular chocolate bars makes him guilty of robbing a vault?"

"It had hazelnuts," I asserted.

Mickey threw his hands in the air. "Big deal. So, it had hazelnuts. You're gonna disparage a war hero over the type of candy he eats?"

I breathed in through my nose. "No, sir. I'm simply stating a fact."

Mickey was glowering. "I don't give a—"

I beat back his black stare with my best fierce look. "When you searched the vault, you recall who checked that shelving unit they cut into?"

"That means nothing," Mickey shot back.

"I bet it was Tony," I said firmly.

"Sara, what's the significance of the candy bar?" Agent Bailey asked.

"You know the Piney Branch outfall Mickey said I

told him about? Where I think the crew gained access to the sewer interceptor network?"

"Yes."

"I found a Shazam wrapper right outside the entrance." I glared at the bristling Mickey Fraser. "With hazelnuts."

Chapter Twenty-Seven

The crew comes together

"It's the most popular candy bar out there," Mickey growled. "That doesn't mean—"

"Did you happen to pick up the wrapper?" Agent Bailey asked.

"Yes, sir. It's in a sealed plastic bag in my backpack."

"Did you touch it?" Agent Mahoney asked, concern in his voice.

"Only to pick it up and put it in the plastic bag."

"We're going to need you to turn it over to us," Agent Bailey said.

"Yes, sir. I'll bring it in tomorrow."

"Very good," he replied. "We're about done here. Anything else you need to tell us?"

I debated bringing up the missing journals because if I said something, they might be able to recover them and get Evy off my butt.

Evy?

Crap.

She falsified that dang report to the Board of Trustees. As far as the Board knows, all the journals are in the vault. If I say something now, that will put Boss Lady in a bad spot. Which means, I'll be in a real bad spot. And unemployed.

"I take it from your silence you have nothing else to say?" Agent Bailey asked.

My gaze bounced around to each man in the room before settling back on the lead agent. I made a snap decision. "Actually, there's one more thing."

He leaned in on the desk. "Go on."

I took a deep breath. "Three days after the power outage, I was in the valuables vault conducting the monthly inventory of Oliver Carlton's observation journals, and I found several were missing. I believe they were stolen the same time as the diamond."

"Based on what?" Agent Bailey asked. "Maybe someone took them for research purposes."

I shook my head and explained about the collection of journals, the mandatory inventories, the restricted access, and what they contained.

"Doesn't sound like there's much interesting info in them," Agent Bailey said.

"There really isn't," I replied. "Unless you're a research historian."

"So, there's really no motive," he said. "What makes you think they were stolen during the power outage?"

"Because they were there before. And if a journal is taken out of the valuables vault, it sets off an alarm at the day gate."

"There's a theft detection device on each book?" Agent Mahoney asked.

"I guess. Evy never said. She just told me the journals needed to stay in the valuables vault or else alarms would go off."

"Okay. How do you know they weren't missing before the power outage?" Agent Bailey asked.

Crap.

I never considered that possibility. As soon as I found those strange pages in the digitized versions of the missing journals, I jumped to the conclusion they were stolen during the diamond heist.

"Um, I didn't notice any gaps in the row of journals until I did this month's inventory, which was three days after the power outage."

"So, you're not really sure," Agent Bailey stated. "They could've been missing prior to the outage."

"I suppose so, but I don't think so," I said.

"Why not?" he asked.

"Because like I said, none of those journals can be removed from the vault without setting off an alarm. The only way out undetected was through the tunnel your guy discovered."

"Hang on now," Jefferson said. "Why would someone with only one minute before the power kicked back on, along with the sensors and cameras, spend precious seconds to steal three random journals?" He looked at Mickey. "Don't make much sense to me."

"Same thing I was thinking," Mickey said. "Don't forget, they also had to get past the electromagnetic locks, pressure sensor under the diamond, and security sensors on the display case, all in sixty seconds."

"In the dark," Jefferson added, his eyes trained on me.

I hesitated. "Beats me. It doesn't seem like a coincidence is all I'm saying."

Agent Bailey addressed me. "Sorry, but it doesn't sound like there's a correlation between those missing journals and the diamond theft. We're going to focus on the diamond."

I edged forward in the chair, preparing to stand. "Can I go then?"

He considered me for a few seconds. "You're free to go, but I would like you to stay and hear what we have to say. It might change your perspective regarding your situation."

"Why? Am I in trouble?"

"You're a person of interest," he replied.

Crap. Do I stay and see where things go regarding my *situation*, or do I get the heck out of here? If I leave, I'll appear uncooperative, which certainly won't help things. If I stay, I might be able to convince them I'm on their side. *Might.*

I scooched back in the chair.

"Wise decision," Agent Bailey said. He looked over to Mickey. "I understand how a pressure sensor works, but tell me about these display case sensors."

"There's two, one on each of the rear corners of the case. If the locks are defeated and the lid is lifted, an alert is sent to Jeff's and my phone and the control room. Same with the pressure sensor under the diamond."

"They all wireless?" Agent Mahoney asked.

"Yeah," Mickey replied.

"With a vault inside a vault, extremely doubtful their alert signals could get out from inside the valuables vault," Agent Mahoney said. "I suspect the case with those sensors was designed to be in an exhibit hall, not a double-vault. The crew knew that."

Jefferson glanced at Mickey. "You know, Mick, that's an excellent point you raised about them locks. How in the Sam Hill did they defeat those? In less than sixty seconds? There's only one fob for each. I got one, and you got the other."

"Those locks have their own power source?" Agent Mahoney asked.

"Correct," Jefferson replied. "Battery powered with a separate backup for each. Power outage would have no impact on 'em."

Agent Bailey shared a look with his partner. "Know what I'm thinking, Mike?"

"Antwerp?" he replied.

The word exploded in my head. First, Jefferson raises the Pink Panthers, and now these G-men bring up Antwerp? Both of which Mrs. Majelksi brought up to me over two weeks ago? Was the old lady that good, or does she know more than she's letting on? Maybe Zoe was right about her all along? She's involved and was keeping tabs on my investigation to steer me away if I got too close. Straight to the Pink Panthers and Antwerp crew. My heart sank. If Zoe's right, that meant Grant was involved, too. She warned me about both, that they were hiding something. I pushed the possibility to the back burner, but not out of my mind. Yet.

"Exactly," the lead G-man said, turning to the two security men. "One of the case studies Quantico teaches is the Antwerp diamond heist back in 2003."

Jefferson's eyes lit up. "I heard of them fellas. I was still with NCSBI. Hadn't joined INTERPOL yet. But those boys pulled off the crime of the century."

"Sure did," Agent Bailey said. "Stole over one-hundred-million dollars' worth of diamonds, gold, and jewelry from the Antwerp Diamond Center."

"From a supposedly impenetrable vault," Agent Mahoney added.

"They busted an Italian crew, I believe," Jefferson

said.

"Correct," Agent Bailey replied. "It was a five-man team. They nabbed the ringleader and three other guys."

"But none of the loot was recovered," Agent Mahoney said.

The lead agent looked at the two security men. "They planned the job for over eighteen months. Sound familiar?"

Jefferson struck a thoughtful pose, a thumb and forefinger cradling his chin. "Why you bringing these fellas up? To my knowledge, the Pink Panthers never collaborated on that job or with anybody outside their group."

"We haven't determined the Pink Panthers are involved in this case," Agent Bailey said.

The exhibit security director pushed off the table to a full stand. "Now hold on, them—"

Agent Bailey cut him off. "And the Antwerp crew defeated a vault protected by ten layers of security." He paused for effect. "Including a magnetic field."

Jefferson's eyes widened. "How's that?"

"One of the measures protecting the vault door was a magnetic field," Agent Mahoney explained. "One metal plate was attached to the inside top corner of the door, a second to the top of the doorframe in line with the first plate. When the system was armed, those plates formed a magnetic field. If a code wasn't typed into a nearby keypad and the door was opened, the magnetic field was broken, triggering an alarm."

"Sounds like the electromagnetic locks on the display case," Mickey said.

Agent Bailey nodded. "That's what I'm thinking."

"How'd they defeat the magnetic field?" Mickey

asked.

"Like any good crew, each member had a specialty or specialties," Agent Bailey replied. "This crew had a mechanical/electrical genius who specialized in alarm systems. He devised an ingenious way to redirect the field away from the door without breaking it, spoofing the system to think the door was closed."

"And you're thinking this crew did something similar with the display case?" Jefferson asked.

Agent Bailey nodded. "It's got to be something like that because of the limited time they had in the vault. Maybe built some kind of device they adhered to both sides of the display case by the locks that redirected the magnetic fields away from the metal plates to these devices."

"So, when the top was lifted, the fields remained active, but the locks were released," Mickey said, amazement in his voice.

"Yes," Agent Bailey said. "In essence, the plate was moved to each device as the magnetic fields were diverted away from the locks."

"Son of a gun," Jefferson said. "That really possible?"

"I believe so, but only a handful of people in the world would think of building such a thing," Agent Bailey said.

"Including this fella with the Antwerp Crew," Jefferson stated.

Crap. And perhaps Mrs. Majelski?

"Exactly," Agent Bailey replied. "If they had a device like that, they could defeat those locks in seconds."

"Greatly boosting their odds for success in less

than a minute," Agent Mahoney added.

I glanced over at Mickey. His head was lowered, thumbs pressing hard into both temples.

Jefferson turned his attention to me. "How we doing, young lady?"

"What do you mean?" I asked.

"We getting close to figuring out your crew and how they done it?" he asked.

"How the heck should I know?" I appealed to Agent Bailey. "I told you guys. I have nothing to do with any of this."

"Darlin', I may have been born at night, but it sure as heck wasn't last night," Jefferson shot back.

Agent Bailey rotated around and held up a hand, signaling Jefferson to cool it as he asked him, "You sure the Pink Panthers never collaborated with anybody outside their group?"

"Not to my knowledge. 'Course, when I was with INTERPOL investigating them fellas, we figured they numbered close to eight hundred."

Mickey's head popped up. "Seriously?"

"Yes, sir. And those are who we considered their core fellas. They got others spread out in a bunch of countries they tap into when they need 'em for a specific job. Best we could figure, these rascals are ex-military out of the former Yugoslavian states. You know, Serbia, Montenegro, Croatia, Bosnia, places like that."

"Who's the ringleader?" Mickey asked.

"Hard sayin', not knowin'. They're a shadowy network. We determined there was no top dawg, more like a committee of big boys. Sorta like the New York Mafia's Commission." Jefferson glanced over at Agent

Bailey. "Whatcha pondering, Moss?"

The agent rubbed his chin. "Is it feasible...possible...that several members went outside the group to pull off this heist?"

My white-haired accuser wrinkled his forehead. "I s'pose. Right when I left INTERPOL to take this job, we had them boys on the run. And their safe havens were disappearing right quick as more and more extradition treaties were being negotiated with them countries. Plus, technology was coming 'round fast, making it tough on them rascals. Maybe their target list was shrinking so fast some of them fellas branched out."

"I'm thinking a few might have become guns for hire," Agent Bailey said.

Jefferson wagged his head no. "Nah, they carried, but they never shot anything or anybody up. They was too smart for that."

"I was using the term more to describe them as independent consultants," Agent Bailey clarified.

"Gotcha," Jefferson replied. "Talent for hire for anybody willing to pay up."

Mickey rubbed the back of his neck. "You know, when I was playing high school football, I was being recruited by colleges all over the country. I—"

Jefferson broke in. "What in the blazes does football have to do with this case?"

"Hear me out, Jeff," Mickey fired back. "College coaches recruit star players to build the best teams they can. They have their own pitches, but the goal is the same. Assemble the most talent they can to win the ultimate prize. A national championship."

Agent Bailey's head kept going up and down as

Mickey spoke. "You think someone recruited the best of the best to put together a crew for this specific job?"

"Yeah, that's what I'm suggesting," Mickey replied. "A mastermind had a plan to hit the exhibit but needed an expert crew to pull it off. So, like a college coach, this person went out and recruited star talent for this one job."

"How much is the diamond worth?" Agent Mahoney asked.

"Fifty million," Jefferson answered.

"A five-man crew pulled the Antwerp job," Agent Bailey said. "Fifty million leaves plenty of leeway when trying to recruit the best of the best."

Jefferson counted off on his fingers. "If you're right, the mastermind recruited this Italian genius to handle the display case. Found another fella to oversee construction of the tunnel. Another to figure out how to bust into the vault. Maybe a muscle guy for the digging and heavy lifting. And a grease man to wriggle through the hole." He looked at his hand. "That's a max of maybe five at the most."

"Plus, himself," Mickey added.

"If so, the mastermind would likely be European to know who to go after," Agent Bailey said. "Maybe the ringleader of the Antwerp crew?"

"Nah, that fella might still be in jail," Jefferson replied. "I'm thinking one of the top Pink Panthers put this deal together for himself. You know, to keep from splitting the profits with the other big boys in the network." He turned his attention to me. "However, there's one person I forgot just now when I was putting the crew together. The lookout gal."

I faced Agent Bailey. "Can I go now?"

His gaze flicked to Jefferson before eyeing me for a few seconds. "I hope now you realize we're going to solve this pretty quick. It's what we do." He leaned forward on the desk. "So, the question is, you ready to tell us what's *really* going on?"

I swallowed. "I've told you everything I know. Can I leave?"

"Yes, but stay in the area."

Crap.

Chapter Twenty-Eight

The message

For the rest of my Thursday workday, the G-men left me alone while they pored over the valuables vault searching for evidence. Mickey and Jefferson hovered around outside it like two nervous fathers-to-be. I couldn't put my finger on it, but something was bugging me about that FBI interview-turned-interrogation. And not just the whole "person of interest" thing, although that was part of it. Something else kept gnawing at me. Something Agent Bailey or Mickey or somebody said. Throughout the afternoon, I kept revisiting things but with no success. And when five o'clock came, I was out the door and laying tracks before one of them got the idea to start up their inquisition again.

When I got home, Mauzzy met me at the door with his usual pitiful "feed me" look, his front paws tapping away on the floor. It was always a good sign when Sweet Handsome greeted me this way, because it meant I wasn't in his doghouse.

I bent to rub his ears. "Handsome, you want some dinner?"

Mauzzy danced around me as I made my way through the hallway into the kitchen.

Mom was at the stove cooking dinner. "Sara, I didn't hear you come in. How was work?"

On the drive home, I decided to keep this whole "person of interest" thing to myself since I hadn't done anything and it will eventually resolve itself. No sense getting my parents worked up over something I didn't do.

"It was interesting," I said before walking into the laundry room to get Mauzzy's food.

When I came out, Dad and Zoe were in the kitchen, having arrived home from work. She was bouncing around like she had been holding it for the whole commute home and had to go bad.

I set Mauzzy's food bowl on the floor and sat at the oak kitchen table. "You okay, Zo? Looks like you're about to burst."

"She is," Dad griped, taking a seat next to me. "I thought we'd never get home."

Zoe's eyes were coming out of her head as she hopped from one foot to the other. "We got something to tell you."

"I have some news, too," I said.

"We go first," she squealed. "We go first."

"Okay, but you gotta sit," I implored her. "You're killing me."

She called over to the family room. "Matt, get in here. You need to hear this, too."

My brother strolled over to the kitchen and sat at the table. "What's up?"

Zoe sat in a chair next to him, her shoulders rocking to the beat of a silent melody. "Your dad has something to say."

Mom rapped a wooden spoon against a pot, turned

off the stove, and leaned up against the island to hear the news. Mauzzy finished inhaling his dinner and sat next to me. Everybody's attention was on Dad, including Mauzzy.

He looked around the table before ending on me. "You know that pigpen cipher you sent me?"

"You solved it," I exclaimed.

A broad smile lit up his face. "I solved it."

"Yaaaaassss," I screamed.

Zoe leaned on the table, her shoulders still rocking. "Tell 'em how you did it, Mr. D. Tell 'em."

"I won't bore you with the technical details, but the number six was the key piece of data I needed to crack it."

Beaming, Zoe twisted around toward Matt. "It was all because of your brilliance."

Matt's pale complexion was no longer as his face reddened. "I didn't do anything."

"Sure you did," Zoe gushed. "You were all over the number six."

He returned her radiant smile with a sheepish one of his own. "Yeah, I guess."

I couldn't wait any longer. "Dad, what's the message? Zoe, did he tell you?"

"Nope. Said I had to wait. It's been killing me ever since he told me he solved it."

Dad grinned. "Longest drive home. Almost caved. Talk about relentless. Now"—he held out a hand—"although I solved the cipher, the message is cryptic."

Zoe drummed lightly on the table. "*Tell us.*"

"Okay. The message is…" He paused for effect. "'*In death all is revealed and then all will make perfect sense.*' That mean anything to you kids?"

Zoe stopped drumming as her mouth dropped open.

I broke the stunned silence. "Seriously?"

"Yeah, why?" Dad asked.

I searched through my phone's photos. "We found the same saying carved in the floor of the chapel at Arcadia."

Dad got a puzzled look on his face. "Why would he go through the effort to encode a message he's already got in English on the chapel floor? His cipher was pretty darn sophisticated. He didn't come up with it in a few hours."

I found one of the pics and showed him. "Right there. The same message."

He took the phone and looked at the pic, then up at me. "Pretty elaborate calligraphy to be carved into marble. Somebody spent some time on it."

I took the phone back from him. "What do you think?"

Dad propped an elbow on the table and rested his chin in his hand. "There's a reason for the message being the same as the floor carving."

"Like he's trying to tell us something," Zoe said, looking over at Matt.

He held her gaze. "That there's significance to the words on the floor. There's a distinct reason for them being there."

I jumped up, the chair scooting back and sending Mauzzy scurrying for his recliner. "Maybe the treasure is under those tiles."

Zoe's head swung around toward me. "Holy... That's it. That's gotta be it."

"We have to go back to Arcadia," I cried out. "Zo,

can you call in sick tomorrow?"

"Sure, so long as Mr. D doesn't rat me out. Matt, are you—"

"Hold on," Dad interjected. "Just hold on. You're not going down there to tear up those tiles."

I jerked my head back. "Pssh. I know that."

His face grew stern. It was a look I've seen *way* too many times to recount. "Sara, you'll be arrested for vandalism. Or worse."

Without taking my eyes off Dad, I slipped back into my chair. "All we're going to do is look around the chapel. Maybe there's a hidden entrance leading to a chamber under those tiles."

Mom spoke up. "This is serious, Sara. You cannot go down there and start tearing things up."

It's like both have been down this road before. Actually, they *have* been down this road before. Many times. Always with me. Never Matt. And things didn't always end well.

"Geez, guys," I said. "We're not going to break the law. Just poke around."

"Don't even try bending it," Dad warned. "Because your *bending* is most people's *breaking*."

My gaze shifted back and forth between my parents. On Mom's face, worry and consternation. Dad's, a stone-cold serious countenance.

"Don't worry," I said.

"Know how many times we've heard that from you?" Dad asked.

"I'm older now. I know better."

From the look on his face, the man wasn't convinced. Yeah, he was a smart man.

"Sara, you said you have some news, too," Mom

said in an obvious attempt to change the subject.

With all the excitement of Dad cracking the cipher, I completely forgot about my big news.

Crap.

I can't go to North Carolina. Can I? Agent Bailey's words echoed in my head. *Stay in the area.* Do I hang back and let Zoe and Matt search for the treasure? Although, I haven't done anything wrong, and what exactly did he mean by the word *area*? That's a very general instruction. Since he didn't define it, how can I be held accountable? I mean, sure, he could have been talking about the Baltimore-D.C. area. But he could also have been talking about staying within a day's drive of D.C. And Arcadia was easily within a day's drive. Problem solved.

"Sara?" Mom prodded.

I refocused. "I do. The FBI showed up at the vault this morning."

Dad groaned as Mom's face went from worried to shaken.

"Not to see me," I said defensively. "They came to inspect the vault, trying to figure out when the diamond was swapped out."

Mom was instantly relieved. Dad, not so much.

"Nothing else?" Dad asked.

"Nope," I lied. "Just there for the vault."

His gaze was penetrating. Intense. Probing. I fought the urge to look away.

Without breaking eye contact, he said, "I hope so."

"What else would they be there for?" I asked nonchalantly.

He set his jaw. "We both know the answer to that question."

"Did they find anything?" Mom asked.

I thankfully shifted my attention. "They sure did. Found a tunnel."

Zoe gasped. "Seriously?"

"Seriously," I replied. "The thieves drilled the vault and cut through a steel plate with some fancy plasma gizmo."

"Son of a… You were right," Zoe said.

Dad's face relaxed, but not his vigilance. "Right about what?"

"She said thieves dug a tunnel and drilled the vault," Zoe said with pride in her voice. "She figured it out when nobody else could."

"How'd you know someone could dig a tunnel in downtown D.C.?" he asked. "Sounds impossible to me."

I told him about the underground interceptor network and how one ran along Constitution past the museum.

Dad locked in on me. "Lemme guess. One of these interceptors dumps somewhere into Rock Creek Park."

The man was good. Real good.

"Piney Branch Creek," I said matter-of-factly.

"Which is in Rock Creek Park," he replied.

"Uh-huh."

"Which is where you went a couple of weekends ago"—he put up air quotes—"to 'catch some sunshine and fresh air,' right?"

"Maybe."

"You know that was your tell," he said.

"My tell?"

"Your desire to get sunshine and fresh air," he replied. "That was your tell."

"That obvious?"

"Very. And now I'm supposed to believe you're going to North Carolina and won't be tearing anything up? Like marble tiles?"

I held up my hand like I was taking an oath. "Yup. Trust me."

From the look on the man's face, he was far from convinced. And rightly so.

Chapter Twenty-Nine

The chapel

Courtesy of a dead car battery, we didn't get on the road the next morning until ten-thirty. Unfortunately, it meant we weren't going to have time to visit Arcadia and the chapel today. It was going to have to wait until Saturday. After four hours of driving, we were at a gas station, wrapping up a second pee and first fuel stop. Matt and Mauzzy slept in the back seat while Zoe leaned up against the hood as I pumped gas.

I pointed with my head toward a fuel pump two aisles away from us. "See that silver sports car over there?"

She craned her neck to see around the fuel pump. "The one with the scraggly-looking dude and skanky chick?"

I hissed. "A little less obvious."

"What? How else am I gonna see?"

I gestured to keep it down. "I think they've been following us."

Zoe closed her eyes and shook her head. "You're so effing paranoid. We left Annapolis four hours ago. No way they tailed us all that time."

"I've seen that car off and on ever since we got on I-95."

Zoe brushed aside my concern. "Doesn't mean squat. If they're going to Florida, they're going on Ninety-Five. And if they drive as crazy-fast as you, they'll keep pace with us."

I screwed the fuel cap on and we got in the car. "If I see that car when we get on I-40, then we're being followed."

"You get a look at those two? No way they're international jewel thieves."

"We'll see."

I started the engine and the car tore out of the gas station onto a service road leading to the highway. In the rearview mirror, the silver sports car exited the gas station traveling in our direction. With one eye on our tail, I lowered the window and tossed my stale gum out.

"Whoa," Zoe cried out. "What are you doing?"

I yanked on the wheel and after several violent swerves, the car returned to the middle of the road. "Sorry. Was making sure my gum didn't stick to the car."

Zoe admonished me. "Watch the road, girl. Not your effing litter."

As always, she had a valid point. *Sorry, officer. I ran into the ditch because I had to see if my litter got stuck on my car.*

I gripped the wheel, focused on the road, and three hours later with no other major mishaps, we pulled into the crappy motel's parking lot.

"Matt and Mauzzy, we're here," I called into the back seat.

"See? We weren't being followed," Zoe said triumphantly. "They stayed on Ninety-Five when we exited."

"Followed?" my brother mumbled as he rubbed his eyes.

"Everything's okay. Just your paranoid sister at it again."

I shut off the engine and turned to my gloating best friend. "Haven't you heard of a handoff?"

"Yeah, in football. Hey, don't roll your eyes."

"During long-term surveillance, there are usually multiple teams working it. The silver sports car could have handed us off to a trailing car when we got on Forty."

"You read too much," she replied.

"Just keep your eyes peeled."

We got out of the car and I tended to Mauzzy, who remained asleep in his milk crate. In my peripheral vision, a white sedan cruised slowly past the motel. I spun around. A strange woman in the passenger seat stared directly at me.

****

The next morning, right before leaving the motel for Arcadia, I had one tiny thing to address. Although Mauzzy was snoring beneath the covers at the bottom of the bed, there was no need for stealth because he was going to figure it out anyway after we left. But I had to give it a shot. I picked up a bulging sealed plastic bag of Mauzzy's food from the dresser top, crammed it into a second sealable plastic bag, and slipped over to the closet. I eased the door open, placed the bag on the top shelf back in the far corner, covered it with a spare pillow, and quietly closed the door.

"You really think that's necessary?" Zoe asked.

"Yup."

"It was safe on the dresser."

My eyes widened. "Seriously? Back in Tuscaloosa he once got up on the kitchen counter and raided the pantry."

"Forgot about that. Ever figure out how he did it?"

"Nope. He covered his tracks. But I'm sure he used a kitchen chair somehow. And speaking of…" I wheeled the desk chair into the bathroom and closed the door.

Zoe slowly shook her head. "Wow. Talk about paranoid."

"It's called scar tissue." I patted the bump at the bottom of the bed. "Okay, Sweet Handsome. We're leaving."

A muffled fart came from the covers, then a groan, followed by the bump moving quickly to the top of the bed. Mauzzy poked his head out, took a deep breath, yawned, and lay on the pillow.

I gave him chin scratches and a big kiss. "Be a good boy."

We left the motel and fifteen minutes later were parked at Arcadia. The silver sports car and white sedan were nowhere to be seen, and I didn't pick up either one in my mirrors on the way over. The only other vehicle in the lot, a mud-splattered jacked-up pickup with oversized wheels, sat in the far back corner.

"Hey, at least we're not smuggling in some stolen books," Zoe sang as she danced alongside my brother.

"Don't remind me," Matt lamented.

We entered the great hall, said good morning to the non-Adonis docent, and made our way toward the south portico. When I passed through the French doors into the parlor, a familiar sound reached me from off to the left, where double doors led to the dining room.

Something scratched at the floor, followed by a double-click and shuffling feet.

"Wait right here, guys," I said.

I approached the dining room and poked my head through the doorway. Standing in front of the fireplace was—

"Good morning, dear."

—a grinning Mrs. Majelski and her walker.

"What are you doing here?" I whispered.

Her slate-gray eyes twinkled. "Why, the same reason you're here."

I glanced around. The place was empty. "How do you know why I'm here?"

The geriatric wonder cackled. "You're cute." Her face grew serious. "I only have a few seconds. You and your little friends need to be careful today. But trust your instincts."

"Careful? Why?"

She winked. "You'll see."

"And what do you mean 'trust my instincts'? I don't know what's going on."

"Just remember what I said, dear." She deftly whipped the walker around and motored toward an arched opening leading to a hallway. "And be careful," she called over her shoulder.

The ancient lady disappeared into the dark hall, the scratching and clicks growing fainter by the second. I returned to the parlor, dumbfounded.

"What's wrong?" Zoe asked.

"Just talked to Mrs. Majelski," I said.

Zoe's hands flew up. "What the *heck* is she doing here?"

"Not sure," I replied. "But I think she's either

following us, or someone else."

"Who's this lady?" Matt asked, a nervous look on his face.

I explained what I knew about her, but instead of relaxing, my brother grew more tense.

"What'd she say?" Zoe asked.

"To be careful today."

Matt went white.

"About what?" Zoe asked.

"Wouldn't say."

Matt made a move toward the great hall's French doors. "I'm outta here."

"Hang on, Matt," I said.

He stopped and faced me. "Us being here sounds dangerous. What if—"

"If it was dangerous, she would've said so," I said. "She just warned me to be careful. That could be about anything."

Zoe stood next to Matt. "I told you a couple weeks ago I don't trust that old lady. Her and Grant. Now she shows up down here? Something stinks."

I took a defiant stance. "She's okay. Have I ever been wrong before?"

"Oh, yeah," Zoe protested.

At the same time, Matt mumbled, "Ask Dad."

I made an exaggerated smile. "Ha-ha. Let's do what she said and be careful, but let's also do what we came here for. Okay?"

They looked at each other, then back at me. "Okay," they replied together.

"Great," I said. "I think we first should go inside the chapel to examine those tiles with the saying."

"Agreed," Matt replied.

We followed the stone path winding through gardens exploding with color, ending at the chapel. I opened the door and stopped short. My heart sank as I surveyed the interior.

Zoe slammed into my back. "Hey, what's the deal? Get moving."

I stepped to the side so Zoe could see inside the building.

"What the...," she whispered.

Matt entered the chapel and stopped. "Whoa." He did an about-face and pushed past us for the door, eyes wide with fear. "We gotta get outta here before we get blamed. This is what that lady was talking about."

I caught the back of his shirt, pulling him to a stop. "We're not going anywhere. We need to investigate."

My freaking-out brother faced me. "It's not just the old lady. You heard Dad last night. Even if we don't get caught, if he hears about this, he'll blame us." He pointed at me. "Actually, you."

If I didn't talk him off the ledge, the mission was going nowhere. "Listen, Matt. We just got here. The docent saw us. No way we could cause this much destruction in five minutes. You with me?"

He looked over at Zoe, his eyes pleading with her for guidance.

She took his hand. "For once, your sister's right. C'mon, let's go inside and see what we can find."

Zoe led Matt inside and I closed the door behind us. The once stunning chapel was ransacked. We crept up the aisle, stepping over and around ripped-up floorboards. The spectacular oak walls were full of gaping holes, as if someone took a sledgehammer to the golden panels. On both sides of the chapel, the ravaged wood walls cried to us. All four rows of pews were upended and lay scattered across the destroyed floor. I checked for ciphers or messages on the bottom of each pew as we passed, but there were none. No doubt that was why they were flipped over. Somebody else did the same thing.

"Let's spread out," I whispered.

Matt and Zoe stepped over to a wall and peered in one of the yawning holes. I approached the tombs, praying the vandals left the deceased alone. Fortunately, the only one that got hit was Oliver Carlton's tomb. Marble panels from all four sides lay shattered on the floor, including the one with the grid of symbols. And many of the marble tiles around the tombs were pried up and lay broken, including the ones with the carved mysterious saying.

The only part of the chapel untouched was the intricately carved wood ceiling.

I left the tombs and worked my way through the destruction over to Matt, whose head was inside a sizeable hole in the wall. "What do you think?"

He pulled his head out and faced me. "Looks to me like someone was searching for something?"

"Oh my gosh, the treasure," I cried out. "You think they found it?"

Matt surveyed the destroyed chapel. "Hard to say. My first reaction is no because of *all* the holes and stuff. It's like they couldn't find anything and kept looking."

Zoe crossed over to us from the far side of the building. "Somebody sure did a number on the place."

I focused my phone's flashlight on the hole Matt had been looking at and examined it. "There's easily a foot of space in here between the outer and inner walls. Plenty of room to hide stuff." I scanned the room. "There are holes in every single panel."

"You thinking that's where the treasure was hidden?" Zoe asked. "In the walls?"

"Yep," I replied. "Unfortunately."

"You could be right," Matt said as he assessed the wreckage. "But I'm not so sure."

"Why's that?" I asked.

His arm swept around the room. "Take a look at all these holes."

I took in both side walls. "I don't get it. Why wouldn't treasure be hidden in the walls?"

Matt shook his head. "I'm not saying it isn't possible. I'm saying the *location* of the holes tells me they probably didn't find what they were looking for. There are too many holes in the panels. Up and down each one. And if you're going to hide treasure, you'll want to be able to periodically access it. It won't be closed inside this type of lavish wall."

"Hope you're right," I said.

"What do we do now?" Zoe asked.

"If anything was here, somebody already found it," I replied. "Let's check around outside. I still think the saying was a marker. Maybe there's a hidden entrance leading to underneath it." I blew out my anger and frustration. "Or where it used to be."

We picked our way back to the entrance and exited outside to the brilliant sunshine and rising humidity.

"Zoe and Matt, you search around outside the chapel. I'll work the gardens."

"What are we looking for?" Zoe asked.

"It could be anything," I replied. "A depression in

the ground. A loose brick in the wall. Possibly a symbol in the brick serving as a marker or pointing to another symbol."

She clutched Matt's hand. "Got it. Let's go."

I left them at the chapel and worked my way through the gardens. With each step, I examined the flagstones in the path. I scrutinized every statue for symbols and hidden messages. And since Oliver Carlton was an inventor, I looked for a hidden switch that could make a statue or bench slide away to reveal a secret entranceway. Even the flower beds were searched. But all I found was a four-foot black snake lurking under a bed of hostas. After that discovery, it took me ten minutes to get up the nerve to resume the search.

When I returned to the chapel, Zoe and Matt were sitting outside on a nearby bench holding hands. "I take it you guys didn't find anything?"

Matt quickly released Zoe's hand and shook his head. "Not even close."

"Me, neither," I said. "Let's head back to the mansion."

"Should we tell somebody about the chapel?" Matt asked as he stood.

I scrunched up my face. "Don't know. My gut's telling me we keep quiet."

Zoe jumped up from the bench. "Your gut doesn't have the best track record. I say we tell someone."

My brother glanced down at her, then at me. "It's two against one, sis. We need to say something."

I sucked in a breath and blew it out slowly. "Fine, but I think it's a mistake."

****

After dropping the shocking news about the chapel to the docent at the information desk, we spent the rest of the day at Arcadia waiting to be interviewed by the cops. They appreciated us hanging around while they first inspected the chapel and quickly ruled us out as suspects. Something about the level of destruction didn't match up with our lack of physical attributes. In other words, we looked weak and pathetic. During our wait, we wandered through the mansion pretending to be tourists, but were really searching for clues missed during the last trip. We found nothing.

"C'mon, let's get outta here," Zoe said. "It's almost five. I'm starving."

Matt put a hand to his stomach. "Can we hit a drug store or something on the way?"

Zoe rested a hand on his arm. "What's the matter?"

"I'm feeling kinda nauseous."

"Those cops rattle you?" she asked gently.

"I don't know," he replied. "I guess."

"We'll get you some ginger candy or something," I said. "That'll calm things down."

Twenty minutes later, I walked into a superstore on a hunt for anti-nausea medicine for my ailing brother. He didn't feel well enough to go in, so Zoe stayed behind in the car with him. As I passed a smiling meeter-greeter wiping down shopping carts, I looked up and stopped dead in my tracks. A white-haired man with a bad comb-over pushed a full shopping cart toward me, accompanied by a pleasant-looking gray-haired woman about his age. I put my back to them and tugged on a shopping cart at the end of a train of carts, praying he didn't see me. He knew I wasn't supposed to leave the D.C. area and, in a heartbeat, would snitch on me to the FBI.

A voice from behind said, "Miss?"

I froze.

"Excuse me, miss? I have a buggy all wiped down for you."

Angling my head to the right, I spied Jefferson Scott pushing his cart through the exit doors. I let go of mine and turned to go inside. To the meeter-greeter, I said, "Thank you, but I won't be needing one today."

I hurried into the store. Why was Jefferson in Brunswick the same time we were? Was he the one following us on the interstate? If so, why? He accused me of being part of the crew who pulled off the heist. Was he surveilling me, hoping I led him right to them and the diamond?

Chapter Thirty

That's not the best answer

The following morning, we packed up and got ready to return home. We were no further along in solving the wall grid or the meaning behind Carlton's mysterious message at the end of his will that was also carved into the chapel's floor. All in all, a disappointing weekend, made worse with the breathtaking chapel being reduced to splintered wood and broken marble.

"I wanna check one thing out on the way home," I said, slipping into the driver's seat. "It won't take long."

Zoe dropped into the passenger seat, tugged the door shut, and angled toward me. "I know what you're up to, and it's not necessary."

I started the engine, backed the car out of its space, and headed for the exit. "You can't believe everything on the Internet. Need to confirm if it's correct."

She slapped her forehead. "The address is correct. You saw an old guy who looks like this dude, Jefferson Scott. Last night, you found an address in Brunswick County under the name Jefferson Scott. How is it not correct? The dude lives there. Probably home for the weekend."

I gunned the engine and the car leaped forward,

tires squealing as we rocketed onto the road. "Need to be sure, because if he doesn't, why's he here?"

Zoe white-knuckled the door. "Cripes, girl, don't hurry on my account."

I checked the rearview mirror. An oversized black or dark-blue pickup swung onto the road from another motel several blocks away. "I'm not."

Twenty minutes later, we were parked on a quiet tree-lined street two houses away from the supposed home of Jefferson Scott. Sitting in the driveway was—a white sedan. It looked like the one I saw Friday evening outside the motel, but I couldn't be sure if it was the same car. And the woman who was with him at the store could have been the woman I caught staring at me from that car, but again, I couldn't be sure.

A silver car with a rear spoiler sped past with two people in it.

I pointed toward the fast-disappearing car. "You see that?"

Zoe leaned forward, peering through the windshield. "See what?"

"I swear that was the car tailing us on the way down here. The one at the gas station."

"You mean the one that just flew by?" she asked. "If they're following us, they're doing a pretty crappy job."

I checked the side mirror. A dark pickup turned onto the street and parked on the opposite side three houses away from us. The brake lights went off, but nobody exited the truck.

With my eyes glued to the side mirror, I said, "That was a handoff."

"What the heck are you talking about?" Zoe asked.

"That silver car was the same one tailing us Friday on Ninety-Five. And they handed us off"—I motioned with my head toward the side mirror—"to that pickup down the street."

Zoe got up on her knees and stared out the rear window. "They're parked in the opposite direction. No way they're watching us."

"Yeah, they are. They're watching us the same way I'm watching them. Through the side mirror."

"How do you know that?"

"Because nobody got out of it."

Matt stopped messing with his phone and also looked out the rear window.

"You two need to quit staring," I said. "Don't want them to know they're made."

Zoe dropped back into her seat. "How do we confirm the old guy is in that house? We could be here all day."

I put my attention back on the house. "I have an idea."

"No surprise," Zoe said. "Question is, is it a good idea?"

I faced my BFF. "I think so, but you might not agree."

She wrinkled up her nose. "I know you. I'm smelling something."

"He doesn't know you."

She shook her head repeatedly. "Uh-uh. No way. No effing way."

I looked in the rearview mirror. What little color Matt had, drained from his face. "All you need to do is ring the doorbell and when somebody answers, say you're new to the neighborhood and ask if they've seen your dog because he jumped the fence this morning."

Zoe squeezed her head. "I don't have an *effing* dog."

I kept my tone calm and steady. "I'll send you a pic of my friend Danielle's pup. It's an Australian shepherd named Wiley."

Matt interjected. "Sara, this is crazy. We don't know who lives there."

"That's precisely why we need to do this," I said. "I need to know if Jefferson Scott followed us here. If he lives here, no problem. But if he doesn't…"

"No fricking way this will work," Zoe argued. "What if the geezer doesn't answer the door? What if it's his wife or whoever she is?"

"That's why I'm sending you the pic of Wiley. I saw a bag of dog food on the bottom of their cart. The lady is probably a dog lover. If he's there, she'll show him the pic to see if he's seen the poor lost thing."

Zoe's phone chimed with my text. She checked the photo of Wiley, then eyed me. "You sure about this?"

"It'll work. Just be your cute energetic self and flash that brilliant smile of yours."

With a groan, she opened the door and leaned back toward me. "I can't believe you roped me into one of your screwed-up plans."

"Just be yourself," I said. "And when you return, walk up the street before crossing over and doubling back to the car. You know, in case he's there and watches you leave, I don't want him later giving me a hard time."

"Hope you don't regret this," she warned.

"Good luck," Matt said, his voice cracking.

Zoe took a deep breath, clambered out of the car,

and bopped across the street toward the house. She rang the doorbell and waited. When the door opened, she showed her phone to—a well-dressed white-haired man with a bad comb-over.

Crap.

Jefferson Scott lived there.

****

The following morning, on my drive to work, I spotted a silver sports car trailing me on Route Fifty. And all the way down New York Avenue, it stayed three car lengths behind me. When it followed me onto Sixth Street, my stomach tightened. And when it turned into my parking garage, right behind me, I became a quivering, shaking mess of adrenaline. Behind it, a black sedan and oversized pickup followed us into the garage. When I got to the third level, they were still behind me. I was working on a plan to get out of there when blue flashing lights bounced off the ceiling and walls.

So not good.

I swerved into a parking space, and the three vehicles, all now with crazy flashing lights, boxed me in. Lowering the window, I put my hands in clear view on top of the steering wheel and waited.

Agent Bailey appeared outside the door, with another man and woman standing behind him. In his hand, several pieces of paper. "Good morning, Sara. Why did you go to North Carolina when I explicitly told you to remain in the area?"

I *knew* we were being followed. Although, not sure if being followed by the FBI was better or worse than being followed by an international gang of thieves. I guess time will tell. Real soon.

"Um, totally forgot. Something urgent popped up and I made a snap decision to go check it out. In North Carolina."

His face remained expressionless. "Brunswick County, to be precise."

"You were following me?" I asked.

"Not me. My team. You were supposed to bring me that candy wrapper Friday and instead bolted the area, despite me telling you otherwise."

"Can I take my hands down?"

"You may."

I let go of the wheel and lowered my hands. "I didn't bolt. I was following up on a lead after my dad solved a strange cipher in the Carlton will."

"You bolted. You were driving fast and erratic."

"I was trying to lose… Um, that's how I drive."

He forced a smile. "They told me. You were trying to lose my team. And despite how it looks for you, I'm going to give you a chance to clear yourself."

Crap. Clear myself?

"Excuse me?" I asked.

He held up the papers. "I have sworn affidavits here from Mickey Fraser and Jefferson Scott attesting to their reasonable belief you assisted with the theft of the Star of Midnight by providing a criminal syndicate with information regarding the vault and its security systems. Their beliefs are based on your deception and actions."

"*What?* I didn't—"

"Hear me out and listen carefully. With your consent, we would like to conduct a search of your car and phone. I don't have a search warrant, yet, so I'm asking for your voluntary consent to the search. It's entirely within your rights to refuse. However, if you're innocent as you claim, this is your opportunity to prove it. Do you understand?"

I swallowed hard. "Yes, sir."

"Good. Do you consent to us searching your phone and car?"

I sucked in a deep cleansing breath and let it out slowly. "Yes, sir."

The man and woman behind him tugged on blue latex gloves.

"And do you understand this is a voluntary consent and you are free to refuse my request?"

"Yes, sir."

He backed away from the car, slipped the papers in his jacket's inner pocket, and snapped on his own latex gloves. "Very good. Please step out of the car, give me your phone, and"—he pointed to a spot by the hood of the car—"stand over there."

I complied with his request and the man and woman went to work in my car. They picked through fast food bags full of trash, empty soda cups, and—dirty socks from my Piney Branch Creek escapades. So embarrassing.

Two hours later, Agent Bailey approached me with my phone in his hand. He showed me one of my pictures. Then he swiped on the phone and showed another. "Can you explain these photos?"

Crap. I completely forgot about those pics.

"Um, that's the Star of Midnight."

"I'm aware. Did you take these?"

"Yes, sir."

"Where?"

"At the Carlton."

"*Where* at the Carlton."

Frick.

I grimaced. "In the vault."

"The one that was drilled?"

"Yes, sir."

"The one where no cameras are allowed?"

I nodded.

"You know how this looks?"

I screwed my face up. "Not good?"

His face was grim. "This is incriminating evidence and supports the affidavits I mentioned earlier. Did either Fraser or Scott know you took these?"

"No, sir."

"Who have you shown these to?"

I fought through the panic that had my head spinning to the point I was about to vom. Right on the man's shoes. I couldn't remember if I showed Mrs. Majelski, and if I did, I had to keep her out of this mess.

"Just my friend at work, Danielle Rollins."

He considered me. "Nobody else?"

I shook my head.

"Were you told no photographs were to be taken inside the vault?"

I briefly closed my eyes. When I opened them, spots danced in front of me. "Yes, I know the policy."

"And yet you still took them. Of a diamond that is now stolen. Why?"

I stared at the G-man. My legs went wobbly. "I don't know," I muttered.

"That's not the best answer."

Chapter Thirty-One

They found him

"Let's try it again," Agent Bailey said. "To a trained eye, these show security features of the display case and the vault. So, why did you take these photos?"

I didn't know what else to say to my inquisitor, so I went with what I've heard my whole frigging life. "Um, questionable judgment?"

A thin smile crossed the otherwise stern agent's face. "After reading your extensive and rather colorful file, *that* statement I believe."

Seriously? That's what he believes? That my judgment sucks? I needed to turn this around. Fast. *Think, Sara.* Those photos were taken…

Hold on. Hold the frick on.

It was right there all along.

I pointed at my phone in his hand. "Look at the date/time stamp of those photos. They were taken right before the blackout and robbery. I mean *right before*. No way the crew could have used those photos because they were about to enter the vault. That proves those aren't surveillance photos."

He studied the two photos on my phone. "Valid point."

"See? I've been telling the truth."

He ignored my fairly accurate statement and handed me the phone. "You're good to go. Besides, we didn't find anything else on your phone. And your car, other than it being a real mess, was clean."

With an embarrassed smile, I collected my purse from the car and locked it. Turning to Agent Bailey, I dug into my purse and took out a sealed plastic bag with the Shazam candy wrapper from the sewer outfall.

"This is for you," I said.

He took the bag and, with a wry smile, said, "Thanks. Although I was expecting it last Friday."

I scrunched my face up. "That was my intention, too."

The G-man held up a hand. "I know, until your snap decision derailed everything. Speaking of which, there's one piece of advice I'd like to give you." He paused. "Make that two."

I was afraid to hear, but what choice did I have? So, I smiled sweetly. "Yes, sir?"

"Stop putting yourself in situations where you feel like you have to evade a cop's question. That's never a tenable situation, and one day it's going to bite you."

I frowned. "Understood. It's a work in progress."

He responded with a restrained smile.

"And the second?" I asked.

"Slow down on the road."

****

When I finally arrived at work, my commute had gone from one hour to three, courtesy of Agent Moss Bailey. I dumped my things and before getting coffee, zipped around to Danielle's cubicle.

"Hey, has Evy been looking for me?" I whispered.

Danielle spun around in her chair. "Where have

you been?" she mouthed.

"Got detained. Don't ask."

She held up both hands. "Don't wanna know. But you're in luck. She didn't come in today."

I did a fist pump and breathed a sigh of relief. "Yes."

"Hey, guess who I saw this morning at the elevator?"

"Gentleman Hottie?"

"How'd you know?"

"Because he's all you talk about." A beat. "But I don't blame you."

"Right? Anyway, you know he wears glasses?"

I shook my head.

Her eyes lit up. "He was wearing them this morning."

"And?"

"Sheesh, I thought he was good-looking before. But when I saw him this morning with those glasses? Bam. Have my baby."

With a short laugh, I said, "Totally get it. I'll let you go on dreaming about GH because it's coffee time for me."

I left Danielle in her rapture, hit the coffee station, and strolled to my cubicle without a care in the world. There was no Evy around to berate me for being late. No Agent Bailey to harass me over my innocent actions. Okay, mostly innocent. And no Jefferson Scott accusing me of being the crew's "surveillance and lookout gal."

As I sipped coffee, my confidence grew. I was on a roll. My seat-of-the-pants plan yesterday to confirm Jefferson's address in Brunswick worked to perfection.

Granted, it resulted in giving him an alibi for being down there. But still. And this morning I handled the FBI all by myself. For once, I didn't need Mauzzy's help. And now, I had a day of peace and quiet with Evy gone, which I planned to spend searching for those dang journals. But first, there was one thing to take care of that was bugging me ever since Agent Bailey showed up outside my car window.

I gulped down the remaining coffee, snagged my phone from the desk, and took off out of the vault. Minutes later, I did something I've never done before. I barged into someone's office when the door was closed. His feet were up on the desk, a newspaper obscuring the rest of his body.

"Reasonable belief I assisted with the theft?" I roared.

Mickey snapped the paper down, and seeing me, yanked his feet off the desk. "Whoa. What's your problem barging in here like that?"

My index finger slashed at the space between us. "What's *your* problem siccing the FBI on me?"

"I didn't sic them on you. Moss Bailey called Friday morning. Said he was working on getting a search warrant and asked if I was comfortable providing an affidavit as the Carlton's chief of security."

I leaned in toward him, working my very best fierce look. My very best. "And obviously you had no problem doing it."

Maybe it was because of the enormity of the man, or he practiced in the mirror like I did, or he got it from his football days, but calling it his fierce look didn't do it justice. He looked ferocious.

"What'd you expect me to do?" he bellowed. "You're caught on camera running all around the vault right before the robbery. You're a college kid, yet you seem to know everything about the theft, before any of us security professionals did. And Jeff had a plausible reason for all that, based on his experience with the Pink Panthers. Plus, you were deceptive with me about who you were working with when you gained access to the interceptor network, among other things."

"Should've talked to me first."

He responded with a short, mocking laugh. "Right. My mistake for not alerting a person of interest regarding the FBI's intention to obtain a search warrant against her."

I crossed my arms and leaned back. "Didn't say that."

"Pretty much did."

"What I meant was, you know my history. My tendency to kinda get into situations that make me look bad." I stuck my neck out. "But that's all it ever is. And you knew that."

He relaxed and stuck a hand out toward a chair. "Sit. Please."

I took a seat and waited for his apology.

Mickey sat back and leaned on the chair's arm. "As a security officer, I couldn't alert you to law enforcement's intentions regarding investigating your role in the case. If I—"

"Which was none," I interjected.

He put up his hands in mock surrender. "Which was none. Moss called after he left you this morning."

"So why didn't you tell him about my past? In 'Bama. Instead of letting him light me up this morning."

He gave me a quizzical look. "I did. Last Thursday. You were there. I told him to read your file."

"That wasn't said in support of me," I snapped.

Mickey sighed and rubbed his forehead. "Look, it was the best I could do. My job isn't to support you. It's to protect the interests of the museum."

"But why didn't you tell him, you know, when he asked you for an affidavit?"

Mickey folded his hands on the desk. "Tell him what? That I believed you? I didn't, entirely. Figured it was best to let things run their course."

I eyed him. "They teach you to say that in secret agent school? Because I've heard almost the exact same line in my past."

That got a chuckle out of the man. "Among other things."

"I'm sure."

The cell phone on his desk buzzed. He glanced at it, then at me. "Speaking of..." He answered the call. "Hey, Moss." Mickey focused on me as he listened, his head bobbing occasionally. "Andorra? Right, non-extradition. Uh-huh." After another minute of listening, Mickey said, "Heavy Russian accent? To the untrained ear, a Serbian accent gets confused with being Russian." He nodded. "Yep, that's what I'm thinking. Sounding more and more like them. I'll call Jeff and let him know. He can reach out to his INTERPOL buddies still working the Pink Panthers. Right. I'll let you know." He tapped off and set the phone down.

"That sounded interesting," I said.

"FBI tracked Merv Glickman to Andorra."

"Where's that? Never heard of it."

"Small country between France and Spain. It's a non-extradition country so Glickman was more than happy to talk. The agent said the guy enjoyed it, like he was boasting. Taunting even."

"I knew he was skeezy. What'd he say?"

"Listen to this. Two months ago, a man with a supposed heavy Russian accent found Glickman in New York City and gave him a briefcase with one million cash in it."

"Cash? Why?"

"In exchange for pronouncing a fake Star of Midnight to be the real deal, if it was ever required."

"They were buying insurance?"

"Exactly. Glickman was Bancroft and Culpeper's senior gemologist in New York. They knew if somebody got suspicious about the fake, he would be the one called in to examine it. And get this, if his services were needed, they would provide him a fake passport and first-class ticket to Andorra, along with a villa and another two million waiting. He howled and said it was a no-brainer."

"What a slimeball," I said. "He say who these people were?"

Mickey shook his head. "No, but in his mind, they were Russian mafia."

"So, he wasn't about to double-cross them and take off with the million."

"Exactly."

"Did he say where the diamond is?"

Mickey picked up his cell. "Nope. And said he doesn't care, either. He got his. Hey, if you don't mind, I gotta make a call."

"Sure." I stood and stepped over to the door.

"Closed?"

With the phone to his ear, he gave me a thumbs-up. "Hey, Jeff. They found Glickman."

Chapter Thirty-Two

Euclid makes an appearance

When I got home Monday evening, not only was I met by Mauzzy doing his usual feed-me dance, Zoe was right beside him jumping from one leg to the other. Her face was bright green fluorescing eyes and brilliant white teeth.

"Easy, Zo, don't land on him," I cautioned.

She took a hop back from Mauzzy but continued her gyrations. "Matt wanted to call, but I told him to wait 'til you got home."

I bent and gave Sweet Handsome some long overdue loving. At least that's what he's been telling me for the past several weeks. "You want dinner?"

Zoe yelled up the stairs, "Matt. She's home."

Then off we went, Mauzzy and Zoe dancing circles around me as I tried not to trip over their excited little bodies. Along with Mrs. Majelski, they were the three teeniest people in my life.

In the laundry room, I scooped food into Mauzzy's bowl, and no sooner had it touched the kitchen floor, he attacked it with his usual starved fervor. Zoe was at the kitchen table kneeling on a chair turned sideways, drumming away.

A rich, comforting aroma filled the room. A

mixture of sauteed garlic and onions, and simmering tomato sauce. That meant only one thing. Mom made her fantastic chicken cacciatore. But she wasn't in the kitchen or family room. And neither was Dad. I spied the slow cooker on the counter set on warm.

"Where's Mom and Dad?"

"It's Monday night," Zoe said, still pounding the table. "They got their summer bowling league."

I slid out a chair and sat. "Totally forgot."

Matt scuffed into the kitchen, an electronic tablet in one hand. "Hey, guys."

With a squeal, Zoe jumped off her chair, met my brother by the island, and dragged him by the hand over to the table. "Tell her. *Tell her.*"

Mauzzy finished his dinner and started racing around us, ears straight out and riding the wind as he circled 'round and 'round.

"Zo, calm down," I said. "You've got Mauzzy way amped."

Matt took a seat next to me, and Zoe was back up on her knees in the chair on the other side of me.

I corralled Mauzzy, cradled him tight, then looked over to Matt. "Okay, what's got Zoe more hyper than usual?"

He opened the tablet and slid it over in front of me. On it was a picture we took of the chapel floor during our first visit. "When I studied the wall grid, then the tomb's grid, then the saying both in the chapel and coded in the will, it all made sense."

I stared back, confused.

Matt continued "Before Carlton died, there were the floor tiles in his office with every sixth one being a diamond, and the first number in the grid was a six. But that was it. I made an assumption the grid on his tomb was carved after his death."

Something from my earlier research of Oliver Carlton resonated in my head. "You know, your assumption might be right. During my research, I found an odd entry. Shortly before he died, Carlton gave his longtime butler five twenty-pound gold bars. Maybe part of that was for the butler to use to commission the grid on Carlton's tomb after his death."

"That fits," Matt replied. "So, prior to his death, there were only two references to the number six, and both in his office."

"Do you get it?" Zoe blurted.

I set a sufficiently calmed Mauzzy on the floor, who scampered for the safety of his recliner. "Do I look like I get it?"

Matt pointed to the tablet's picture of the chapel floor. "Just like the number six was the key to Dad solving the will's cipher, the resulting message he came up with matched the one on the chapel floor."

I stared at the pic. "Which told us this message was a key to something. And the coded message was—at the end of his will." I glanced up with eyes wide. "Nobody would know about the coded message until *after his death* and the will was read."

"Exactly," Matt said. "Oliver Carlton was leaving breadcrumbs all along the way. The saying is really a two-part message, and him carving it in English on the chapel floor was one of the clues. The first half of it, '*In death all is revealed*,' told us that after he died, look to the diamond pattern carved in the grid on his tomb. It tied back to the office floor and became the third reference to the number six, which we picked up on and allowed Dad to solve the cipher in his will."

I could see it coming together, but I wasn't quite there yet. "And by having the deciphered message from his will match the one on the chapel floor, he's telling us there's a message within the message."

"Nope, *two* messages within the one," Matt said.

Zoe was back to rocking. "Right? I had the old dude all wrong. He was brilliant."

I studied the saying. "This is a two-part message? I don't see it. Wasn't he saying that after he died, it would all make sense regarding the number six being the key to solving the puzzle?"

My brother rarely showed excitement. He was pretty even-keeled, like Dad. But right now, he looked like he just hit the lottery. Which for Matt would be more like him proving Einstein's Theory of Relativity or solving some famous math problem.

His gaze bounced to Zoe, then me. "Almost everybody would see the saying as you do, that it's just one message." He paused and exchanged a knowing glance with Zoe before focusing back on me. "But a mathematician might see it as a two-part message."

"Like you," I said.

"Yep, like me," he responded, beaming.

I read the message again. "I assume the second half is what you're referring to as the second part of the message?"

"Correct," Matt said. "By itself, it meshes with the first half of the statement. It's a logical finish and provides no reason for anybody to think more about it." He took the tablet, brought up the office wall grid, and slid the tablet back in front of me. "Until you take into consideration how the number six keeps showing up."

"More breadcrumbs," I said.

"More breadcrumbs," Matt echoed. "With Carlton's death, the tomb grid was the final piece of the puzzle signaling the number six was key. However, he also placed the number six in the wall grid's first position for another very specific reason."

"You won't guess it in a million years," Zoe sang.

"Obvis, since I hate math," I groused. "Specifically, subtraction."

"Zoe's right," Matt said. "Only a mathematician *might* pick up on this very special breadcrumb. But only if he or she was looking for it, because Carlton buried it in all those numbers in the grid. It goes back to Euclid."

"Euclid?" I asked. "I know that name, and now you're confusing me. How does geometry fit in all this?"

Matt feigned shock. "I'm impressed my non-math sister knows about Euclidian geometry."

"Didn't say I know about it. Just recognize the dude's name."

"Get on with it," Zoe begged.

"Euclid discovered the concept of perfect numbers," Matt said. "In—"

"Oh, my God, perfect numbers," I exclaimed. "All will make *perfect* sense."

"Now you're on it," Matt said. "A perfect number is a whole number equal to the sum of its whole number divisors, excluding the actual number."

I rattled my head. "I'll take your word for it."

Matt continued. "Euclid discovered the first four perfect numbers."

"Based on Carlton's breadcrumbs, I assume six is one?" I asked.

Zoe's head swiveled toward me. "Whoa. I didn't get that when Matt explained it to me. Maybe you have a bit of math geek in you after all."

"Ha, doubtful," I said. "Go on, Matt."

"So as Zoe just confirmed, six is indeed the first perfect number." He pointed to the wall grid pic on the tablet in front of me. "When I was working through the grid, I noticed the very last number."

"Twenty-eight," I said.

"It's the second perfect number," Zoe shouted.

I looked up at Matt. "Seriously?"

He smiled broadly. "Yep."

"What's the third one?" I asked.

"Four ninety-six," he replied.

I scanned the wall grid pic before my head jerked up and I stared at my brother. "Holy crap. It's the center number."

"Yep. Wanna know the fourth?"

"Hit me."

"Eight thousand one hundred twenty-eight."

I searched the grid but couldn't find the number. "Am I missing it?"

He shook his head. "Nope, it's not there. And that's another breadcrumb. The phrase *'and all will make perfect sense'* is referring to the first three perfect numbers. Six, twenty-eight, and four ninety-six. So, we've made progress, but I don't yet know how those numbers fit into the big picture."

I stared at the wall grid and those three numbers. "Six, twenty-eight, and four ninety-six," I mumbled.

There was something about those numbers. I've seen them before, in that very order. I closed my eyes. They were banging around in the back of my head. In fact, they've been knocking around back there for over two weeks.

I opened my eyes and stared at Matt, openmouthed.

"You okay?" he asked.

"I know why those numbers are significant."

Chapter Thirty-Three

The missing journals

I arrived at work early the next morning, right after the vault opened, because I had a huge mission to pull off, and the fewer people milling around, the better. What I was about to do violated museum policy in so many ways, but I saw no other option.

After getting situated in my cubicle, I accessed the digital archives of the Carlton Papers. Navigating my way into the folder with his journals, I brought up journal six, then rolled to the edge of my cubicle and took a quick look around. All clear. I rolled back to the desk, slipped a flash drive out of my pocket, and inserted it into the computer. With another quick check over my shoulder, I saved a copy of the journal to it, then quickly did the same with journals twenty-eight and four ninety-six. I yanked the USB out of the computer and stuffed it in my pocket.

Leaning back in the chair, I closed my eyes and took a moment to relax. So far, so good. At least two major museum policies were just violated, both punishable by mandatory termination. And I was wasting time chilling because I still had a couple more to violate.

I grabbed my purse and headed for the main vault's

day gate.

A voice called out from behind. "Sara, where are you going?"

I wheeled around. Boss Lady stood outside her office, hands on hips. "Um, left my phone in the car. I'll only be gone fifteen minutes."

She checked her watch. "Make it quick. We have an eight o'clock meeting, or did you forget?"

"No, ma'am. I'll be back by then."

She shooed me away. "Very well. Get moving."

I gave a thumbs-up, dashed through the day gate, and took off for the garage. Five minutes later, with perspiration dripping off me, I removed a backpack containing a laptop from my car's hatch and hot-footed it for a nearby coffee shop with free Wi-Fi. Soon after, the three journal files from the flash drive were winging their way through cyberspace in an email to Matt.

A check of my phone showed just five minutes remained to get back to the museum before Boss Lady devoured me. No time to return the laptop to my car. I stuffed it in the backpack, exited the shop, and about jumped out of my skin.

"Everything okay, dear?" came from inside a parked black SUV with heavily tinted windows. A silhouette with white hair sat in the driver's seat.

I peered across the space between us and into the open passenger window. "Everything's fine, but I gotta get to work."

"Back to work is more like it," floated out from within the darkness of the vehicle.

This woman never stopped amazing me. And freaking me out.

I glanced around. Nobody was on the sidewalk. I

took a step toward the car.

"Don't come any closer and don't stare," she warned. "Pretend you're talking on the phone."

I pulled out my phone and held it to my ear. "What are you doing here?"

She chuckled lightly. "Keeping an eye on you, dear. I thought you knew that."

My head whipped around toward the car window. "Still?"

Her white hair bobbed up and down in the dark. "*No staring.*"

I looked down the street. "Well, everything's fine," I said out of the corner of my mouth.

"Sure, now that the FBI cleared you."

"How'd you know about that?"

"You're cute," she said with a short laugh.

"Then I guess you know we're making progress."

"I do. Well done. Just remember what I said Saturday. Trust your instincts, dear."

I took two steps toward her vehicle. "Yeah, about that. What specifically—"

"Him," she said as the window slid up and the SUV slipped away from the curb.

Him? Who him? Mickey? Grant? Carlucci? Barton? All of them? None of them?

With the clock ticking, I shook off Mrs. Majelski's words and hustled back to the museum.

When I swiped through the day gate, Boss Lady was waiting. "You're five minutes late, and I have a very tight schedule today."

"Sorry. I hit traffic?"

Judging by the dark look on her face, that attempt at levity was ill-advised. "You didn't have that backpack when you left. I thought you were getting your phone?"

Crap. Time to think fast.

"Um, I was. But when I got to my car, I saw this in the back seat. I was over at some friends last night and forgot to bring it into the house when I got home. It has my tablet, and today is supposed to be a scorcher. Didn't want it getting ruined."

She eyeballed me. "You are well aware that other than phones, personal electronics and thumb drives are not permitted in the vault."

"Yes, ma'am, I understand. But I couldn't leave it in my car."

"Well, it's not staying here, either," she said with a huff. "Let's go. In my office. Bring that thing with you. After our meeting, take it upstairs and leave it with security." She stuck a bony finger out at me. "And don't ever do this again."

I followed the fast-moving Boss Lady into her office. She sat behind the desk and gestured for me to close the door.

"Let's make this quick," she said. "Where are my journals?"

I couldn't tell her about our discovery last night, but I could give her hope. "I don't know, but I'm getting closer to finding them."

She clasped her hands on the desk and gave me a good, long stare. "How close?"

As the words left my mouth, my brain couldn't believe what I was saying. "I'll find them by the end of the week."

"You better."

"No worries."

A suspicious look came over Boss Lady's skinny face. "How can you be so sure? Last week you hadn't a clue."

"I ran across some information yesterday that shows promise."

"Information? Have you told anybody about these journals?"

"No," I lied. If she knew I told the FBI, she'd blow a gasket. And then fire me on the spot.

With a withering glare, she said, "Because of your little calling-in-sick ploy a couple of weeks back, I was forced to stick my neck out with this month's report to buy *you* time. You and I are the only people who know those journals are missing. But the day is coming when I can't and won't cover for you." Out came that dang finger again. "And if I hear about this from somebody else, it's your job."

I swallowed hard. "You won't."

I hope.

****

Late that afternoon, I sat in my cubicle sipping on the third coffee of the day and mulled over my pending termination. Perhaps I made an unwise snap decision to promise finding those journals for Boss Lady by Friday, but at least it got her off my back today. I'll deal with her on Friday if I don't come up with the goods. Which the way it was looking, I might be calling in sick to buy me the weekend. Nothing like kicking that can *all* the way down the road. Hopefully, it was a very long road.

As I ran various possibilities through my head regarding the journals' whereabouts, for some reason I kept returning to the FBI's interrogation of me last Thursday in Mickey's office. I may have been under duress fending off their accusations, but still, somebody said something I wasn't expecting. By one of the agents? Mickey? Jeff—

Jefferson Scott.

It was him. He said something that was, oddly, one hundred percent accurate. And that stuck with me. Why would him being right about something bug me? Other than the fact I didn't care for the man. At all.

I revisited this morning's meeting with Evy. Something she said had me focusing on Jefferson's statement last Thursday. What was it?

Her words resonated in my head. *You and I are the only people who know those journals are missing.*

Before my FBI interrogation, her statement was accurate. But during their interrogation, I told them several journals were missing right after the diamond was stolen. And Jefferson questioned my—

I snatched up the phone and entered in a four-digit extension.

"Security, Mickey Fraser."

"Hey, it's Sara. Can I see you?"

"Kinda busy. Can it—"

"It's urgent," I whispered.

"Come on down."

Minutes later, I entered Mickey's office and closed the door. "Thanks for seeing me."

"What's so urgent?"

"I figured out who's behind the heist."

Mickey leaned on his forearms, his eyes locking onto me as skepticism screamed from the man. "How's that possible? The FBI doesn't even know, and they were able to track down Glickman."

"Because they don't know much about the missing

journals. They only know what I told them."

"I'm not following."

"Before that interrogation of me last week—"

"Interview," Mickey stated.

"Whatever. Nobody knew about the missing journals except me and Evy. When I told you guys about them, I didn't say how many were missing."

The security man leaned back, crossed his arms, and studied me. "Okay, you didn't say how many were missing. Who cares? How does that have anything to do with who stole the diamond?"

I put up a hand, asking for patience. "When you guys were pushing back on my conclusion the journals were stolen the same time the diamond was, Jefferson challenged me. He asked why would someone with only one minute to steal the diamond, and I quote, '*steal three random journals.*' Make sense now?"

"I don't remember him saying that," Mickey said cautiously, his eyes slits under bushy eyebrows. "Just so we're clear, you saying the *Fire and Ice Exhibit*'s *director of security* is complicit with the robbery?"

"I'm not saying he's complicit. I'm saying he's the mastermind. The ringleader. The boss man." I looked Mickey in the eye. "He's the ultimate inside man."

He slowly shook his head, appearing unphased by my bombshell accusation. "Not buying it. You're accusing Jeff of a major heist, in fact, one of the biggest robberies of the century, based on some missing journals? The guy's a former decorated cop. He worked for INTERPOL for cripes sake. No way."

"It's not just some missing journals. It's—"

He leaned in. "You're missing the point. Why would he, or anybody for that matter, care about those journals? It's the same thing we were trying to tell you last week. Someone stealing a fifty-million-dollar diamond isn't gonna give a second thought about those books."

There was only one way to convince him about Jefferson. I sized Mickey up. He's never really done anything to hurt me. Other than the whole affidavit thing, and if I was being honest with myself, I probably wouldn't have entirely believed me then, either. Plus, he's always made time for me, like today. In the end, like he said the other day, he was just trying to do his job and protect the Carlton's interests. And Mrs. Majelski told me this morning to "trust my instincts" about "him." She might have been referring to Jefferson, but maybe also Mickey. Unlike my snap decisions, this was a well-reasoned one. Mickey Fraser, the Carlton's chief of security, was worth the risk.

I inched forward to the front of my seat. "What if I told you this heist was *all* about those journals?"

That produced a short, derisive laugh from him. "I'd call you crazy."

I paused to allow the moment to build. "I have good reason to believe those journals are the key to finding a legendary treasure in North Carolina from a wrecked Spanish galleon. Worth billions. Oliver Carlton found it, and that was the source of his wealth."

Mickey sat back and stared at me for several seconds before erupting in laughter. "What's this, some kind of April Fool's joke in July?" He looked around the room, then gave me the once-over. "This one of those TV prank shows? You got a hidden camera or something on you?"

"Rest assured, this is no joke."

His laughter subsided. "Sounds like one to me."

"It isn't."

His eyes worked me over, any prior amusement replaced by a serious intensity. "If those journals are worth billions, why take the added risk and go through the effort to steal the diamond? They had to defeat the display case, both its locks and sensors. Why not just grab the books and run?"

"Jefferson worked for INTERPOL for years, correct?"

"He did."

"And he was very familiar with the Pink Panthers, their methods, and stuff. Right?"

"Apparently."

My finger shot out. "And you even suggested it last week."

"What's that?"

"A mastermind recruited an all-star crew to bust into the vault."

Mickey's eyes bulged as he leaned forward. "*To steal the diamond*. Not a bunch of old journals."

I shook my head. "Nope. You're wrong. To steal both."

He angled his head. "Why?"

"I happened upon Jefferson over the weekend in Brunswick, North Carolina. Apparently, he lives there."

"He does. Been going home on weekends. How's that make him guilty?"

"It doesn't, but that's the same place where the treasure is rumored to be buried, so I'm sure he knows about the legend. And because of his time with INTERPOL, he knew who to recruit from the Pink Panthers and the Antwerp crew. He put together a team, gave them the intel they needed, and their payment was the Star of Midnight. They just needed to grab those journals for him."

Mickey's mouth turned downward. He wasn't buying it. "That's one helluva theory."

"*Amore*," I said.

"Huh?"

"Remember? That's what someone spray-painted along the weld lines on the Piney Branch steel plate."

"Yeah, so?"

"It's Italian. I think they were trying to hide the weld lines."

"How do you know it wasn't some kid who tagged it later?"

Now it was my turn to look skeptical. "I don't. But I find it suspicious the crew who pulled off the crime of the century, the Antwerp Diamond Center heist, was all Italian."

Mickey sat quietly, chin in hand, as he considered me. After a good ten seconds of silence, he spoke up. "That diamond could easily be recut for a crew of four to five to divvy up. They just needed to steal some books along with it."

"That's correct."

"And the big payday for the mastermind could be billions."

"Yes, sir. According to the legend, the ship had seventy-five tons of gold and emeralds. My brother calculated the value to be around four billion."

Mickey's eyebrows arched high. "How sure are you about this treasure?"

"Can't say I'm one hundred percent certain, but it's getting there. All the evidence I've uncovered points to the legend being real. And this past weekend when Jefferson was in Brunswick, somebody ransacked the chapel holding Oliver Carlton's tomb."

He rubbed his chin without taking his eyes off me. "Like someone was looking for a treasure?"

"That's what I think."

"They find it?"

"Hard to say, but I don't think so."

He sat back, shifted his considerable weight in the chair, and looked off to the left for a few seconds before addressing me. "Tell me again why you're certain Jeff is involved."

"Because when you guys were *interviewing* me, he questioned why someone would take the time to steal *three* random journals."

"And nobody knew the number missing?"

"Just Evy and I. When I told you guys about them, I only said *several* journals, yet he knew three were missing."

He twisted his mouth up. "You know, I have a vague recollection of him saying that, three random journals."

"Trust me. He said it."

He sighed. "Fine, leave this to me. Not a word to anybody. Got it?"

"Yes, sir."

"I mean it. Not to anybody."

"I understand."

As I headed to the door, Mickey placed a call. "Moss, need to see you. Fast."

I returned to the main vault, but right before I swiped my card to open the day gate, my phone chimed.

"Hey, Matt. What's up?"

My brother was breathing heavily. "Sara... Sara, I..."

Chapter Thirty-Four

Shakespeare?

Matt sounded close to hyperventilating. "I think…
It's…"

"Everything okay?" I asked in a hushed tone,
walking away from the day gate.

More heavy breathing. "Yeah… Yeah. I'm… I'm
fine."

"You don't sound fine. Take a breath and calm
down."

He blew out several times.

"Doing better?"

After a big exhale, he replied, "I'm good."

"Okay, what's going on?"

"I think I figured it out."

I glanced around. "You solved the wall cipher?"

"No, but pretty sure I've got the sequence."

"What do you mean?"

"I figured out the methodology. How to use the
journals."

I became weightless as a sudden warmth erupted
throughout my body. "You figured out the message?"

"No, it's going to take some time. But I've got the
first six words, and it isn't nonsense."

"What are they?"

"It's kinda weird, but because it's so weird, that tells me I got it."

With a quick check over my shoulder, I hissed. "Matt, what's it say?"

"*Astride him the sun grows hot.*"

"What?"

"That's the first six words. *Astride him the sun grows hot.*"

"What the heck does that mean?"

"Dunno. Told you it's weird. But it's legit. Sounds like poetry or something."

Terrific. What I expected was going to be map directions to a billion-dollar treasure turns out to be the whimsical poetic ramblings of an eccentric genius.

I checked the time. "It's four-thirty. I'll sneak out early. Keep working it, and when I get home, I can help."

"Okay. I'll be in my room."

I tapped off, swiped through the day gate, and gathered up my things. Evy wasn't in her office, so I slipped out of the vault and headed for the parking garage. An hour later, with the rare cooperation of the traffic gods, I was home. Per usual, Mauzzy waited at the door. After feeding him, I dashed out of the kitchen.

"Sara, what about dinner?" Mom called from behind me.

"I'll eat later," I shouted from the hallway.

I charged up the stairs and ran into Matt's room. He sat at his desk using a pencil to count something on his laptop. An open electronic tablet lay next to it.

"Have you—"

"Shhhh. Don't wanna lose count."

I sat on the bed and waited, my brother

methodically counting away as he mumbled numbers to keep track.

Ten minutes later, he exhaled and wrote something on a piece of paper. "Wow. That was the biggest number yet. Three thousand one hundred fifty-six."

"Seriously? How long it take you to count that?"

"Over an hour."

"An hour?"

He picked up the paper he wrote on. "Yep. That's the only word I got since I called you."

"That was an hour and a half ago."

"Said it was going to take time."

"With that word, is it still making sense?"

"Yep. And it's still weird. Here's what I got so far. *Astride him the sun grows hot on.*"

"That's not even close to being directions to a treasure," I whined.

"Still sounds like poetry."

A high-pitched screech from downstairs cut through the air.

"Zoe and Dad are home," I said.

Five seconds later, she burst into the room and wrapped her arms around Matt from behind his chair. "I'm so proud of you."

My brother took a peek at me out of the corner of his eye. "Thanks, but I haven't solved it yet."

Still squeezing him, Zoe said, "But you will."

"Not if you strangle him," I said.

She released Matt, who spun around in his chair to face her. "I only got one more word since I called you. It's taking forever."

Zoe was electric, bouncing from foot to foot, her eyes alive with excitement. "It'll go faster now 'cause we're here."

"Don't get your hopes up, Zo," I cautioned. "You may have been right way back when you said Carlton might be playing a joke on us."

Her little shoulders sagged. She turned to Matt. "Still sounding weird?"

"Like I said, only got one more word, but, yup," he replied.

"And not directions to anything, let alone treasure," I grumbled.

Undeterred, Zoe perked back up. "Okay, how do we do this?"

"Go get your tablets, paper, and a pen. We'll each work from one of the journals," Matt said. "I already forwarded you Sara's email with the files."

Zoe skipped to her room as I walked to mine. When we returned to Matt's room, the two of us sat on his bed while he remained at the desk.

"Okay, listen up," Matt said. "Sara, you bring up journal six on your tablet. Zoe, you take four ninety-six. And I'll take twenty-eight. Carlton used a reversed sequence for the book order, and a forward sequence for the numbers using every sixth as the applicable number."

"What do you mean a reversed sequence?" Zoe asked.

Matt rolled his chair over to the bed and showed us his tablet with the pic of the wall grid. "See the last number, twenty-eight?"

"Uh-huh," she muttered.

"That's the book I used to get the first word, which was the two hundred fourteenth word in the book because two fourteen is the sixth number counting at the top of the grid from the left."

I took his tablet and studied the grid. "So, the second book is four ninety-six?"

"Exactly," Matt replied. "And book six is the third. Then we start back at twenty-eight for the fourth, and so on."

As Matt spoke, I recalled the first time I went through the digitized missing journals a few weeks back. "Hang on. The first word came from book twenty-eight? Then four ninety-six, which is in the middle of the three-number sequence? And then six?"

"That's right," Matt said with a knowing smile.

"That's gotta be the correct sequence," I said. "I found a cryptic page in each of the missing journals. On the first page of book twenty-eight. The middle page of book four ninety-six. And—"

Matt finished my last sentence with a broad grin. "The last page of book six."

"He was telling us the sequence," I blurted.

"Oh, my God, Matt," Zoe gushed. "How'd you figure this all out?"

I thought she was going to plant one on my brother right there in front of me. So gross.

My brother's face transitioned from pale to pink to ruddy. "Um, just lucky, I guess."

"Well, I think you're brilliant," she murmured.

I waved a hand between the two lovebirds. "Hey, still here. And we got a puzzle to solve."

My brother flinched, took his tablet from me, and rolled back to the desk. "Okay, you guys ready?"

"What book do I have again?" Zoe asked Matt.

"Four ninety-six," I said. "Focus."

She flashed a coy smile. "I am."

I pursed my lips and tapped her tablet. "Right here, girl."

"We ready?" Matt asked.

"Let's go," I replied. "Just remember, take your time. Accuracy over speed."

Matt gave us the next two numbers for our books and we got to work. For the next several hours, the room was silent as we counted away. It was mind-numbing work that took extreme patience because you didn't want to lose track of the count when you got up in the thousands, and each of us had one number way up there. Mine, three thousand six hundred ninety, was by far the smallest of those three.

When Matt finished his first count, he looked up and saw us waiting on him. "My second number is only three twenty-two, so let me count that off and then we can put the words together."

Five minutes later, my brother raised his head. "Let's see what we got. Zo, what's your first word?"

"*My*."

Matt wrote the word on the paper. "Sara?"

"*Face*."

Matt jotted the word down. "And I got *as*. Back to you, Zo."

"*Earth*."

"Finally a word coming close to map directions," I said. "And mine has promise, too. *Falls*."

"Sorry, sis. I know you're thinking waterfall, but my next word scuttles that possibility. *Away*." Matt read from the paper. "*Astride him the sun grows hot on my face as Earth falls away.*"

"That isn't sounding any better," I complained.

"Let's press on," Matt said. He gave us our next

two numbers and the room fell silent again.

This time, I was the last one to finish. "Whew, that was a tough count."

"Whatcha got, Zo? Matt asked.

"*I*."

He looked to me.

"*Feel*."

"And I got *like*," he said.

"If the next two words are *an idiot*, then Carlton got the last laugh," I groused. "Because that's how I'm gonna feel if this is just an eccentric old man waxing poetic."

"Only one way to find out," Zoe sang, her sparkling eyes taking in my brother. "My word is just the letter *a*."

"*Bird*," I said.

"*Weightless*," Matt said. "*Astride him the sun grows hot on my face as Earth falls away. I feel like a bird weightless*." He looked up. "Still weird but also making sense."

Mom appeared in the doorway. "It's getting late. You kids want any dinner?"

"Yes, please," Zoe begged. "I'm starving."

"Okay, I'll bring up some plates," she said, before disappearing into the hall.

"Thanks, Mom," I called out.

Five minutes later, Mom returned with a tray holding three heaping plates of pasta primavera. After scarfing down dinner, Matt gave us more numbers and we got back to counting. When we finished and he had the newly deciphered words written down, Matt read from the paper. "*Astride him the sun grows hot on my face as Earth falls away. I feel like a bird, weightless and free. Yet when Pegasus returns.*"

I shook my head. "This isn't good. It reads okay so you've cracked it. But it sure isn't telling us where a treasure is hidden."

Matt picked up his tablet and counted. "We have twelve words left. Let's grind through it and finish."

The next count for Zoe and I was brutal because both our numbers were in the thousands. Since Matt's two numbers were both under one thousand, he reluctantly agreed to take Mauzzy out for me while Zoe and I continued to count. Eventually, we had another six words. Unfortunately, the pasta was putting Matt to sleep.

I clapped my hands. "C'mon, guys, six more words and we're done."

Zoe perked up. "Let's do it. Matt, give us our numbers."

With renewed energy, we dove back into the count. At three-thirty in the morning, we finished decoding the message. We were beyond exhausted but the final piece of the message gave us a boost.

"Read it again, Matt," I said wearily.

"*Astride him the sun grows hot on my face as Earth falls away. I feel like a bird, weightless and free. Yet when Pegasus returns me to her, I once again treasure the ground beneath my feet.*"

"What the heck does it mean?" Zoe asked, her wee body stretched across the bed. "Sounds like Shakespeare."

"It seems like some kind of poem or something," Matt said, turning to his laptop. "Lemme search on it."

"I don't know about you guys," I said, "but I'm grabbing onto the word *treasure*."

Zoe hauled herself up off the bed and tottered to the door. "It's way past three, and we got ourselves an effing poem. I'm going to bed."

"Thanks, Zo," I said.

She stuck a hand in the air as she exited into the hall.

"Nothing turns up," Matt said. "It must be something he wrote."

I stepped over to the desk and stared at the message scrawled on the paper. "That last bit of the message, *I once again treasure the ground beneath my feet*, could mean buried treasure."

Matt pushed back from the desk and stood. "It could. But Earth is a big place. And I gotta go to bed. I'm wiped out."

I picked up the paper and staggered toward the door. "Me, too. At least you don't have to be up in a couple hours."

"Good night, sis."

"Night, Matt. Thanks for all the help. No way we could have done this without you."

With a tired smile, he replied, "You mean discover a new poem for the world?"

I didn't even try to muster up a witty comment. "Yup, something like that. Night."

I dragged myself down the hall into my bedroom, where Mauzzy was snuggled under the covers and snoring away. After getting ready for bed, I read the message one last time.

Astride him the sun grows hot on my face as Earth falls away. I feel like a bird, weightless and free. Yet when Pegasus returns me to her, I once again treasure the ground beneath my feet.

Easing Mauzzy over, I fell into bed. I was drifting off to sleep when my eyes flew open.

I solved the meaning of the message.

Chapter Thirty-Five

X marks the spot?

The following morning that came *way* too early, I spent the first coffee of the day sitting in my cubicle trying to sort out how we were going to get back down to Arcadia. Today was Wednesday and I couldn't risk waiting until the weekend to go down there in search of the treasure.

My desk phone rang. When I saw the caller ID, I had my solution. "Good morning, Mickey."

"Hey, morning. Got a few minutes?"

"Sure."

"Come on down."

I hesitated. "You don't have the FBI there waiting for me, do you? Because I thought Agent Bailey cleared me."

Mickey chuckled lightly. "Man, you're paranoid."

"Trust me, it's not without good reason."

"Well, it's all good. Just come on down."

"Okay. And I've got something to talk to you about, too."

Five minutes later, I sat across from Mickey with the door closed.

The security chief stood and came around the desk, his hand extended. "I wanted to personally congratulate you."

His paw swallowed my hand as we shook. "Thanks, I guess. What'd I do?"

He ambled back to the desk, his beleaguered chair protesting loudly when he plopped his bulky frame into it. "You put us onto Jeff."

I sat up straight, a spark of energy boosting my exhausted body. "I was right?"

"Sure were. Moss Bailey and his team visited him last night at his apartment. Moss got Jeff to voluntarily consent to a search of the place along with his phone."

"He pulled the same trick on me."

Mickey looked sideways at me. "It's not a trick. It's a legit way to shortcut the process if the target agrees to a search."

"I guess it depends on if you get busted as a result."

A grin spread across the man's wide face. "Then I guess Jeff got tricked."

I jumped out of the chair, that little spark of energy turning into a jolt. "Seriously? He got busted?"

"Sure did. They found those journals of yours hidden in the canister of an old vacuum cleaner. He must've figured no way anybody would find them. It's probably why he consented to the search, figuring he'd be in the clear when they didn't find anything."

I pumped a fist. "Yaaasssss."

"Thought you'd be happy to hear that."

"Nothing sweeter to hear than your accuser got arrested for the crime he accused you of." A frowning Boss Lady from yesterday's unpleasant meeting popped into my head. "And finding those journals makes it doubly sweet. You don't know how big a deal that is for me."

Mickey raised an eyebrow. "Bigger than finding the diamond?"

"Big time. Did they find it?"

He shook his head. "Not yet. But they're working on Jeff. Knowing him, he'll leverage the missing diamond to cut a deal and save himself some jail time."

"Hope they haven't recut the diamond."

Mickey scrunched up his face and gave a little head shake. "Nah, doubt it. I'm sure they know from Jeff the fake was discovered, so they'll wait for the heat to die down before doing anything."

"Fingers crossed."

He brightened. "Look, I wanted to see you to personally thank you and apologize for not believing you. If it wasn't for your persistence about the diamond being a fake, doubt we would've uncovered the heist."

My face stretched into an oversized smile as a warmth seeped into my cheeks. "You're welcome, and don't worry about not believing me earlier. I'm kinda used to it."

Mickey grinned. "Explains your tenacity."

I let out a short laugh. "Sometimes it can be a good thing. Other times"—I wiggled a hand—"not so much."

The smile on his face disappeared. "You said there was something we needed to discuss?"

"There is. You're the chief of security. Grant says I can trust you."

"You can, as long as you're not breaking the law."

"This is about museum business," I said. "Big business."

"What's on your mind?"

"Did Jefferson say why he had the journals

stolen?"

"Not really. Said he's been an Oliver Carlton buff his whole life. He was obviously lying. Why?"

"Him being a Carlton buff makes sense. He's probably been researching the guy for decades and somehow figured out the same thing we did."

The security chief cocked his head, a perplexed look on his face. "Figured out what?"

"That those journals are the key to locating the treasure."

Mickey sat back in the chair and studied me. "Yesterday afternoon you weren't certain it existed. But now those books are suddenly the key to finding the treasure? What changed?"

"With the help of my brother and a friend, we used the digitized versions of those journals last night to solve a wall cipher in Oliver Carlton's office."

"And it gave the location of the supposed treasure?"

"Mmmm, not exactly."

Mickey cracked a smile. "That's a definite maybe."

"The deciphered message was a poem or verse Carlton wrote to point us to the treasure."

He dropped his enormous head and stared at me. "But you're not sure."

"Pretty sure. The end part of it talks about him treasuring the ground beneath his feet. So, the treasure is buried or underground in a cavern or something. And the first part talks about him riding Pegasus."

That got a roar out of the security chief. "*Pegasus?* Unless there's a statue of a winged horse on his property, how does that tell you anything?"

"There's not, but it does."

"Then where is it?"

I stared back. This was the tricky part. I needed to stay firm. "I can't tell you."

Mickey howled. When his laughter subsided, he asked, "Then why are we doing this dance?"

"Because I need your help?"

"You have a funny way of asking."

"I need you to arrange for a security team to travel with me to North Carolina. To Arcadia."

"Why?"

"Because if I'm right about the treasure's location, and pretty sure I am, we're going to need armed guards."

His eyes bugged out. "Armed, too?"

"The treasure is worth billions."

He leaned forward on the desk, his thick neck sticking out. "Lemme get this straight. You want me to send an *armed* security detail with you to North Carolina to *search* for a treasure. You understand what you're asking?"

"It's the only way."

"But you won't tell me where it's hidden."

"You don't need to know. I just need security."

With chin in hand, his eyes dug into me. After seconds of silence, he spoke up. "You're asking me to stick my neck out based on a hunch."

"It's more than a hunch. I was right about the diamond, wasn't I? And Jefferson Scott? I'm right about this, too."

More staring before he let out an exasperated sigh. "There's that damn persistence of yours. I'm doubtful, but there's too much at stake for the Carlton for me not to listen to you." He looked off before turning back to me. "I'm gonna have to clear this with the Executive Director. If she says no"—he flipped his palms upward—"there's nothing I can do."

"I understand. Make sure she knows how much this can be worth to the Carlton."

Mickey picked up his desk phone and punched in a four-digit number. "Good morning, this is Mickey Fraser. Is Director Doyle available to meet with me? Uh-huh, right." He checked his watch. "Two o'clock it is. Thank you."

He replaced the handset and looked at me. "I'll call you."

****

I tapped on the open office door. "Excuse me, Evy?"

Boss Lady looked up from an open three-ring binder. "Yes?"

"Can we talk?"

"Only if it's about those missing journals."

"It is, partly."

She waved me in. "Close the door."

I entered the office, closed the door, and sat in a guest chair. "I just came from Mickey Fraser's office. The FBI recovered the journals."

Her head jerked back. "FBI?"

"Yes, ma'am. Jefferson Scott had them in his apartment."

"*Excuse me?* Jefferson Scott?"

"Yes, ma'am."

"Why on earth would he have them? And what's the FBI doing searching for those books? Yesterday you said you didn't tell anybody about them being missing. And now they're in the hands of the FBI?"

I explained about the treasure, the wall grid, and Jefferson masterminding the diamond heist to get his hands on the journals. I skipped the part where I told the FBI about them going missing. That little tidbit was no longer important since the journals were found. And she would go ballistic if she knew, meaning I would be unemployed. So that little secret will stay buried.

Her fingers drummed the desk as she gazed at me. "With those books over at the FBI, I suppose this could put me in a bit of a quandary." The drumming stopped. "Unless we can get those journals back discreetly."

"I think they're going to hold them as evidence."

With an icy smile, she said, "We'll see. I'll call Moss Bailey and give his arm a good twist."

That was the easy part, telling her about the journals. Now came the hard part.

I swallowed. "Um, there is one other thing I need to talk to you about."

She raised her pointy chin. "Yes?"

"You know that treasure I told you about?"

No response.

"I'm waiting for a call back from Mickey Fraser, but I'm going to need tomorrow and Friday off."

Boss Lady stared at me with unblinking eyes. "Why?"

"To go search for the treasure."

"A treasure hunt? Poppycock."

"Pretty sure I know where it is, and if I find it, billions will go to the Carlton."

She arched a perfectly manicured eyebrow. "Billions?"

"Yes, ma'am, depending on how much Carlton spent when he was alive. But it's gotta be at least one to two billion."

"And this is why you're waiting to hear back from Mr. Fraser? For security?"

"Yes."

She angled her head, eyes narrowing. "So, he believes you and this dubious legend?"

"He's skeptical, like you, but said there's too much to lose if he doesn't check it out. He's meeting with the Executive Director this afternoon to clear it with her."

"I see." Boss Lady lowered her gaze to the open binder. "It appears to be out of my hands, then. If Director Doyle approves Mr. Fraser providing the security, I guess you're going." She glanced up. "Keep me apprised."

"Yes, ma'am."

I spent the rest of the morning and well into the afternoon downing coffee while poring over maps and aerial photos of Arcadia to see if any other spots could remotely match the deciphered message. I found none, meaning I was right. *Pegasus* was the keyword. Those tiny angel wings with the praying hands above the corner stall in the stable weren't angel wings after all.

They were the wings of Pegasus. And a discreet X-marks-the-spot.

My desk phone rang, and with all the coffee in me, it about caused an accident.

"Hey, Mickey. Good news?"

"Yes and no. She approved me going with you, but I can't take any of the Carlton's security team."

"No offense, but that's useless," I complained. "We need armed guards. Not just you."

"Hang on, hang on. I can bring my firearm and—"

"You may be big and all, but one little pistol isn't

going to protect"—I dropped my voice to a harsh whisper—"a billion-dollar treasure."

"Let me talk," he barked. "If we find the treasure, she's authorized me to hire an armored truck service from down there to secure the treasure and haul it to one of their vaults until the Carlton can sort things out. She also approved me purchasing digging tools."

"Start making those calls because we're leaving around five tomorrow morning. And we'll need way more than one or two trucks."

Chapter Thirty-Six

Is it all about symmetry?

We arrived at Arcadia Thursday afternoon just before one. Mickey drove a shiny black pickup with an extended cab, the digging tools in its bed. The monstrosity of the truck was a perfect fit for the mountain of a man. In contrast, Zoe, Matt, and I were crammed in my tired little hatchback, made all the smaller when he parked beside us in the Arcadia lot. Mauzzy stayed home because we were driving straight to Arcadia and he would only be in the way during the hunt. Of course, that's not how I put it to him.

The truck's passenger window slid down and Mickey leaned over, gesturing for me to lower my window. "You guys need to get in my truck."

"Why?" I called up to the open window.

"Just get in and I'll explain."

We got out of my car and climbed up into the behemoth. I took the front passenger seat, while Zoe and Matt clambered up into the back seat.

I faced Mickey, waiting for his explanation.

He put the truck in reverse and backed out of the parking space. "I spoke to Arcadia's managing director on the way down. Since we don't know if we're going to find anything, she wants us to be discreet. We'll take my truck to wherever we're going on the property. It can pass as a work vehicle."

"Works for me," I said, adjusting the air vent to blow directly on me. "Anything to keep out of that heat and humidity."

Mickey laughed. "Trust me, you're gonna be hot and wet soon enough. Where to?"

"The stable," I replied.

I directed Mickey to the edge of the grounds and the dirt road that ran along the property. Kicking up a cloud of dust as we slowly bounced along, the truck eventually stopped in front of the stable at the far rear corner of the estate.

"Tools are in the bed," Mickey said. "Just in case someone decides to hike down here, I'm gonna put some cones out and run tape to set up a work zone perimeter."

We climbed down from the cab and sorted out the tools. There were shovels, pickaxes, a heavy iron rod with a flat sharp end, and a similar iron rod with a sharp pointy end, along with orange work cones and a roll of yellow caution tape. There were also two oversized coolers loaded with bottles of water. By the time we lugged the tools to the stable's door, I was past glistening and just plain sweaty.

I dropped my tools and took off through the structure to the corner stall with the wings and praying hands above the split-door. The top half of the door was open. I unlatched the lower half and stepped inside. The stall was maybe a ten-by-ten or twelve-by-twelve square with a dirt floor.

Zoe poked her head in. "This it?"

"It's gotta be," I said. "Check out the little wings

above you."

She leaned back and looked up. "Whoa."

I slipped past the wide-eyed pixie and headed back to the stable's entrance. "Let's bring those tools down here and get started."

Matt shuffled toward me with a shovel over each shoulder.

"Back left corner," I said.

After several trips, we had the digging equipment inside the stall.

Zoe wielded a shovel that appeared supersized in her wee hands. "Where do we start?"

Slowly turning around, I took in the stall. "He built this structure after he discovered the treasure. The question is, would he have centered the stall directly over it, or off to a side?"

Zoe and I looked to Matt.

He rubbed his chin as he glanced around the space. "If it were me, I would offset it as an added measure of security. How many chests were there?"

"Seven hundred fifty," I replied.

"That would easily take up this entire space," Matt said, looking around the stall. "And unless he got help, that's an awful lot of digging to bury the entire thing. I think we're looking for a cave entrance."

"A *cave?*" Zoe exclaimed. "Where? There's just dirt."

"There's a huge surficial aquifer system starting here in southern North Carolina and running to southern Florida," he said.

"How do you know that and what does it mean?" she asked.

"In addition to math, he's also a geology geek," I

said dryly.

Zoe gaped at Matt, adulation spreading across her face. The girl loved smart guys. Not so sure how I felt about her loving this particular smart guy, though. I was moving toward acceptance, but clearly, I wasn't there yet.

"It's true," he said. "Geology is one of my interests. A surficial aquifer is a shallow subterranean water system, and with limestone deposits being in the area, the likelihood of the shipwrecked crew discovering a subterranean cave to hide the treasure is high."

"So, no digging by them?" Zoe asked.

"Maybe not, but definitely for us," I said. "Where would you start, Matt?"

"I think we're looking for a horizontal door of some kind in the floor," he said, roaming around the stall. "And assuming from time to time he needed to get to the treasure, it had to be easy to access and cover back up."

"So where?" I asked.

He stopped near the stall's entrance where the tools were dumped and whipped around to face us. "I bet the entrance is no more than six inches deep. That would allow—"

"*Matt*," I cried. "Focus. Where?"

He looked down at the floor, then up at me. "I think we start in the center with an exploratory hole and if at six inches we find nothing, we move a foot in each direction and dig two more holes."

Zoe immediately attacked the middle of the floor with her shovel, but it barely penetrated the dirt. She jabbed at the earth a second time, the shovel coming away with a paltry bit of dirt. "It's hard as a rock."

"Looks like mattocks first, then shovels," Matt said, picking up what I thought was a pickaxe, but apparently was called a mattock.

"Hold on," I said. "Let's think about this for a sec. If there's the possibility we'll be digging holes everywhere, where do we put the dirt now? We don't want to later be digging out double the amount of dirt."

Matt pointed to a wall shared with the next stall. "I say we dump it along there. The probability of the entrance door along that wall is low."

Zoe tossed away her shovel and picked up a mattock. "Let's dig."

I took a mattock, raised it high, and hammered at the ground. After the vibrations in my hands and arms stopped, it only took that one big swing for me to realize I was a shovel girl. I picked up the shovel Zoe tossed away and scooped up the dirt loosened by their mattocks, chucking it toward the wall.

Fifteen minutes later, Mickey showed up carrying one of the oversized coolers that he placed with a grunt inside the stall. "Make sure you stay hydrated. Don't want anybody collapsing on my watch." He surveyed the small two-inch-deep hole in the center of the stall. "That the spot?"

I leaned on my shovel, wiped matted hair out of my eyes, and scowled. "No, we're digging for the fricking fun of it."

He backed up with hands out front. "Dumb question."

I gave him an exaggerated smile.

He responded with an awkward smile. "Got the place taped off. I'll be in the truck keeping an eye out.

Lemme know if you need anything."

Mickey left and we got back to digging. Eventually, and I mean eventually, we had a one-foot-wide hole dug six inches deep. And there was no hint of an opening, a door, or anything else for that matter. Except more dirt.

I dragged my shovel over to the cooler, dug out a bottle of water, and took a big hit of the ice-cold liquid. "Looks like our first hole is a bust."

Matt and Zoe joined me at the cooler, each getting a bottle of water.

"Let's expand the dig," Matt said, taking a slug from his bottle. "But also keep digging the original hole. Zoe and I will dig a new hole to the left of the first. Sara, you keep taking the first hole deeper."

"Deeper?" I asked. "You said the entrance would be no deeper than six inches. Why keep going?"

"Why not?" he replied.

"Because I'm doing the digging," I said. "And that dirt is hard."

My brother picked up the heavy iron rod with the spiked end and handed it to me. "Every couple of inches, ram this into the ground to see if it breaks through or you hit something."

I took the rod and about impaled my foot as its weight caught me off guard. "Here's an idea. How 'bout *you* keep digging the first hole and jabbing it with this pike thingy, and Zoe and I will dig the next hole?"

Matt finished his water and picked up a shovel. "Sure, no problem."

We continued digging, Zoe and I working on the second hole, Matt expanding the first. Each time he stabbed the earth, I prayed he would hit something. But each time, all he hit was more dirt.

By the time Zoe and I reached six inches, it was pushing three in the afternoon. Our second hole appeared to be a bust, and Matt had gone a few more inches on the first with no success. As my legs and back complained to no end, I found myself questioning why in the heck we were doing this instead of having the Carlton handle it. After all, it was their fricking treasure. All my talk yesterday justifying us finding the treasure as our payoff for solving the puzzle seemed pretty lame right about now.

I dropped the shovel and staggered over to the cooler, followed by Matt and Zoe. My arms were leaden, my back aching, and my clothes filthy wet. Just one disgusting dying mess. I snared a bottle of water from the cooler and chugged it, waterboarding myself in the process.

"Smaller sips," Matt cautioned as he cracked open a bottle from the cooler.

Sputtering and choking on insurgent water in my lungs, I glared at my brother. "I'm…thirsty."

He shrugged. "Suit yourself."

After one long hacking cough, I successfully cleared the remaining water.

"Nice," Zoe said.

I hunched over with hands on knees, head bowed, and eyes closed. When I opened them, a small puddle had formed in the dirt. I was disgusting. Straightening, I looked at my motley crew. Both their faces were smudged with dirt, and they were a sweaty mess, but they also had bright eyes full of expectation. How was that possible? We've been at it for hours with no success.

"Maybe I was wrong," I said. "We should've found it by now. Let's leave it up to the Carlton."

"No way," Zoe protested. "It's only been a few hours. Besides, you may have suspect methods and questionable judgment, but you're usually right. Eventually."

I looked around the torn-up dirt floor and sighed. "I don't know, Zo. This time—"

"We're finding that dang treasure," she said, punching the air for emphasis. "I believe in you. And I believe in Matt. Now let's get going."

With renewed energy, courtesy of my best friend, I found myself thinking clearer. "Matt, I think we should focus all our efforts on the first hole."

"Thoughts?" he asked with eyebrows raised.

"Carlton was into all kinds of things, including architecture and engineering," I said. "He designed all of Arcadia. If you look at it, everything about the place is symmetrical."

Matt's eyes lit up. "Meaning he couldn't help but center this stall directly above the entrance to the cave."

"That's exactly what I'm thinking," I said.

Zoe hoisted a mattock and swung it into the hole. Matt did the same and I picked up a shovel. Every five minutes, Matt jammed the iron pike into the ground. Thirty minutes later, the hole was over a foot deep.

"If we don't hit anything this time, I think we move on," Matt rasped as he raised the heavy pike high over his head and launched it toward the hole.

"Have faith," I said. "It's here. We just gotta —"
Clang.

Chapter Thirty-Seven

Vindication, finally

"Do it again," Zoe yelled.

Matt yanked the pike out of the hole, raised it high, and sent it screaming downward.

Clang.

We looked at each other, eyes wide, mouths open.

"I think we found it," I said in a hushed tone.

Zoe let out a high-pitched squeal, dropped her mattock, and danced around the stall, her arms waving wildly in the air.

"Hang on, Zo," Matt urged. "We need to excavate this. For all we know, I hit an old horseshoe."

She stopped dead in her tracks, arms straight up. "What?"

"He's right," I said. "The hard part has just begun. We need to dig out whatever made that sound."

Zoe zipped over to the hole and retrieved the discarded mattock. We immediately set to work on expanding the hole, Matt periodically jabbing the ground as we searched for the edges of what was hopefully a buried door. By the second stab of the pike, we realized it was no horseshoe. Whatever the pike was hitting, it was substantial. The excitement of the find had us so energized, dirt flew everywhere, the hole expanding in all directions at a rapid rate. In time, a two-foot square metal plate set within a two-inch metal frame sat at the bottom of the hole. Attached to one end of the plate, a heavy metal ring.

"How do we get inside?" Zoe asked, bouncing up and down. "How do we get inside?"

The girl had unlimited energy. I was exhausted yet she was jumping around the place like a first-grader at her birthday party.

Matt got on his knees, extended an arm into the hole, and tugged up on the ring. "Oof. It didn't budge." He tried again, this time using both arms. "Nope."

"Maybe it's stuck after being buried all those years," Zoe offered.

Matt sat beside the hole. "And then some."

I dug my phone out from my shorts and called Mickey. "Hey. Come on down here. And bring a flashlight. Uh-huh. I think we found it."

Minutes later, the giant Mickey Fraser filled the stall door. Strapped to his right hip, a holstered gun. In his left hand, a foot-long blue metallic flashlight.

"What'd you find?" he asked.

"Looks like a metal door," I replied.

Zoe came up behind me. "Why's he got a gun?" she whispered.

Mickey lumbered up to the hole and peered down before glancing over at Zoe. "For protection."

She stuck her head out from around me and addressed Mickey. "Whose?"

"Ours," I said.

"You tried opening it?" Mickey asked.

Matt raised a hand, still sitting beside the hole. "Couldn't budge it."

Mickey looked around the stall. "Might be rusted shut." He zeroed in on the other iron pole with the flat edge and stepped over to pick it up. "Maybe we can pry it open."

"You might be right about it being rusted shut," Matt said. "Because I'm sure he engineered some way using hydraulics to lift it without much exertion."

Mickey positioned the flat portion of the rod up against the door's seam. "Hydraulics? Back then?"

"Easily," Matt replied. "Hydraulics has been around for over two hundred years."

Mickey aggressively wiggled the iron pole back and forth while pushing down with his heavily-muscled arms, working the flat edge into the space between the door and the frame. "Okay, ready?"

Matt lay prone, extended his arms into the hole, and grasped the ring. "Uh-huh."

The security chief gasped as he leaned his monstrous frame onto the pole. Matt tugged and tugged, but the door didn't move.

"Okay, move out of the hole," Mickey said. "I'm gonna try and loosen it up." He took the pole and with short, quick movements, chopped down around the edges of the door. Then he worked the flat edge back into the slim gap. "Let's try it again."

Matt got back on his stomach and stuck his arms into the hole. "Ready."

Mickey drew his body up and exploded down onto the pole. His face turned dark red as the man put his prodigious bulk to work. As Mickey grunted, Matt's torso jerked up and back as he yanked on the ring. Suddenly, with a hiss, the door raised, sending Mickey face-first into the ground.

"Oh my God, are you okay?" I cried out, scrambling to assist the fallen security chief.

He rolled off the iron pole and sat up, rubbing his ribs. "Haven't taken a shot like that since my playing days."

"Are they broken?" I asked.

He stood and carefully brushed off his shirt. "Nah, but I'll feel it for a while."

Matt peered into the hole. "Hey, guys, look at this."

We surrounded the hole where the door was opened, with some kind of hinge system on its inside supporting the weight. Steep metal stairs led down into darkness.

Mickey picked up his flashlight and handed it to me. "The honor is all yours."

I clicked on the flashlight and aimed the beam down the stairs. It was so grody. Going through the interceptors was nasty, but that paled in comparison to what waited for me down those steps. And without my nose clip.

Turning back to Mickey, I said, "You should go first. After all, you're security."

His eyes widened. "Look at the size of that hatch, then look at the size of me."

"You can do it," I urged. "You're an athlete."

Mickey put his hands out and took two steps back. "Look, even if I could squeeze through, there's no telling if I could get back out. Sorry, but you're up."

I looked back down the stairs. There better be a dang treasure down there, and it better be fricking huge. I took a deep breath, then a second, wriggled into the hole, and descended the steps. A stifling dank mustiness reached up to me as I went deeper into the hole. After the tenth step, my foot hit a rough stone floor and…

What was on…

"Oh, my God," I screamed. "*Oh, my God.*"

Mickey's voice boomed from above. "Sara. *Sara.*"

I screamed again, battling invisible hands roaming all over my face.

"I'm coming down," Zoe yelled.

"It's okay," I called up. "Sorry. Spiderwebs."

If I wasn't so excited and nervous at the same time, Zoe's reaction would have cost her five to six dollars for the curse jar. Easily five to six.

I flashed the light back up the stairs. "Hey, I said sorry."

The glaring visage of my best friend stared back. "What'd you expect? He had maid service going down there for the last hundred fifty years?"

I pawed at my face, clearing as best I could the remaining felonious strands of webbing, before turning back to proceed into the space. The place was damp and cool. I put the light on a wall. It was gray rock.

I was in a cave.

A voice spoke from behind me, causing me to fumble and drop the flashlight, sending it clattering and rolling away on the rock floor. "Thanks for clearing out those spiderwebs."

I fetched the fallen light and swung it around. There stood a smiling Zoe, her new blue and purple streaks shimmering in the light's beam. Gone were the neon green ones. Behind her, Matt was halfway down the stairs.

"Don't scare me like that," I scolded.

"Ditto," she replied with attitude.

My brother came up to us, shining his phone flashlight around the space before examining a wall. "Yep, limestone."

I pointed the flashlight forward. "There's nothing

here. Let's keep moving."

We crept along a narrow tunnel barely six feet high. I knew that because my hair kept brushing against the ceiling and God knows what else. A picture of hanging bats popped into my head, sending a shiver through me. After thirty paces, the tunnel opened up into a circular cavern. When the light's beam hit the far wall, it reflected back to us.

I stopped and stared in complete and utter amazement.

"Holy crap," Zoe whispered from behind me.

Matt let out a gasp. "Whoa."

Lining the wall and protruding out into the space were stacks of gold bars.

"Sara, you did it," Zoe whispered. "You fricking did it."

On another wall were five small chests. I hustled over to them and lifted one of the lids. Cut emeralds filled the chest.

"Guys, check this out," I said, holding up a handful of emeralds.

Zoe left Matt and rushed over to the chests. "They're effing beautiful."

I lifted the lids of the other four chests. Two were filled with cut emeralds and two were filled with chunks of uncut ones.

"I expected chests of gold coins," Matt said from over by the gold bars.

I put the light back on the gold. "He must've melted the coins into bars."

"Probably did it to keep people from realizing he was sitting on a treasure," Matt said.

"Makes sense since he went to great pains to keep it

hidden," I said.

Matt surveyed the stacks. "There must be four thousand, easy." He picked up a bar. "This could be twenty-five pounds."

"The ones he gave his butler were twenty," I said.

"Four thousand twenty-pound bars are worth two and a half billion," he said.

Zoe spun around. "And that's not counting all these emeralds."

I headed toward the tunnel leading back to the stairs. "We're wasting time. I gotta get Mickey to call those armored trucks in."

When I got to the entrance door, I yelled up the stairs. "Better make that call."

Mickey's head appeared over the doorway. "Seriously?"

I smiled the biggest smile ever. "Seriously. Tell them to bring an army because they're moving over four thousand bars of gold. That's forty tons."

Despite his size, Mickey almost fell down the hole.

****

The same day we found the treasure, a convoy of armored trucks hauled it away to their vault, finishing up late at night. We drove home the next morning, arriving mid-afternoon, and were celebrating around the kitchen table with pizza and soda. Plus, beer for Dad, who took the day off when he heard about our discovery.

"I can't believe you kids found a treasure worth over two billion dollars," Mom said, shaking her head in disbelief.

Zoe's fists pounded the table. "It was fricking amazing."

"Matt, what was the final count again?" I asked.

My brother clasped his hands on the table, a faux academic look on his face. "That would be precisely four thousand three hundred twenty gold bars. A total of forty-three point two tons. Worth just over two point seven five billion dollars."

"Don't forget the emeralds," Zoe squealed.

Dad took a swig of beer. "That will make for one hell of an endowment for the museum."

"Sure will. And Boss Lady said the Board of Trustees will be meeting next week to discuss a reward for us."

"Reward?" Matt and Zoe said in unison.

"Yep," I said, turning to Dad. "We couldn't have done it without your help. You solving that filthy cipher was huge. It put us on the right track to bust things wide open."

A proud smile lit up his face. "*Pigpen* cipher."

I grinned. "That's what I said."

"Sara," Mom said, "did they—"

My phone chimed. When I looked at the caller ID, a flash of heat radiated through my chest. "Grant," I shouted into the phone.

"Congratulations," he said warmly.

"Oh, my God. It was amazing." I paused, glancing at Dad, who was paying close attention. "Hey, how'd you find out? I tried calling several times but you never picked up."

"Sorry, wasn't in a position to talk. But a mutual friend got the word to me."

"Mutual? You mean—"

"Yep. Hey, only got a sec. Just wanted to tell you congrats, I'm so proud of you, and I'll never doubt you again."

I laughed. "Until the next situation I get myself into."

He returned my laugh with one of his own. "Probably. How 'bout you tell me everything next Saturday?"

"Sure. What time you want me to call?"

"I'll pick you up at eight. For dinner."

"Dinner?" A second passed, then another, before it hit me. "You're coming back to D.C.?"

"I am. We caught a break. I'll be wrapping things up here next week. Hey, gotta run. See you next weekend."

"Deal. Can't wait." I tapped off.

"Okay, so I was wrong about him," Zoe said. "But still not so sure about Mrs. Majelski."

"You were wrong about both of them," I said. "Again."

Zoe wagged a hand. "Mmmm, not so sure."

I glanced around the table. "You heard. He's coming home. That will give us one week together before I head back to school."

"One week is better than nothing," Mom said. "But I've been dying to ask the entire time you've been on the phone with Grant."

"Yes?" I asked hesitantly, not sure where she was going, and not sure I wanted to hear.

"Did they find the diamond?"

I breathed out a sigh of relief. That's a question I could handle. "They did," I replied. "Yesterday. The FBI told Mickey that Jefferson Scott took a one-time deal and squealed on the crew. He handpicked them for this specific job from his INTERPOL days. The diamond was their payment to steal the journals. Italian police caught the lead guy at his girlfriend's apartment in Turin. Had the diamond hidden in a jar of eggplant caponata. They're still looking for the others, but Mickey said it was just a matter of time. INTERPOL has something called red notices out on them."

Dad stared at me in disbelief. "I can't believe you solved a jewel heist *and* found what is probably the biggest treasure in the United States."

"What do you think of my persistence now?"

He chuckled. "Can't speak to that, but for once your stubborn hardheadedness came in handy."

As if on cue, a pitiful whine floated up from beside my chair. Staring up at me was the plaintive feed-me face of Sweet Handsome.

"Mauz, you ate two hours ago."

He sat, set his jaw, and eyed me hard. Apparently, if we were eating and celebrating, he should be allowed the same gastronomic indulgence, too.

I lifted a piece of vegetarian pizza and took a glorious bite.

Another whine.

I looked down. The little guy continued to stare at me.

Unrelenting.

Unblinking.

Unwavering.

He was the most persistent, stubborn, hardheaded, devious, master manipulator on the planet.

But he was my Sweet Handsome.

And I loved him.

A word about the author...

B.T. Polcari is a graduate of Rutgers College of Rutgers University, an award-winning mystery author, and a proud father of two wonderful children. He's a champion of rescue pups (Mauzzy is a rescue), craves watching football and basketball, and, of course, loves reading mysteries. Among his favorite authors are D.P. Lyle, Robert B. Parker, and Michael Connelly. He is also an unapologetic fantasy football addict. He lives with his wife in scenic Chattanooga, Tennessee.

www.btpolcari.com

Thank you for purchasing
this publication of The Wild Rose Press, Inc.

For questions or more information
contact us at
info@thewildrosepress.com.

The Wild Rose Press, Inc.
www.thewildrosepress.com

www.ingramcontent.com/pod-product-compliance
Lightning Source LLC
Chambersburg PA
CBHW051133030726
47504CB00004B/844